Hann

D0858545

The Lighthouse Girl
of Newfoundland

Hannah

The Lighthouse Girl
of Newfoundland

Don Ladolcetta

Tranquility Press 2021

Copyright © 2021 Donald Ladolcetta

All rights reserved. No part of this book may be reproduced or used in any manner without the prior written permission of the copyright owner, excepting brief quotations in a review.

For information:
Tranquility Press
723 W University Ave #300-234
Georgetown TX 78626
tranquilitypress@gmail.com
tranquilitypress.com

ISBN 978-1-950481-29-3

Library of Congress Control Number: 2021939809

Cover design by Teresa Lynn using photo by Yakov Oskanov/ Shutterstock.com.
Unless otherwise specified, all photos herein are from the personal collection of Donald Ladolcetta and used with permission. Beached Iceberg photo on page 336 courtesy of Doreen Dalley, Twillingate, Newfoundland. Used with permission.
House photo on page 336 courtesy of Library and Archives Canada/National Film Board. Used with permission.

This book is dedicated
to Mom, Joan Greene Ladolcetta
(also called Hannah or Johanna).
I love you and miss you dearly,
and would have loved to see the look on your
face if I had written this book while you were
still alive.

Acknowledgements

I want to thank and acknowledge the following for assisting me or inspiring me in the writing of this book.

I need to acknowledge the role Covid-19 or the coronavirus has played. Without it there would be no book. I was self-isolating and social distancing within the confines of my house and staring at four walls in the midst of the pandemic when my son Frank suggested I use the time to write the great American novel. Thank you, Frank, for the idea.

I wish to thank my wonderful, loving wife, Patty, for being my muse, my sounding board, my first editor, my cheerleader and best friend. I want to thank my son David and friend Stephanie Rivers for being secondary but very valuable follow-up editors. Thank you Linda Ladolcetta, for your feedback and memories. Of course my last and final editor, Teresa Lynn, deserves kudos for her skill in guiding a blind man through the dark.

I wish to thank my many cousins who not only shared stories with me about my Mother's homeland, but also opened their homes to me in my many visits to their beautiful country.

I wish to thank my aunt Angela (Baby Angie), who is the only surviving human featured in the book. Your memories were valuable sources in a number of places within.

A Note from the Author

This story takes place in Newfoundland. The title character, Hannah, was born and grew up there. She later became my mother. I have visited her home place many times, both as a child and as an adult. The story incorporates many true-life experiences of Hannah as well as her family. It also incorporates a little fiction for these characters as well, so for anyone who is acquainted with better details of these people that differ from my depiction, please forgive me for taking some poetic license.

I have incorporated Newfoundland culture and history into the book so you can better understand the setting behind the stories. All these references are actual fact. The culture of the place is different than many other places you read about. These differences make Newfoundland extremely interesting and fun.

The novel also contains several Newfoundland words. Newfoundlanders are famous for having invented a lot of words not found in the dictionary. The glossary on the following pages gives the meaning of unique words.

I hope you enjoy this book. It was fun to write.

~*Don*

Glossary

Newfoundlanders speak English, but due to years of isolated life on the island prior to World War II, they have invented many words that only an islander would know. This glossary contains words I used in the book or words my mother used when I was growing up.

Avalon Peninsula: A peninsula on the southeast corner of the Island of Newfoundland. Point Verde, Placentia, and the capital city of St. John's are located here.

Bad'n arder: A naughty boy.

Banker: A boat employed in cod fishing off Newfoundland; or, a Newfoundland fisherman.

Bazz: Kiss.

Best kind, b'y: An expression meaning "It's good" or, less frequently, "That's right" or "I agree." B'y is short for boy.

Bodhrán: A shallow, hand-held drum used in Irish and Newfoundland music. It's a little larger than a tambourine, and is played with a short drumstick that uses both ends of the stick in a seesaw type motion.

Boil-up: A common method of preparing dinner in which meats, vegetables, and sometimes dessert, are boiled in the same pot at the same time. Also called Jigg's Dinner.

B'y: Boy.

Capelin: Tiny fish about 3 or 4 inches (5 cm) long and ½ inch (1 cm) wide.

Cartel ships: Ships that engage in humanitarian efforts.

Chile (also chil'): Child. Used by elderly people as a term of endearment when addressing a child they are fond of.

Cod britches: Male sex organs of a codfish, which are black in color and shaped like pants (hence the name britches). An acquired taste, but many Newfoundlanders love fried cod britches.

Cod tongue: Not actually the tongue, but a piece of fish flesh cut from the underside of the fish's mouth between the jawbones.

Cold plate: A dish served at weddings consisting of sliced cold cuts (turkey, roast beef, and ham) and cold salads (macaroni, potato, and coleslaw).

From away (also "Come from away"): Not from Newfoundland.

Commonwealth Realm: An independent country with a written constitution and the King or Queen of England as its monarch, as Canada and Australia are today.

Corned: Drunk.

Dole: Give, usually by the government. "On the dole" means collecting government welfare.

Dory: A small but seaworthy rowboat used by cod fishermen.

Feller/fella: Fellow; a young man.

Figgy pudding (also called lad in the bag and figgy duff): A dish made by putting flour, molasses, and raisins in a bag—often a pillowcase—tightly tied closed with string. The bag is put into a boil-up pot of corned beef and cabbage so everything cooks together into a pudding-like cake. Frequently covered with either turkey gravy or molasses sauce.

Fish and brewis: A Newfoundland meal consisting of hardtack bread, pork scrunchions, and codfish all boiled together into a mush.

Fishing planter: See Planter.

Flake: A wooden rack set in the sun where salted codfish is laid out to dry.

Gatching (also gatchin'): Showing off.

Guff: Impertinence. "I'll take no guff from you."

G'wan: Short for "go on." Used to mean "Stop kidding me."

Gut: A wide river's end where it meets the sea; a narrow channel. Placentia Gut.

Hardtack: Extremely hard and dried bread or cracker. Nearly impossible to eat without soaking in liquid first.

Ice pans: Flat sheets of ice. Jumping from pan to pan to traverse the ice is known as ice panning.

Jib: A triangular sail at the front of a boat.

Jigging: The act of setting baited fishhooks attached to fishing lines in the sea and jerking the fishing lines up and down repeatedly to catch fish.

Jigg's dinner: A boil-up. Jiggs was a comic strip character from "Bringing Up Father" whose favorite meal was a boil-up, so the dish became known as Jigg's dinner.

Kitchen party: A typical party in Newfoundland held in the kitchen.

Lad in the bag: See Figgy pudding.

Lops: Waves on the ocean.

Lard tunderin' Jayzus: An expression of excitement. A mispronunciation of Lord thundering Jesus.

Make or Break engine: An old style, one-cylinder boat engine so simple that a fisherman can easily *make* the repair if anything should *break*. It made a familiar noise: putt, putt, putt, putt, putt, putt.

Mauzy: Foggy.

Molasses coady: A sweet sauce made from molasses and butter that is poured on cakes and figgy pudding.

Mummer: A costumed person who strolls the streets at Christmas to friends' houses, dancing and pulling pranks until the friends identify them. The act of mummering meant that all parties involved would engage in drinking alcohol and feasting throughout the evening.

Noke: A dunce or a fool.

Outport: A small, isolated fishing settlement in Newfoundland.

Packet Boat: Medium-sized boats designed to carry domestic mail, passengers, and freight between outports and mainland ports.

Pans: See Ice pans.

Place names: Newfoundlanders have a sense of humor. They have given crazy names to many towns. Some examples: Tickle Cove, Tickle Harbour, Blow Me Down, Come by Chance, Conception Bay, Cupids, Dildo, Exploits, Happy Adventure, Heart's Delight, Little Heart's Ease, Muddy Hole, Tilting, and Jerry's Nose. These are just a few.

Placentia: A village in Newfoundland on the Northwest point of the Avalon Peninsula where much of this story takes place. This village was the capital of Newfoundland when the French ruled the colony.

Planter: The name given to the owner of a fishing plantation. See "The History behind Her Story" at the back of this book for more information.

Peas pudding: A cross between pea soup and a boil-up, made by putting hard yellow split peas in a bag—often a pillowcase—and placing the bag into a boil-up pot with corned beef and cabbage to make a smooth consistency similar to mashed potatoes.

Point Verde: French for "*Green Point*." A village in Newfoundland on the Northwest point of the Avalon Peninsula where the story begins. It is not far from Placentia.

Quintal: A measure of dried salted cod equal to about 112 pounds.

Regatta: A rowing race using six-man, fixed-seat, rowing shells. The boats are long, low, and lightweight, designed only for racing.

The Rock: Nickname for Newfoundland, as it is a rocky island.

Rooms: A spot on the beach or shoreline reserved by inshore fishermen. See "The History behind Her Story" at the back of this book for more information.

Saltbox house: A box-shaped house. These were very typical of the homes built by Newfoundland fishermen and were named because they resembled the shape of the boxes that were used to store salt.

Scoff: A big feast, frequently a boil-up.

Screech: A 140-proof rum of Newfoundland, named

for the shout made when drinking it. Capitalized, it refers to a brand; otherwise, it is slang for any cheap but strong rum.

Screech-in: The act of initiation that turns a person into an honorary Newfoundlander in a ceremony that requires drinking screech, kissing a codfish, and speaking like a Newfoundlander.

Scrunchions: Pork fatback or salt pork cut into tiny cubes and fried crisply to render the fat. Both the crispy chunks and fat are ingredients in many recipes.

Snaz: An old maid who likes to poke her nose into everybody's business.

Techy (also tetchy): Peevish or cranky.

The Triangle Trade: The trade pattern between Newfoundland, Jamaica, and Boston. (In some uses of this expression, Boston is replaced by England.)

Toutons: Risen bread dough flattened and fried like a pancake, served with molasses.

Ugly stick: a musical instrument made from a mop or broom handle with bottle caps, tin cans, small bells, and other noise makers attached. The instrument is played with a stick and has a distinctive sound.

Vamp: Bottom of socks. "My stocking vamps are wet."

Yank: Short for Yankee. An American.

Yes, b'y: Yes, boy, meaning "You got that right, boy."

Prologue

Hannah's Ancestor

April 30, 1794

Michael Green stared into the darkness, his brows pulled together in worry. He had sailed Placentia Bay many times before and always enjoyed the calm and beautiful waters. But today thick, dark storm clouds piled into the sky. At the first sign of them, Michael prayed they would make the port of Placentia, Newfoundland before the storm arose to its full fury and the winds and waves grew fierce. Yet the storm seemed to build faster than the three-masted ship sailed.

As a ship captain, Michael knew his business well. He could take charge during any tempest, giving orders to his crew with confidence. But he'd sold his merchant schooner, the *Mason's Apron*, three weeks ago. Now his role as a mere passenger, with no control, left him uneasy.

"If I was on the *Mason's*—" he started to mutter to himself.

"Talking to yourself now, are you?" John Corbin, a wealthy merchant returning with his wife and daughter from the family's Jamaican trading operation, approached and gave Michael a friendly slap on the back.

"Just looking at the storm coming in. It's going to be a big one."

"Eh, maybe it won't be so bad. You never can tell."

"John, I'm a captain. I know what I'm talking about. We're in for a big storm. Sure would be good to make port before it strengthens."

"I'm sure Captain Bell is doing his best to get us there quickly," John replied. "The ship can only sail so fast."

"We can't reach land too soon as far as I'm concerned." The men stood silently in the rising wind a few moments, then Michael continued, "I need to get back to Point Verde anyway. I've been gone too long and I'm sure my workers are taking advantage of my absence and business is suffering."

"Tell me something, Michael. I know Point Verde means *green point* in French. I always thought the French gave it that name because there's so much greenery on the land. But now that I know you have business there, I wonder if the place is named for you."

Michael's chest puffed up in pride. "It's named after my family. We've been fishing there since many years before the French turned Newfoundland over to England in 1715."

"I'm surprised to hear that. The king made it illegal to own land in Newfoundland. How can you possibly still be there after all this time?"

"We ignored His Majesty. We refused to abandon our fishing rooms out there on his say-so and have been squatting there ever since. As long as we filled our fishing quota, the governor and the admiralty just looked the other way. Besides, we aren't the only ones doing it. Look around at all the other fishing villages. Illegal squatting is going on everywhere. No one is stopping it."

"That can't go on forever. Surely someone will come along soon and evict you."

"I'm fixing that problem right now. Luckily, the laws are changing. I intend to stake my claim and buy permanent rights to it. I just sold my ship, and I'm going to use the money as a down payment on the purchase of land in the Point Verde area near Placentia. The family has planned this ever since we sold our American properties in Boston. We left there as soon as they started that war for American independence. God save the king!"

A wave swamped over the railing, drenching the men and turning their thoughts back to the storm.

"I better go check on the wife," John said. "She's not used to such rough weather." He disappeared into the darkness.

Michael remained on deck. The wind and sea pounded the vessel. As the storm picked up, Michael contemplated the ship beneath his feet. Owned by his friend Captain John Bell, the *Commerce* was a beautiful and sturdy 365-ton, 16-gun, copper-bottomed sailing vessel with a complement of 121 seamen and a few passengers. Like Michael's old ship, the *Commerce* engaged in the Triangle Trade, sailing between Jamaica, Newfoundland, and Liverpool, England. Today it carried a load of dry goods, sugar, molasses, rum, and livestock destined for sale in Placentia.

Michael stood cold and wet at the ship's rail, staring in the dark. He couldn't see anything, but he smelled land on the port side. He clung to the rail as the ship tossed back and forth from the waves.

If the ship had guidance from a lighthouse, everyone would feel safer knowing the ship's heading, he thought. Lighthouses on the English Channel were common, and Michael had grown to appreciate them when he sailed those waters. No lighthouses existed on this part of the Newfoundland coast.

He prowled the deck. If only he could be of some use to the captain and crew! Being a passenger, Michael had no job to perform, nothing to do which would assist the crew in this maddening storm. His only option left him praying that Captain Bell would make good decisions and that the crew could hold fast.

The storm raged into the night, continuing to beat savagely upon the *Commerce.* Hours later, the ship suddenly lurched sideways in a way much differently than it had been doing—a way no wave could ever achieve. Immediately after came the dreaded call, "Man overboard!"

Then many voices screamed out in a cacophony of disasters. "We've hit rocks!" "He disappeared!" "There's a hole in the hull!" "The ship's beached on the rocks!" "We're taking on water!"

Pandemonium broke out among the crew. They raced this way and that and back again, not seeming to know what to attend to first. The storm continued its fury and the ship now listed sideways at a steep angle. Waves washed over the low side, causing the vessel to lurch.

A broken mast had strewn rigging about the deck, and Michael navigated the ropes as he raced forward to take stock of the situation. One third of the aft section ripped into splinters on the port side. The vessel lay hopelessly grounded on a rocky outcrop jutting up from the end of a strip of land. It rapidly took on water, and the violent surf beat the remainder of the ship against the crags.

"Abandon ship! Abandon ship!" The crew spread the captain's call throughout the ship. Michael quickly jumped off the deck onto the treacherous rocks below. Up and down the side of the ship, other passengers did the same, followed by the crew. They helped each other cross the ragged rocks amidst the crashing waves and wind to the nearby shore.

Michael had made it halfway across when a gust of wind knocked him off his feet and onto his left side. "Ouch!" For a moment stars swam before his eyes so he couldn't tell which way was up and his brain seemed filled with cotton.

"Here, let me give you a hand." A deep, friendly voice broke through the fuzziness. A warm grip under his elbow helped him to his feet and stayed until he could stand steady on his own. By the time the stars stopped swirling, the man had gone and Michael didn't know whom to thank.

The crew and passengers gathered and huddled in misery on the rocky beach at the base of a cliff bordering the shore. Rain and wind kept them company. Noise from the storm made it impossible to talk; besides, most of them remained in too much shock for conversation. Poor visibility from both the darkness and the rain ruled out the idea of seeking shelter. Michael and the others waited out the long stormy night for what seemed like an eternity.

The storm ended along with the night. As dawn

broke, the captain reached into his pocket and pulled out a sheet of paper.

"Roll call," he announced, and then called the names of each passenger, followed by the crew.

"Impressive," Michael said to the man standing near him. "Only a great captain would remember to bring the passenger list in all that chaos."

The roll call accounted for all the passengers and every crew member except one—the seaman who first fell overboard. The angry sea claimed his life. It also took most of the cargo. All that remained of the ship itself were a few pieces of lumber and debris floating around the rocks.

Little by little, the shock wore off and the survivors started to look after one another. Michael walked around the rocky beach looking for ways to lend a hand. He found John with his wife and daughter. They sat together on the pebble beach, leaning against the cliff. The women shivered despite John's coat draped over them.

"Good morning, friends. Mrs. Corbin, I hope you and Emma are unharmed?"

Mrs. Corbin lamented, "Oh, it's been a terrible night. Emma and I were frightened out of our wits. We're cold and wet, and all of our clothes and nice things are gone."

Emma added, "I'm fine. I think I sprained my ankle jumping off the ship, but it's not too bad."

"Ladies, have no fear," Michael said. "We're not far from the mainland, and we're very near the shipping lanes. Help will come quickly, and in no time you'll forget all these sad thoughts."

Mrs. Corbin seemed determined to remain

disconsolate. "In Jamaica, I bought beautiful handmade lace and colorful shawls. I intended to give them as gifts to family in Placentia."

"It's only material goods. Praise God, you and John and Emma are alive, and you'll all get home. Focus on that, and your other worries will go away, I promise you."

Then he turned to John. "Walk with me a bit." Once out of the ladies' hearing, he said, "This shipwreck should never have happened. The storm was a bad one, but navigating in the dark is what gave birth to the disaster. A lighthouse on the coast would've given Captain Bell a beacon to follow, and he surely would've missed the reef we grounded upon. I have experience with lighthouses on the English coast. They're invaluable. We need to tell the governor about this and beg him to make plans for a lighthouse system."

"That's a good idea, Green. I encourage you to do so. But right now, the more urgent order of business is survival and rescue. Let's find Bell and see what his plan is."

Others had the same idea. Several men gathered around the captain.

"This bit of land is approximately a thousand meters long and a thousand meters wide," Captain Bell told them. "There's little food to scavenge and no obvious shelter. We can make use of a few dozen trees and some shrubs in the center of the island, but that's it. I did see a pig in the shrubs—it must have managed to swim here from the ship. Catching it will be a priority, as it may be our only food source. But there are a few crates trapped in the rocks, and we need to bring in every one. Some may contain things we can use. If nothing else, the wood itself can help fuel a fire. The good news is that we're near the seagoing lanes. Someone will find us soon."

The men divided into teams and the captain assigned them to various tasks. Some men gathered driftwood to build a signal fire. The effort took quite a while due to the lack of dry wood and fire-making materials; but man's ingenuity and perseverance won out and they finally built a smoky fire visible for many kilometers.

Some men worked away at trees and shrubs to gather enough material to build small shelters from the weather. Others scoured the island for food and water, or salvaged crates. Michael and John volunteered to round up the pig.

They set out for the brushy area of the island. Rustling and grunting gave away the animal's location right away. *This will be easy*, Michael thought. The two men cornered the hog between some rocky outcrops and started to close in on the animal.

"You cover the beast on the right. I'll take the left side," Michael instructed.

John whispered, "Move slowly...slowly... that's it. We got him!"

They crept within a meter of the huge pig. Just as they leapt toward the animal, it unexpectedly charged right at them. Michael never knew pigs could run so fast.

"Watch it, now, watch it," he shouted. The hog shot out like a bullet and bowled them both over. They looked at each other with surprise and began roaring with laughter.

Michael and John chased the hog further down

the beach and cornered it once again. This time the hog stood with his back against a small cliff with nowhere to go. The men knew the pig was theirs.

"He won't get away with it this time," said Michael.

"I'm not too sure. He's awful big and fast."

Again they whispered and slowly inched their way to a position surrounding the beast. The pig let out a big yelp and, to the surprise of the hunters, jumped high off the ground and hurled its big body against their chests, knocking both men down hard onto the sandy beach. This time it hurt.

"Okay, pig. Fun's over. I ain't laughing now," Michael said darkly.

After several repeated bowling tournaments, which the pig always won, John and Michael fashioned a snare and used wild berries as bait to lure the pig into the trap. It took two days to finally capture the ornery animal, and not a minute too soon.

The castaways languished in hunger. Now they added rations of roast pig to the meager portions of shellfish and berries they'd been surviving on. They found a freshwater spring not far from the site of the shipwreck.

Having attained reasonable comfort, boredom became the main theme on the island, with very little resources for the fight against it. Some created a game similar to horseshoes to pass the time away. Instead of horseshoes, they threw big rocks toward a sand target on the beach, giving points for the closest rock. One sailor broke out a harmonica while others sang along. Despite these weak attempts at distraction, most of the survivors moped about in depression at the thought of their plight.

On the eighth and last day, a passing ship named *The Two Friends* spotted their fire. Even though they suffered with exhaustion from their experience, every castaway on the island danced with elation and joy at the sight of the ship.

In short order, everyone boarded the rescue ship. *The Two Friends* carried 250 French prisoners for transport from Canada to their home country. It took a detour and immediately transported the rescued passengers to Placentia.

Michael Green celebrated his homecoming. He could now purchase the land his family for generations had occupied in Point Verde.

Chapter 1

A Fishing Family

1927

"Hannah, I need you. Get your little brothers dressed, please."

Hannah heard the baby crying in the other room and sighed her agreement. She'd never complain to Mother—dear Mother worked too hard, taking care of all twelve members of the family—but it wasn't fair that she, at only nine years old, had to work harder than thirteen-year-old Madge.

Lazy Madge. Wish we could trade her for a maid. As soon as the thought crossed her mind, Hannah tried to snatch it back. She wouldn't really trade any of her family. She just wanted Madge to do her fair share.

"Gus and Freddie, let's play a game to get you ready. We'll pretend that Gus is a maid helping Freddie. Then Freddie will be the maid helping Gus."

"What's a maid?" the boys wanted to know.

Hannah told them all about how rich people have maids and other servants to help them get dressed, and do their chores, and serve their meals, and everything.

The three of them entered a kitchen warm with the aroma of fresh bread and coffee. Mother brought baby Angie from her nursing and handed her to Hannah to burp while she entertained Gus and Freddie, then started slicing loaves of bread. Madge sat idly at the table, licking a spoon of molasses.

"I thought your stomach hurt," Hannah couldn't help saying. She hadn't heard Madge say anything about her stomach this morning, but her sister often used that excuse to get out of work.

"Molasses helps it feel better," Madge replied, without the least hint of guile.

"You'll never get a husband if you don't learn to keep house."

"What does a little girl like you know about getting husbands?"

"More than—"

"Girls." The one word from Mother closed the mouth of both Hannah and Madge.

Hannah's sisters Monica and Bridie brought in the milk and eggs from the farmyard. Monica poured the milk into the churn and began the laborious process of butter churning, while Bridie took out a skillet and prepared to cook the eggs for breakfast.

Hannah loved this time of day, when most of the family gathered together and weren't yet all tuckered out, and Grandma Murphy hadn't come down. Grandma Murphy was Father's mother, and a most disagreeable old woman. Mother treated her kindly and made the children act gentle and sweet to her, too. Grandma Murphy's beady eyes and perpetual scowl made Hannah nervous. She shivered. *Ugh!* She'd think about something else.

Father was out fishing, of course; he left in darkest part of morning that comes before dawn to get out to sea before the sun rose. And Mary, her oldest sister, worked in town and only came home on weekends. But Leonard should be there.

"Where's Lennie?" Hannah asked, and just then he burst in the door with a grin as big as a crescent moon, carrying something wrapped in brown paper.

"Guess what?" he asked the room, then answered before anyone could. "I just helped Uncle Will slaughter a pig, and in exchange he gave me half a pork leg and a slab of fatback." He winked at Hannah. "You'll get the biggest piece, dearest sister. I'll make sure of it, and then you'll forgive me for that Christmas, won't you?"

Hannah smiled. "It's not quite enough, Lennie. You'll need to do more."

"What C'istmas?" Gus asked.

"I've told you that story. The Christmas Lennie played a very mean prank on me." They called it a prank although it had not been done in jest.

"I don't 'member. Tell me again."

"When I was only your age—" Hannah began.

"Free?"

"Yes, three. When I was only three, I got an orange for Christmas."

"All for your own?" asked Freddie.

"All for my very own. Have you ever had an orange?"

"I had a piece at Peter Greene's party."

"That's right. So you know how good they are. Well, so I got an orange for Christmas, all for my very own, when I was three years old. Lennie was six. I wanted my orange to last and not be over right away, so I put it under my pillow. Then I went to listen to Mother read the Christmas story from the Bible. When she finished, I went back to taste one piece of orange. But... guess what? It was all gone!"

"Like Goldilocks!"

Hannah giggled. "Well, really like the baby bear. But it wasn't a curly-haired girl that ate my orange up; it was a boy. A boy named Lennie! He was still standing there with juice running down his chin."

"Now, Hannah, someday I'm going to make it up to you." A slight catch in Lennie's voice gave away his fondness for his sister.

She smiled lovingly at him once again. "I'm waiting. So where's that pork? I'm hungry." If they had breakfast on the table soon, perhaps they could eat before Grandmother Murphy came down to darken the mood.

Soon the rashers of cooking fatback sent a delicious aroma throughout the kitchen, combining with the scent of fresh bread and coffee. Hannah set the table with a growling stomach. Soon she and her siblings sat with Mother at the table. Before they ate, Mother thanked God for the bread, eggs, molasses, milk, and pork they had to eat that morning.

Breakfast had mostly disappeared by the time Grandma Murphy came downstairs. She complained about being left out, and demanded that Hannah bring her toast and tea.

While Hannah prepared the requested items, Mother and the older girls cleared the table and washed the dishes. Then Mother laid out the chores for the day.

"Monica, you and Madge do the laundry. Madge, you do your share. Bridie can clean house. The garden will be Leonard's responsibility. Hannah, please keep an eye on Angie and the little boys."

The other children disappeared to their chores, but Hannah followed Mother outside. She set the little boys to a game so she could watch Mother make fish.

Mother stopped at the well and filled two big pails with water. She lugged those down to the salt pond into the family's little shed known as a fish room. Inside, barrels and bins held all the fish Father caught all season. The fish he caught yesterday were in a special bin. Mother started her work with those.

She reached into the bin and took out a codfish. With water from the pails, she washed it well, then set it on the end of a table and sprinkled it with salt. Then she reached into the bin and took out the next piece, which received the same treatment. She piled all the clean and salted fish one on top of the other. They would sit there until tomorrow.

Now Mother turned to the pile of fish on the other end of the table. She had washed and salted those yesterday. Today they were ready to go outside on the flake. Father had built the flake from a bunch of tree limbs tied together, like a raft but with more room between them. It stood outside the fish room next to the water.

Mother laid yesterday's fish out on the flake where the sun and air would dry them.

The other women in the village of Point Verde had flakes at the pond, too. All around, Mother's cousins, neighbors, and sisters stood at their own flakes laying their fish out, just like Mother was doing. They all talked and joked and told wild stories and laughed with each other as they put out the heavy cod.

Then Mother went back in the fish room and took all the fish out of the barrel and bins and put them on the flake, too. If there were too many fish to fit on the flake, Mother hung the extras on the clothesline. She made sure it didn't touch any laundry, though.

Every morning, Mother put all the codfish in the fish room out on the flake to dry. Each piece of fish had to dry on the flake several days to remove every last drop of water from it. If the fish got left out overnight, it might get wet and spoil. So every evening, Mother had to lug it all back into the fish room.

With all the fish stowed away for the night, Mother grabbed the pails of tongues and britches and headed back to the house to make supper for her husband and family.

~#~

After supper Father went outside. When he returned, he brought in his whetstone and his fishing knife and hooks. He sat at the table and pulled the knife across the whetstone over and over again, until it was razor sharp. Then he sharpened the hooks the same way.

When he was finished, Leonard said, "Can I sharpen a knife? I want to try."

"Wish you'd said so before," Father answered. "You could've sharpened mine, saved me the effort."

"It ain't hard, is it?" Lennie said.

"No, it's not hard. But I'm tired."

"What's so tiring about fishing? You just sit in a boat all day."

Father's face flickered between disbelief and anger. Disbelief finally won out. "Just sitting in a boat all day? Is that what you think? It's time for you to go out and start learning what cod fishing's all about."

"What is it about?" Hannah asked. She'd never thought to wonder exactly what Father did out there on the sea every day.

Father looked around. All the faces were watching him expectantly.

"Well, the first thing it's about is getting up early. You gotta be at the fishing spot as dawn breaks—that's when you get the most fish. So you get up real early and have a cup of tea, then put on your oil slickers so you don't get too wet, and gather your tools."

"Like that knife and hooks?" Bridie asked.

"Yeah, those. Plus the line, bait bucket, and pail. Don't forget the hard tack to gnaw on later; that's all you'll get to eat all day. Put it all in the dory, then get to rowing. It'll take about an hour of rowing to get to where the cod swim."

He looked at Leonard. "Think you can row for an hour straight?"

Leonard grimaced and shook his head. "I'm pretty strong, but don't reckon I could."

"Then does it get easier?" Hannah asked.

"Well, then you get to stop rowing, but you gotta start jigging. So you put a weight and two hooks on the line, put bait fish on the hooks, and toss it all over the side of the boat. You hold onto the end of it and jig it up and down, up and down, until something tries to eat the bait and gets hooked."

"How do you know when a fish is hooked?" Lennie asked.

"Oh, you can feel it. You know how big cod can

be—a meter long, and weigh forty kilograms. When that chomps on your line, it don't jig easy anymore."

"So what do you do?" Hannah asked.

"You pull up the line, hand over hand, hand over hand, with all that weight pulling the opposite way. It's back-breaking work. And when you finally get the fish up and pulled into the boat, you start the process all over again. You can't take a break, or you might not get enough fish to feed your children or pay your bills."

"There's got to be an easier way," Madge said, at the exact same time that Leonard asked, "How does the fish pay bills?"

Father looked at Madge first. "I wish to God there was. That's the way my father fished, and his father before him, and back 300 years. If there was an easier way, they'd have found it."

Then he looked at Lennie. "You understand business better'n most, so I'll tell you. At the start of the season, a fisherman has to borrow supplies for the year, plus the things the family needs, like flour and seeds for Mother's garden and cloth for clothes. At the end of the season, you take the dried fish to the merchant and sell it. You just hope you caught enough to pay for all the things you borrowed; otherwise you end up in the hole."

"What happens if you get in the hole?" Leonard asked.

"Well, it partly depends on the merchant. If he knows you and likes you, he might give you more time to pay him back. If not, you have to come up with the money somewhere else. But you can't borrow more until you pay back what you already owe. That means no new supplies for the next season, and no flour or cloth either."

No one spoke for a few moments, then Father added, "And that's if the merchant is honest. If he ain't, he might have crooked scales. Then you never get out of the hole. A good fisherman has to know what he caught, so he can't be cheated. Hard for a fisherman to ever get ahead."

"What about the planters?" Lennie said. "They don't work like that—they have people to do it for them. How do you get to be one of those?"

Father humphed. "You gotta own enough land and boats to run a planter's operation. None of our kin has enough land or money to work like that," he said. "Our ancestors did, but that was long ago and they had too many kids. The land was divided among all the children, then the next generation did the same, and so on. Now none of us has enough land to build a room that would handle much fish, nor enough money to hire anybody."

Everyone remained silent again, until Mother spoke. "None of that is the worst part."

Monica asked what all of them wondered. "What's worse?"

"The weather, and the sea itself. Besides a hard living, it's a dangerous one."

Hannah sighed. *Poor Father. A fisherman sure has a lot against him. No wonder they're always poor.*

Chapter 2

Plans

Hannah twiddled her pencil. How was she supposed to concentrate on arithmetic with the other kids making all that racket only meters away? They all finished their homework some time ago, then got together with a deck of cards. Even Mother joined them, helping little Gus learn the game. Now they laughed and teased each other, while Hannah was stuck trying to finish this boring math page.

"Tomorrow I'm going to get right to my homework, instead of drawing a picture first," she muttered to herself. "Then I'll get to play with them."

"In my day we always put work first," Grandma Murphy squawked from her rocking chair in the corner.

Hannah ignored her. *How'd she hear me, anyway? From now on I'm keeping my thoughts to myself.*

Grandma Murphy continued to scold and complain between slurps from her ever-present cup of tea. Just what Hannah needed. More noise to distract her. No one else seemed to notice the old woman's ramblings. Hannah leaned her head on her hand, covering one ear.

"I win!" Madge suddenly shouted.

The other children started to protest, but Mother spoke over them. "Okay, that's enough for now. It's time to set the table."

The kids scrambled to collect their books and tablets from the table. Hannah slammed her arithmetic book shut and gathered it with the rest of her things to take to her room. Then she helped Madge set out the bowls, plates, napkins, and silverware. It was Madge's turn, but if left to do it herself, she'd take forever. Hannah's rumbling stomach urged her to help get the job done.

Meanwhile, Mother sliced a fresh loaf of bread. "Leonard, run see if there's a couple onions ready," she said. "We'll have them sliced on the side if you can find one or two." He ran to the garden.

Monica filled the water glasses and Bridie carried them to the table. Mother put out the bread and a bit of butter. She left the fish and brewis in the oven. No one liked cold fish mush so that dish would stay put, keeping warm, until time to serve it.

The kitchen door flew open just as Hannah set the last knife and fork in place. Father came in, heavy and sagging. His deeply furrowed forehead and sad expression showed his worry.

Hannah knew why. She worried too. The whole village suffered from hard times and Father had twelve mouths to feed. Meals were sparse and luxuries unheard of. Everyone in the house wore hand-me-downs; Hannah's dress had been made from the patterned fabric of flour sacks for Monica. It became Bridie's when Monica outgrew it, then finally Hannah's.

The Greenes weren't alone. Everyone Hannah knew talked about the hard times. Especially for fishing families. Why did her family have to rely on fish? She guessed they'd always be poor.

Shame! Father works hard. Don't blame him for the

times, she chided herself. She stepped forward to give him a welcome-home hug. His eyes shone at her with love and Hannah felt it flow into her, into the entire room. She squeezed him long and hard. Hard times were unimportant at moments like this.

When he'd hugged all the children, Father turned to Mother and gave her a kiss.

"Louise, that dish smells like heaven." Father loved the mush of blended hard tack, fatback, and codfish. Hannah hated the poor man's meal. So did her siblings. But if they didn't eat what Mother put on the table, they wouldn't eat at all.

Mother smiled and turned to lift the pot from the stove. "Sit down to table, Joe."

"Don't be daft, Louise. I smell awful bad, like dead fish."

"We don't care about that, Father. We're just happy to have you home," Hannah said. Many fishermen went out in the morning and never came back. *That won't happen to Father. He knows how to handle his boat.* Still, she knew she wasn't the only one who breathed a little sigh of relief every time he walked in at the end of the day.

"You're some sweet, little Hannah," Father said as everyone found a place at the table. He said grace, then continued, "Tell me, daughter, how was school today?"

Mother spoke before Hannah could. "That scalawag ripped her dress again today. I'll be spending my evening mending her only dress so she can go back tomorrow." Hannah knew by her playful tone that Mother wasn't really angry. Hannah couldn't help it that the hand-me-down dress she wore was getting scragglier and scragglier. Besides, Mother's skill with needle and thread meant she'd have the sewing completed in minutes.

Mother dished up the mush as Hannah explained. "I couldn't help it. At lunchtime that rascal boy Soggy Greene grabbed my lunch pail before I could stop him. I chased after him through the woods and a branch hooked my dress. Soggy got away and ate all my lunch. I really hate that boy."

"Soggy Greene, eh?" Father blew on a spoon of mush. Not until he'd swallowed it did he continue. "That family's had a rough go of it since their father drowned last year. Widow Greene has too many mouths to feed and no way to earn. He's probably half starved. You need to be more charitable to that young fella, sweet child. God wouldn't want you to hate him."

He looked at Mother. "Think I'll stop by there Monday morning before I head out to sea. Maybe chop some wood for her. Winter comes fast."

Mother patted his hand. "You're a good man, Joe Greene."

Father folded a slice of onion into a piece of bread. "Why do you kids call him Soggy, anyway?"

"That's just how he looks," Leonard answered. "His clothes are so ragged, and don't even fit. He came to school with a safety pin holding his fly closed 'cause the zipper was busted, and somebody said he looked soggy. Ever since then, that's what he's called."

"I want all you children to be kinder to that boy," Mother said.

They agreed, then the table became noisy as the children pattered about this and that. Mother and Father ate quietly, smiling often. Grandma Murphy spooned mush into her mouth as fast as she could swallow it, smacking after each bite. At least she couldn't complain while she was that busy eating.

After supper Hannah finished her homework while Monica and Madge helped Mother clean up and wash and dry the dishes. The rest of the children got ready for bed. Grandma Murphy went to her room, and Father snoozed in his chair.

The last dishes were put away by candlelight. "Everyone into bed quickly now," Mother said. "We're low on candles, so put them out as fast as you can."

Hannah slipped out of her dress and handed it to Mother to mend. She pulled on a nightgown and climbed into bed with her sisters. All three girls slept in one bed. When Mary came home to visit, there were four piled into it. Hannah's three brothers shared another bed.

Bridie blew out the candle, but the sisters didn't go to sleep right away. They always gossiped and giggled for a while first.

Suddenly Mother's voice carried through the wall. "Boston!"

Hannah looked at her sisters, and they looked at her and at each other. Why was mother yelling about Boston? They stopped talking so they could hear what Father and Mother said.

"I can't sit by and let my children starve," Father said. "We're leaving Newfoundland. I'm taking a job building boats with my cousin Leonard in Boston. It's all set."

Mother's voice became more angry than surprised. "Joe Greene, you are not dragging me away from my mother and family. I won't have it. Who are you to decide? You're not the king!"

"I am the man of this house and you will do as I say. I cannot let my family starve."

"Since when does the wife have no say? We've always made big decisions together. You have no right to take me away from my family." Her voice got smaller. "You plan on taking me to some strange and foreign place without giving me a say-so. Joe, I can't do this. I'm too scared."

Hannah couldn't make out what Father said next, but the tone sounded comforting—or maybe pleading.

"Get away from me." Mother's voice grew loud again. "I want nothing to do with you. You are not sleeping in this bed tonight, Joe Greene. Get out of my sight. Get out, get out, get out!"

Hannah gasped. The door to her parents' room opened, then closed. Father's footsteps went down the steps. Hannah pulled the covers over her head. She didn't want to talk to her sisters anymore. They must have felt the same way. No one said anything.

Hannah lay awake long after her sisters fell asleep. She heard Father tossing and turning on the kitchen floor downstairs. It couldn't possibly be comfortable, even with blankets.

Surely Father knew the right way. Hannah thought hard about their predicament. *Fishing will never take care of our big family. We need a way out.* The idea of leaving Newfoundland for a foreign place felt scary, but it seemed exciting as well. She'd heard so much about America. The very idea of the place seemed magical and promising.

At the breakfast table Father and Mother looked tired and haggard. They resumed the conversation about America, although this time, in front of Hannah and the family, they talked in a more civilized fashion.

Louise looked hard at Joe. "I'm going to visit Mother today and ask for her help. She'll have an answer."

"Louise, I will not take charity from your family. As man of the house, I will solve this problem."

"I'm not going to ask for charity. What do you take me for? Mother's a smart woman, and she has resources far beyond our little village. I know she'll have an idea. And Joe Greene, I'm telling you: you are not dragging me to Boston."

After breakfast everyone got ready for church, as they did almost every Sunday. Father hooked up the horse and wagon and the family headed to Placentia, the next town over. Grandma hated the long ride so she stayed home. This morning Mother left baby Angie with her. "I need to focus on the conversation with my mother."

The ride took close to an hour. Hannah's brothers and sisters sat in the back of the wagon, laughing and telling stories all the way. She sat on the plank seat between mother and father, enjoying the pleasant journey over winding roads past an isolated farmhouse or two. Usually she took the opportunity to talk to her parents, but this would be one of the last nice drives. Even if they didn't head to Boston right away, the weather would soon change. Winter would be frigid, with lots of snow and ice. When the snow got deep, a sleigh would be the only way to get to town. The trip to Placentia would be rare and uncomfortable for several months.

When they came to the place where the woods

spread close to the edge of the road, Hannah snuggled closer to Mother. She didn't like this place. The trees grew so close together that little light got in. Girls could easily get lost there.

Father and her uncles said fairies lived in the woods. The fairies didn't like people coming near and would haunt and terrorize anyone who got too close. What if one touched her? People said Uncle Ned had been touched by the fairies and that's why he was off in the head. So far she'd been lucky and never even seen one of the creatures. She wanted to keep it that way.

A tree branch brushed close to the roadside. Hannah shivered. She closed her eyes and prayed to the Sacred Heart of Jesus to protect her and her family.

Hannah knew all about the Sacred Heart. She learned about it at church—the Sacred Heart Catholic Church. She loved her little church. When she walked in, she felt protected.

Sacred Heart sat in the heart of Old Placentia and it was a beautiful place. A church had stood at that site for hundreds of years—since Placentia stood as the capital of the French Colony of Newfoundland. The French left long ago but the deep history made the little village an important place on the island, even after the English turned St John's into their capital.

Sacred Heart Church was not the only church in town. Another one stood nearby that served the Anglican faith. It seemed a lot smaller, although Hannah couldn't say for sure because, as a good Catholic girl, she did what the nuns in Sunday school taught her. They said she committed a grave sin if she set eyes on that heathen church. So Hannah took different streets and stayed away from the lane where the Anglican

Church stood. That way she wouldn't accidently look upon what the nuns said was a cursed place.

The nuns also forbade associating with any of those unbelieving Anglicans, for surely their ways would lead you astray with all their heresy. Luckily, everyone in her little village of Point Verde was Catholic, so even at school she didn't break the rule.

Today promised to be a beautiful day. Mother said Hannah could go with her to visit Grandmother Maggie Flynn. Everyone loved Grandmother Flynn. She was a sweet, refined, and educated lady. She came from "good stock" and had many stories about the deeds of her well-connected family.

After church, Father took the rest of the children to visit his brother's family while Hannah and Mother walked home with Grandmother Flynn and Mary. Hannah's oldest sister lived with Grandmother and Hannah looked forward to catching up with her.

"I'll get the tea," Mary said when they arrived at Grandmother's cottage. She disappeared into the kitchen. After some debate with herself, Hannah decided to stay in the parlour and listen to Mother and Grandmother's gossip instead of going to the kitchen with Mary. She could visit with her sister after tea.

The ladies talked about the latest comedies and tragedies of various cousins and other family members. Clinking of dishes drifted in from the kitchen. Soon Mary brought in a tray filled with tea, rice pudding, and date squares. She served Mother first, then Hannah, since they were considered company. Then she served Grandmother, and finally herself.

"Mother, the desserts are delicious. I'm so glad you thought of us," Hannah's mother said.

"I would never let you and Hannah visit without having something special."

"Give me some credit; I'm the one who made them." Mary's playful voice wasn't really insulted.

"Yes, chile. And you did a marvelous job," Grandmother replied.

"You're a young lady now," Mother added. "Practically grown up. I'm proud of you."

"Grown up enough for a boyfriend," Hannah said. "I heard about you and somebody named Jack."

"Jack?" Mother perked up. "Who's this?"

Mary smiled. "Jack Stapleton. He's from Marystown. He's really sweet and so good to me. I think he may be the one."

Mother's brows drew together. "It's surely too soon to say that, dear. You shouldn't fall head over heals with someone you just met."

"It's been longer than you think. We've been together now for almost six months. I met him when Mrs. O'Reilly took me with her on that train trip to St. John's to go shopping." Mrs. O'Reilly was the magistrate's wife. Mary worked as her lady's maid.

Hannah quickly swallowed a bite of date bar to ask, "Is he handsome? Tell us more!"

"He's more than handsome, and he has a great job. He's the conductor for the railroad. Now every time the train arrives in town, the two of us escape for a couple hours until he has to return."

"Why are we just now hearing about him?"

"I wanted to make sure he was serious first. Besides, when would I tell you? I hardly see you except at church these days, and that's hardly the place to discuss such things."

Mother had no answer to that, so she just said, "Well, I hope you don't get too serious with him too fast. But Joe will be here soon to pick us up, so I better get to the point."

Hannah and Mary enjoyed more pudding and bars as they listened to Mother tell Grandmother the details of the calamity facing the family because Father intended to move them all to America. "It's true he can't support the lot of us fishing, and Leonard won't be able to help him for too many years yet," she concluded. "But I don't want to go to America and leave you and all our friends and our home."

"I'd go. If you move to America, I'll quit my job and go with you," Mary said.

Mother stared at her. "Why on earth would you want to move all the way to America?"

Hannah asked, "You'd leave Jack?"

"It sounds like a lovely place to live. Your own sisters say so," Mary said to Mother. "Every time Aunt Rita or Aunt Angela write, their letters are full of things we could never have here." She tossed her head. "Aunt Rita has even offered to put me up in her little apartment in New York."

Mary looked at Hannah. "And no, I wouldn't have to leave Jack. He has family in America, too, and they tell him terrific stories of life over there. He'd like to live there as much as me."

"Heavens no, Mary," Mother exclaimed. She looked ready to go on but Grandmother interrupted.

"Let's take one thing at a time, Louise. Mary and Jack aren't even engaged. Right now we have enough to deal with, what with Joe's problem."

She looked thoughtful a moment, then said, "Don't

worry, child," Grandmother said. "You know my uncle Thomas has power as the archbishop. I'll telegram him first thing tomorrow. I'm sure there will be something."

"I can't imagine what. Joe doesn't know anything but fishing."

"Uncle Tom will never let family down. Besides, on his visit last summer he said I was his favorite niece. He'll find a good government job. Now, tell me about..."

They gossiped about neighbors and relatives. Hannah ate several more date squares and talked quietly with Mary. All too soon Father showed up outside with the wagon.

~#~

Five days later Grandmother pulled up. Before she'd even stepped down from the buggy she started calling, "Louise, Louise! Wonderful news!"

Hannah ran after Mother to meet Grandmother. "What is it?"

As they walked into the house, Grandmother said, "Uncle Tom came through. His cousin Eddie is the Director of the Royal Commission on Lighthouse Administration, and there's an opening at Point Verde Lighthouse. He's giving Joe the lighthouse job right here in Point Verde."

"Praise God, a government job! Joe is sure to like that."

Grandmother sat at the table and gave all the details. Mother and the children gathered around and hung onto every word. Even Grandma Murphy was quiet, listening. "The lighthouse has large living quarters. Larger than this house. And there won't be any rent—it comes with the job."

Mother's smile widened. "Wonderful. Maybe we can rent out this house for extra income."

"The government will also supply some free food, and the rest you can buy from them at wholesale discount. It comes with a barn and two milk cows, many chickens and several pigs."

"Two cows! And pigs—we'll live like royalty. And I know that place has a big plot of land suitable for a vegetable garden."

"It doesn't end there," Grandmother continued. "Joe will get a regular salary. He'll earn twice what he could make with fishing all year."

"We'll be rich!" Madge exclaimed.

"Maybe I can get a new dress," Hannah said to her sisters. She wrinkled her nose as she looked at her much mended, handed down, flour-sack dress. The girls and boys started talking about all the things they wanted to buy with their riches.

"By all measure, the family will be rich," Mother said. "But best of all, worth more than any money, Joe will work on the safe land and not face the daily dangers of fishing at sea."

"There is one drawback," Grandmother said. Everyone went silent. What downside could there possibly be?

"You will be isolated out there. The lighthouse is the only residence on the peninsula. Eddie told Uncle Tom it could take close to an hour to walk to town, and that's if the weather's good. Joe will have to drive the children to school most days. Their friends and cousins won't be close enough to drop by. The lot of you could get lonely."

"No friends?"

"How will I ever find a boyfriend?"

"Who will I trade stuff with?"

Hannah joined her brothers' and sisters' exclamations, but instead of a complaint she had a hope. "Maybe we won't have to go to school every day, if Father can't take us."

"Our friends and relatives will still be a lot closer than they'd be if we moved to America," Mother said. "That's a small price to pay for all we'll be getting in return."

"I'd better go," Grandmother said. "I want to get home before dark."

After Mother saw Grandmother off, she came back in and led the children in a prayer of thanks to God for providing for them. She hummed as she started supper.

When Father came in, everyone started talking at once.

"Wait, stop—I can't hear you all at once. Hush, children. Louise, what is this?"

Mother told him all the good things Grandmother said about the job, while the children took turns interrupting with comments about the distance from town and not seeing their friends and cousins.

Father acted as happy as Mother about the job. Finally, he said, "I know what you children need. A send-off party. We'll have a good old-fashioned kitchen party!"

Shouts of joy met this announcement.

"What a wonderful idea," Mother agreed. "I'll

clean out the root cellar and cook it all to make the biggest scoff Point Verde's seen in many a year!"

"Will you make lad in the bag with molasses coady?" Hannah asked. She hadn't had her favorite treat in ever so long.

"Yes, indeed. And salt beef with cabbage, and mashed turnips, and peas pudding, and who knows what else."

Chapter 3

Kitchen Party

The night of the party soon came. They expected the entire village. Mother had the family move all the furniture except the dining table and chairs outside. Those she set up around the main room, against the walls. She laid out all the food she cooked on the table.

Father borrowed a punch bowl from a neighbor and made a big batch of partridgeberry juice. He added a little of his own homemade moonshine. He only put a bit because each guest would add their own, too. Tradition told them that by night's end the bowl would contain almost pure alcohol, with only a bit of berry flavor.

That evening neighbors filled the kitchen. Ladies brought additional baked goodies and fixings until the table overflowed. Children weaved their way through the thick crowd to sneak sweet and savory treats when the stern eyes of their mothers looked the other way.

The crowd kept growing. Soon it spilled out the back door under the stars on a beautiful night. Just about every neighbor had some kind of musical talent, so they brought their instruments and began to play as the party got into full swing.

Desi and Ken Murphy started it off with fiddle and accordion. Joe Greene tapped on his bodhrán. Tiny children bounced to the music. Don Greene broke out his tin whistle. The music intensified. Brendan Flynn played mandolin. Jeff Greene strummed his guitar and someone else played harmonica. Soon a dozen musicians played.

They had no sheet music. After each song finished, someone would strike up a few bars of a tune and the rest of the group jumped in. Newfoundland music filled the house and wafted out into the yard. Even crabby Grandma Murphy stomped her feet and sang to the music.

Uncle Din and Cousin Eddie spent a lot of time at the punch bowl. Hannah knew what to expect. They never failed to step up their game after tying on a few.

"Come on, Din, let's do our thing," Eddie shouted over the noise.

"Yes, b'y. I'll see you to it!"

The band played *I'se the B'y*, a fast-paced jig, and the two men jumped into the middle of the floor. No one could step dance like Din and Eddie. Everyone in the village looked forward to the coming excitement these two men were famous for.

"Yay, Uncle Din," shouted Hannah. "Go, Eddie."

The rest of the guests, drinks in hand, shouted and encouraged the men. "Give us your best, Din. Come on, Eddie. Don't let him show you up." Everyone circled around as the dancers took the middle of the floor.

Din and Eddie danced a furiously fast foot-stomping jig and the crowd cheered and clapped. The applause encouraged the musicians to play even faster and louder. Watching the dance, Hannah couldn't decide if the men were crazed lunatics having a fit or skilled artisans whose feet moved so fast no one could follow.

Other guests joined in and started dancing on the edges of the circle, but no one ventured to the center lest they bring a woeful comparison to the work of Din and Eddie. After two songs the tousle-haired dancers breathed heavy. Din shouted to the band, "Play *Ode to Newfoundland* while we catch our breath."

The band changed tunes and Mother, who loved this song, sang the lyrics.

When sun rays crown thy pine clad hills,
And summer spreads her hand,
When silvern voices tune thy rills,
We love thee, smiling land.

The room quieted as Mother sang.

We love thee, we love thee,
We love thee, smiling land.

When she finished with,
God guard thee, God guard thee,
God guard thee, Newfoundland.
tears wet the eyes of several listeners, Hannah among them. She loved the way Newfoundland music always told a story. Many of the tunes told of life in the fishing ports. Some ballads made her cry, but others caused her to burst out laughing.

When *Ode to Newfoundland* ended, Hannah shouted, "Play *The Star of Logy Bay*." She loved that song about a couple from the town of Logy Bay—but she had an ulterior motive as well.

Guests shouted, "Louise, you have to sing this song. You make it sound so beautiful." As Hannah planned, Mother complied.

This was Hannah's chance to dance with Father. Mostly he danced with Mother, but she couldn't dance while she sang. Hannah ran to Father. "Dance with me, Father. Please." The two entered the dance floor as the waltz began.

Ye ladies and ye gentlemen, I pray you lend an ear,
While I locate the residence of a lovely charmer fair.
The curling of her yellow locks first stole my heart away,
And her place of habitation is down in Logy Bay.

There were five more verses to that sad song. Hannah hugged her father tightly. She felt small against his chest, but there was no more comfortable place in the world to be.

"Oh, Father, what a wonderful kitchen party."

"Yes, sweetie. It's a lot of fun. Our world's going to change soon. We have lots to be thankful for."

"Father, do you think we'll be lonely out there at the lighthouse?"

"How can we be lonely when we have each other?"

Hannah squeezed him tightly and thought about nothing but the beautiful waltz they danced.

No sooner did the waltz end than Eddie started singing *The Ryans and the Pittmans*, an old sailor's ditty. The band joined him.

We'll rant and we'll roar like true Newfoundlanders.
We'll rant and we'll roar on deck and below
Until we strikes bottom inside the two sunkers
When straight through the channel to Toslow we'll go.

I'm a son of a sea cook, I'm a cook and a trader.
I can dance, I can sing, I can reef the main boom.
I can handle a jigger, I cuts a fine figure
Whenever I gets in a boat's standing room.

We'll rant and we'll roar like true Newfoundlanders.
We'll rant and we'll roar on deck and below
Until we strikes bottom inside the two sunkers
When straight through the channel to Toslow we'll go.

Farewell and adieu to ye young maids of Valen,
Oderin and Presque, Fox Hole and Bruley.
I'm bound for the westward to the wall with the hole in't
I can't marry all or it's yokey I'll be.

We'll rant and we'll roar like true Newfoundlanders.
We'll rant and we'll roar on deck and below
Until we strikes bottom inside the two sunkers
When straight through the channel to Toslow we'll go.

We'll rant and we'll roar like true Newfoundlanders.
We'll rant and we'll roar on deck and below
Until we strikes bottom inside the two sunkers
When straight through the channel to Toslow we'll go.

After the dance with Father, Hannah visited with all the guests. Conversations and good jokes flowed. The music and drinking continued and she danced a few reels with her cousins and neighbors.

A little before midnight, Cousin Eddie, who was a little drunk, asked Leonard for permission to sleep in Leonard's room for the night. Even before getting an answer he began his way to the upstairs bedrooms.

A moment later, Grandma Murphy shrieked at the top of her lungs as if a murderer stood in her bedroom. The musicians stopped playing and everyone ran to the stairs. Father leaped quickly to the second floor to investigate with Hannah right behind him.

There lay Grandma, in her nightgown, face up in her small, single brass poster bed—with Cousin Eddie sprawled face to face on top of her, passed out. His dead weight pinned Grandma down, and her arms flailed about helplessly as she screamed and shrieked.

Hannah yelled down the stairs that everything was all right. She and Father—mostly Father—managed to get Eddie off Grandma and into Leonard's room. By the time she got back downstairs, the music had started again and the guests returned to their merriment.

Hannah enjoyed the party another hour or so. By then she could scarcely keep her eyes open, so she went up to her room even though the party still raged downstairs. She lay in bed wondering and worrying about their new life ahead at the lighthouse, and fell asleep fretting.

Chapter 4

The Lighthouse

Hannah woke early. "Get up, Madge and Monica. It's moving day!" She scrambled out of bed and got dressed. She brushed her hair quickly and scurried to the pail in the kitchen to wash her face.

Mother bustled around, packing last-minute things into a basket. "Have a piece of bread and butter for breakfast," she said. "You can put some jam on it. Then help the boys."

Father came in whistling. He whirled Mother around with a laugh, then grabbed the basket and carried it out to the wagon. The other girls and boys trooped into the room. For a while all was chaos, but finally Mother said they were ready.

Father helped her and Grandma into the buggy. He took baby Angie from Hannah and handed her up. The other kids climbed into the back of the wagon, finding spots among the boxes and furniture. Hannah sat next to Father on the wagon seat. Father clucked to the horses, and they began moving.

Hannah looked back at the house she'd lived in all her life. It grew smaller and smaller with each step of the horses. A sense of longing filled her, overtaking the excitement of the day. Hannah loved her old home. She had so many good times there. They rounded a curve and the house disappeared.

"Goodbye," she whispered.

She faced forward again when Father patted her knee. "Look ahead," he said cheerfully. "This is a good move. You'll soon love your new home as much as you did that one."

Look ahead. She would do just that.

In a bit they passed between two small, calm ponds. The road made a bridge of earth between them.

"Our ancestors built this land bridge," Father told her. "The early fishing settlers dropped rocks across the channel to form it. Then they filled the rocks in with enough dirt to build fishing rooms on it, and flakes for drying cod. Greenes have lived and fished in this area since the 1600s. Their little fishing rooms were the only houses until the lighthouse was built in 1878. And see how the land bridge makes a tidy little harbor? It sheltered their dories from the open sea."

Hannah felt better knowing Greenes had history out on the peninsula, too. It must still be home if family lived there.

On the other side of the land bridge, the scenery began to change. Beautiful grasslands rolled with a gentle slope.

Father swept his hand out to indicate the slopes. "That's the downs." They rounded a curve and he said, "Look ahead. What do you see?"

"The bay."

"Aye, it's Placentia Bay. What else?"

Hannah studied the expanse of water and sky before her. Sea birds soared through gorgeous blue sky decorated with puffy clouds, occasionally diving to the water as they attempted to catch their dinner. The fresh breeze blew briskly in Hannah's hair. Dotted across the bay, many dories bobbed up and down on the water.

"Fishermen," she said. "Like you. And our ancestors."

"Like I was," Father corrected. "They have hard work to make the day's catch. What do you see across the bay, there?" He gestured to the narrow side of the bay.

Hannah squinted. "I don't know. Squares of color. Maybe buildings."

"That's right. Those're the towns of Freshwater, Jerseyside, and Placentia. The bright colors are fishermen's homes. They all use different colors so each man can spot his own home while he's out on the water. Reminds him why he's working so hard."

"They work for colors? Why don't they just paint it white? Then they wouldn't have to work so hard."

Father burst out laughing. It took a minute for him to catch his breath enough to explain. "No, they're working for the families they know are in the colorful houses." He chuckled again.

"Oh."

The horses rounded another curve and climbed a low hill. The lighthouse came into view. It sat right on the edge of a cliff that dropped fifty meters down to Placentia Bay. A smaller building had been built onto its side.

"Is that our house?"

"No, that's where the generators and fog horns are kept."

"What's in those barrels?" Adjacent to the small building, a platform held huge barrels.

"Those are fuel drums. They're filled with acetylene gas that's used to power the lighthouse lamp. Stay away from them, understand? That's not a play area."

"I understand."

Thirty meters behind the lighthouse stood the house. The grounds also boasted a wooden barn topped by a water tower, a small storage shed, and a small workshop. These buildings sat in a great open space of billowing grass.

"What are those giant ropes over them for?" It looked like giant metal ropes had been tied to the ground on one side, thrown over the roof, and tied down on the other side.

"Not ropes; cables. They keep the buildings strapped down so they don't blow away. The wind here can get up to a hundred sixty kilometers an hour. If they weren't fastened down, they'd blow down the hill."

Just then a wind gusted. The cables strained and groaned with a ghostly sound that made Hannah's skin crawl.

A footpath led from the lighthouse to the residence. The path was lined with metal stakes tied to each other by heavy rope.

"What's that rope for? That one is a rope."

"Yep. That's for the lighthouse keeper to hold onto in the wind. Or if there's too much fog or rain or snow for him to see which way to go. That way he won't wander off the cliff."

Hannah shivered. She thought Father would be safe with this job, but it was dangerous, too. Just a different kind of danger than fishing in the sea.

"Why are they all painted that way?" She'd seen

white houses and red barns, but all these buildings were white with big red stripes. She'd never seen anything like that.

"The Royal Lighthouse Commission says how all lighthouses are to be painted. Each one is different, but they all have a design that makes it easy to see from ships and boats on the water. Any sailor or fisherman can tell by the design which lighthouse it is, and know where they are."

"That's smart."

"Yes, it is. Not only that, but each lighthouse has its own foghorn sequence to blow, and its own speed to turn the huge lamp that makes the light. That way, even if it's too dark or foggy to see the paint, they still know where they are. No other lighthouse in the world is just like this one."

Somehow that made Hannah proud.

The wagon pulled up next to the residence. Grandmother had said it was big, but Hannah didn't imagine anything this huge. She jumped down and ran in to explore.

The front door opened into a parlour. The first thing Hannah noticed were the lights. Bright electric lights! A door on one side of the parlour opened into a big bedroom. Off the other side was a large kitchen with a potbelly stove and roomy pantry. A stairway next to the pantry led down to the root cellar.

The most magnificent wonder of all: indoor plumbing provided water to the kitchen sink and the bathroom—the indoor bathroom off the kitchen. Hannah wouldn't have to go outside to the outhouse in the cold and dark, or hold it all night, anymore.

She couldn't resist pushing the handle to flush the

toilet. The water in the bottom magically disappeared, and fresh water filled it. Hannah pushed the handle again and watched with delight as fresh water replaced the old a second time. She pushed the handle once more.

"Hannah!"

She jumped.

"Stop flushing the toilet." Mother stood in the bathroom's doorway. "You'll have plenty of chances when you use it. Right now we need to get this house in order."

"Let me look upstairs first. Please?" She brushed past Mother and ran up the stairs in the parlour before Mother could stop her.

The second floor had five bedrooms, smaller than the one downstairs. The other children were already unpacking, so Hannah knew right away which two rooms belonged to the boys, which two were for the girls, and which was Grandma Murphy's. And—Hannah could hardly believe it—there was a bathroom upstairs, too. That alone made the move worth it.

The entire family worked busily to get the house in order. Well, all except Grandma Murphy. She sat rocking with a cup of tea and complaining that she didn't recognize anything and the bright lights hurt her eyes. By mid-afternoon everything had been put in place.

"I'm going to make lad in the bag for supper, to celebrate," Mother said.

Cheers rose from all the children. Hannah had been hoping for it, since she saw Mother put some salt riblets on to boil a couple of hours ago.

"Can I help?" she asked.

"Of course. Start by pouring flour in this bowl." She set it in front of Hannah on the counter.

"How much?"

"Look at the size of your fist. You want to have enough flour so it looks like four of your fists are in that bowl."

When Hannah and Mother agreed the amount of flour in the bowl looked right, Mother said, "Now get a heaping teaspoon of that baking soda, and half as much salt, and mix them into the flour."

Hannah followed the instructions, then said, "I know what comes next." She grabbed the spice cans with the ground nutmeg and ground cinnamon. "But I don't know how much to put in."

"Three booms of cinnamon and two booms of nutmeg."

"What's a boom?"

Mother laughed. "My own mother taught me that a boom is a heavy shake of the can into the bowl."

Hannah shook the cinnamon can three times and puffs of spice wafted up from the top of the can. "Like that?"

"Maybe a tad more...that's perfect."

When Hannah finished with the spices, Mother set a slab of salt pork out and handed Hannah a knife. Hannah cut the salt pork into the tiniest little cubes until she had a pile the size of her fist. "Do I need to do more salt pork?"

"That's just the right amount. Do you remember what's next?"

"Yes, but not how much." Hannah followed Mother's instructions to add two fists of molasses, two fists of milk, and two fists of raisins.

With the last ingredients added, Mother said, "Now mix it up all good. That pudding should feel a little thicker than applesauce, so if you have to add more flour or more milk, you go right ahead."

No sooner had Hannah finished mixing to the right texture than Bridie and Freddie both ran in, shouting, "Let me lick the spoon!"

"No, me!"

"No, let me lick the spoon!"

"I can't choose between you," Hannah said, and licked the spoon clean herself. "You two can fight over the bowl when I'm done."

Mother handed Hannah the cotton pillow case she used as a pudding bag. "Now pour the pudding into the bag."

After Hannah filled the bag, she tied a tight knot to close it off and dropped the whole thing into the pot with the boiling pork riblets. "We don't have any turkey gravy to pour over the lad in the bag pudding, do we?"

"No, chile, but we'll make molasses coady. First we need to get the potatoes, carrots, and cabbage ready to add to the meat."

Mother helped Hannah wash and cut up the vegetables. When they were done, it was time to add them to the pot.

"You've done well, Hannah. The coady is all that's left. It's easy. Melt a fist of butter, then stir in an equal amount of molasses. When we serve the lad in the bag, you can pour the coady over it."

Hannah thought she might bust with pride when Mother bragged on her at supper. "Hannah made most of this meal herself. She's getting to be a good cook."

They all agreed the meal tasted delicious.

BLEAT!

Everyone at the table jumped. Grandma Murphy shrieked. Mother jumped up and ran to her.

"What was that?" Monica cried.

"The foghorn," Father said. "Better get used to it. It'll sound every day at sundown. And when it's foggy, or poor visibility on the sea for any reason, it'll sound all day long."

"Every day? Sometimes all day?" Hannah shuddered. "It sounds like...like it's telling us somebody's going to die. It sounds like death."

"It'll be the death of me," Grandma said.

"What about at night? It won't sound at night, will it?" Mother's voice sounded more anxious than Hannah had ever heard it.

Father hesitated, then spoke in a soothing tone. "Only when it's foggy." He spoke quickly and loudly over the whole family's claims that it was almost always foggy at night. "We'll get used to it. Think of all the people that live in cities with trains and sirens and all kinds of noise. After a while they don't even notice it. This'll be just like that."

Hannah wasn't so sure.

~#~

The next day they didn't go to church. Mother wanted time to "feel settled" and Father needed to acquaint himself with the lighthouse and the duties he'd take over the following morning. The children ran outdoors to explore their new environment.

"Let's roll down a hill in the downs," Bridie suggested. The others shouted agreement and they all ran to the grassy hills. They tried to see who could roll down fastest, but no one could agree on the winner.

After her third roll down, Hannah lay in the grass and looked up at the sky. "Look at that cloud. It looks like a fish."

"Which one?" her siblings asked at once. They lay with their heads close to Hannah's and she pointed out the cloud.

"More like a shark," Leonard said.

"That one looks like bunny ears." Madge pointed to another. For the next half hour they compared shapes in the clouds.

Leonard suddenly jumped up. "I'm tired of this. Let's go look around the pond and see if we can find a frog."

"Yes, let's!" They ran to the pond and splashed in, wading around the shallow edge. Hannah made sure to watch the little boys closely.

"Something's prickling my toes," Freddie said.

"It's just little fish," Leonard said. "Look, I think they're baby trout." They all stood still and peered in the water. Soon the small fish nibbled all their toes.

"It tickles," Hannah laughed.

"It prickles," Freddie said again. "They're prickly fish."

"Let's catch some." Leonard bent down and thrust his hands in the water over and over. The rest of them followed his lead, but the little fish were too fast.

"I know!" Hannah ran to the house and into the kitchen. "Mother, can I have a hairnet?" She ignored Grandma Murphy's scolding about not being ladylike.

"A hairnet? Whatever for?"

"To catch the prickly fish. They nibble our toes."

"I suppose. Wait there; I don't want you dripping through the parlour." Mother brought Hannah four hairnets. "You'll have to share. And don't let me catch you taking them without asking!" she yelled after her daughter as the girl ran back to the pond.

"Here, look. Nets! We can take turns catching the pricklies with these." Hannah held out three hairnets, keeping one for herself. She spread it out between her hands and pulled it through the water. The little fish swam away from it.

Several minutes later Leonard made a sound of disgust. "They see it coming. This won't work." He thought a minute. "It needs a handle. Let's find some sticks." Four sticks were soon procured, and a hairnet tied to each.

"I got some!"

"Me, too!"

"I want a turn!"

They took turns with the nets until all the children caught some pricklies and all the nets were ripped. Then they went in to have lunch. After lunch, they trooped back outside to explore and play until supper.

Chapter 5

A New Life

Mondays were laundry day, one of Hannah's favorite days. She had fun running clothes through the mangle, but she enjoyed even more the time spent with Mother as they hung the wash on the clothesline and later took it down.

The first Monday in the new house, Mother began, as usual, by washing the least-dirty items—hers and the girls' petticoats, or slips, and nice blouses, and most of baby Angie's clothes. She rubbed them gently on the washboard and let Hannah squeeze the soapy water from them in the wringer. Then she rinsed the items in another tub, and Hannah ran them through the wringer again.

"Careful, now." Mother said that many times on wash day. Hannah knew the wringer was also called a mangle because it would mangle any fingers that got caught in it, so she was careful. But mothers always worry.

When a basketful of laundry had been washed and rinsed, they went outside to hang it on the line to dry. Mother carried the basket of clothes and Hannah took Angie by the hand and helped her walk.

As soon as they stepped outside, a gust of wind caught a stocking on the top of the pile and carried it away. Hannah chased after it, but the wind took it up out of sight.

Mother walked on to the clothesline, which stood halfway between the house and the cliff, with the basket under one arm and Angie in the other.

"We have to keep a close eye on Angie," she said. "If she falls off the cliff..."

Mother didn't finish the sentence. Hannah couldn't imagine anything more awful. "I will," she promised.

The wind continued to whip. It pulled Madge's slip right out of Mother's hand as she lifted the garment from the basket. Again Hannah ran after the airborne item, but it disappeared into the sun.

"I can't believe this," Mother said. "I've never lost a single piece of clothing, and now that's two in one day." She shook her head, then laughed. "I wonder what someone will think when a stocking or a petticoat falls on them from the sky." Hannah laughed, too.

Suddenly Mother stopped laughing and panic entered her face. "Where's Angela? Angela!"

"Mama." Angie stood next to one of the posts holding the clothesline up. Hannah whisked her up and Mother wrapped her arms around them both.

"There goes one of Angie's dresses."

Mother released the girls and hurried to the basket. "Bring Angie over here and watch the basket. Don't let anything else blow away. And don't let Angie wander off!"

Somehow Mother got the basketful of clothes hung, as well as the rest of the laundry done.

At supper that evening Hannah and Mother told the rest of the family about the day's laundry fiasco.

Father laughed with everyone else but then said,

"Don't know what to tell you, Louise. The wind blows up here. That's just a fact of life we have to accept."

"I can deal with the wind if I have Hannah to help. But we have to do something to keep little Angie from wandering off the cliff."

"Let me think on it."

The next morning Father came in after completing his tasks at the lighthouse. He held a harness from the horse barn, a thin rope, and a few tools. Hannah sat next to him at the table and watched him take apart the harness and put it back together a different way.

When he was finished he held it up. "I think that'll work. Bring Angie here."

Hannah brought her little sister to him, with Mother following. Father put the harness on Angie. "Tie the rope to the harness here," he showed them. "I'll attach the rope to the house. It's a twenty-foot rope, so she'll never be able to reach the cliff."

"Ingenious." Mother hugged Father.

"Let's try it out, make sure it works." He grabbed the rope and Hannah carried her sister.

Outside, father attached the rope to a ring he'd nailed onto the corner of the house. He handed the rope to Mother, and she tied it onto the harness. Hannah put Angie down, she stood next to them.

"Hannah, go to the clothesline," Mother said.

When Hannah headed that way, Angie followed her. When she got to the end of the rope length, she kept making steps but couldn't move forward, like someone running in place. Hannah laughed at the confused look on her face.

"That's one problem solved," Mother said. "Wonder what else we'll run into."

~#~

"This is abuse, I tell you," Grandma Murphy said suddenly one evening a couple of weeks later.

Father lowered his newspaper. "What on earth are you talking about, Mother?"

"You're keeping me stuck out here in this lonely place. My friends with their old bones live too far away to visit me now. And with that blasted horn! You did this on purpose. You want me to wither away of loneliness, or die of fright, so you'll be rid of me."

Father started to object, but Hannah interrupted. "Grandma, you're not alone. You have all of us." She didn't add that she was getting used to the foghorn, just like Father said they would. At least, she was beginning to. She hardly ever jumped at it anymore.

Grandma glared at her. "What kind of company are you? You're no good. All you want to do is play cards. I hate games."

Hannah felt tears in her eyes. *She doesn't have to be so mean about it. Even if it is true.*

As Father and Mother tried to placate Grandma, Hannah thought about what Grandma said. She hadn't realized Grandma Murphy's life changed so much with the move. The old woman still spent her days sitting in her rocker, drinking tea and commenting on—mostly complaining about—the activities of the family.

But now, like the rest of them, Grandma Murphy lived far from the little town where her friends lived. Hannah and her siblings still saw friends at school, and had each other to play with the rest of the time. Grandma didn't get to go to town to see friends. When they lived in Point Verde, people she'd known all her life often stopped by for a bit of gossip. The long walk from town made that impossible.

Grandma's lonely, but it's her own fault. We'd spend more time with her if she acted nicer. Who wants to be around a mean old woman you can't ever please? Besides, coming here has been good for Mother and Father.

Since moving, Hannah hadn't seen the furrowed brow that used to live on Father's face. When he came in to supper, he was lighthearted and quick with a laugh instead of heavy with worry. His new job was simpler and much less back-breaking than fishing, but everyone knew its extreme importance. He called it "meaningful" and said the word with pride.

The move benefitted Mother, too. No longer consumed with making fish, she now focused completely on making a happy home for her family. With the increased income, she'd already bought fabric and made Hannah a new dress and Gus and Freddie new shirts. Now she spent time each afternoon sewing a dress for Bridie. They had plenty of food so she could serve a variety of meals. Like Father, Mother had time and energy to join the children in a game or two after supper each evening.

Mother's voice interrupted Hannah's thoughts. "Hannah, do you want to get up early enough to help me make toutons in the morning? It's your turn if you want to."

"Oh, yes! I love toutons."

"Okay, then. Madge, come help me make the dough for tomorrow's bread."

"You better learn to make the bread, too, Hannah," Madge said as she passed. "You know every good wife has to know how to make good bread. Besides, you can't have toutons without bread dough."

"She'll learn in good time. No girl grows up in Newfoundland without knowing how to make bread. She can make toutons just about perfectly by now." Mother smiled at Hannah.

"Too bad I only get the fresh bread on Sunday," Father commented. "If you got up earlier to bake it, I could have it warm from the oven other days, too, before I have to go to work." His tone told Hannah he was teasing.

"Yes, but then you wouldn't get to enjoy toutons with molasses for breakfast," she said. Father agreed with a wink.

The next morning Mother gently shook Hannah awake earlier than usual. She scrambled out of bed and got to the kitchen even before Mother, but not by much.

"Go ahead," Mother said as she got down the coffeepot. "You know what to do."

Hannah set a cast-iron skillet on the stove and dropped a teacupful of lard in it to melt and heat. Then she grabbed a hunk of the risen but uncooked bread dough Madge and Mother had prepared the evening before. She gauged its size—about the same as a lemon. Perfect.

Rolling and pressing gently, Hannah flattened the dough to about a half-inch thick. The fat in the skillet sizzled as she plopped the piece of raw dough in the pan. The aroma wafted irresistibly as she fried both sides to a lovely golden brown.

She dipped it out onto a plate and covered it with molasses. "Mmm." Nothing beat a hot touton for breakfast. They were good warm, too, but Hannah never passed the chance to eat the first one piping hot.

Every time she ate one of the tasty treats, she remembered all the good times the family had enjoyed at various festivals. The texture of toutons reminded her of the soft pretzels such events always sold. Pretzels didn't taste nearly as good, though.

Hannah wasted no time finishing her breakfast. Father would be ready to eat soon, and the other kids might show up. They'd complain about being left out if she didn't make them a hot touton like she had. So she put her plate in the sink and grabbed another piece of dough.

Father came in and sat down to the table just as Hannah lifted the next touton from the skillet onto a plate. She handed him the plate and dropped another piece of flattened dough into the skillet. As each touton fried, Hannah prepared the next one. She made a large batch. It took many toutons to feed their large family.

"Think you can get up early two days in a row?" Father asked after he drained the last of his coffee and set the cup down. "If you want to, you can go with me to the lighthouse tomorrow."

So the next morning Hannah again got up early, though not as early as the day before. She had hot toutons for breakfast, made by Mother this time. Then she and Father set out down the path to the lighthouse. The sun peeked over the horizon as they arrived.

Hannah started to climb the stairs but Father stopped her.

"We start down here. First thing is to put out the light." He turned a large, flat knob on what looked like a huge, square barrel. Father said it was a tank.

"The lamp runs on gas. It can go a few days, but I have to make sure it never runs out. See? The tank is over half empty." He tapped on top the tank and a hollow sound rang out.

"So I have to refill it." He rolled one of the fuel drums from the adjacent platform to the tank and poured it in.

An elaborate mechanism sat on top of the tank. "This is an old-fashioned revolving mechanism that uses gravity for power. The turntable works much like the big grandfather clock in the parlour. I hoist this weight to the very top." Father pulled and pulled on a length of rope that went through the mechanism then over a thick beam near the ceiling. A weight hung from the other end of the rope.

"Gravity pulls the weight down slowly. This mechanism keeps it from falling too quickly, and keeps it swinging back and forth. That makes the lamp spin."

"Do we go up now?"

"Not yet. The next step is to oil and lubricate all the flywheels and gears that power the light." He let Hannah pour and rub oil on some of them.

"Before we put the oil away, we go next door and oil the foghorn."

They waited until after the horn sounded, then ran to the horn-house. Father turned the foghorn off quickly, before it sounded right in their ears and made them deaf.

A weight hung from a rope, just like in the lighthouse. "Does the foghorn work the same way as the light?"

"Similar. See these bellows? They pump air through those pipes. They're the foghorn's vocal cords.

The same kind of weight and pendulum machinery as the light powers the bellows." They repeated the procedure of raising the weight and oiling all the moving parts.

"Now we go up." Back in the lighthouse, they climbed up the many stairs to the very top.

"Here I inspect the lamp and polish it up. It'd be big trouble if it broke or got moisture in it." Father looked over every inch of the lamp. Then he handed Hannah a rag and took another for himself. As they polished the giant glass, they chatted about all the wonderful things in their new home.

"That's it," Father said when the entire glass had been rubbed.

"You get paid all that money, and a free house and everything, just for that?" It wasn't even lunch time yet.

Father grinned. "It's easier than fishing. But no; I mean that's it for now. There's the evening work to start the light and horn again. Besides that, I'm responsible for keeping the entire property, including the house and all the buildings, in good shape. With all these moving parts, things break down often, and it's up to me to fix them. Lighthouse keepers have to be resourceful and self-reliant. There's no one else to turn to way out here. So the pay is as much for the responsibility as it is the work."

"Do you have to fix anything today?"

"Today I'm going to start making a crane."

"A crane?" How could Father make a bird? Would he carve one from wood?

"Not a bird." Father must have known what she was thinking. "A winch. A machine that can lift things. The supply boat will be here in a week or so. It'll have all our supplies, for the lighthouse and our home—the fuel for the light, our food, everything. They'll unload the crates and barrels on a dock at the bottom of the cliff. It's up to me to get them up here."

"Oh. That'll be hard. Can't you leave them on the dock and just bring up what you need when you want it?"

"No. What if a storm comes, or a tidal surge? All our supplies could be washed out to sea. No, I must bring them up as soon as possible. They're too heavy for any of you to help. But a winch will help. I'll be able to stand on the top of the cliff and turn the crank on the winch. It'll pull a long rope, on the end of which will be a crate or barrel on a little platform.

"Like the weight in the light and horn houses?"

"Smart girl. Very similar. Now run along and play. I've got to get the winch made before the supply boat comes."

~#~

As it turned out, Father was right. Hannah soon learned to love her new home. She and her siblings did have to walk 45 minutes to—and from—school every day, but Hannah didn't mind walking, and the time was made up for in freedom.

Since Mother no longer had to make fish, she took over many of the chores the children did before. Sure, they still had minor chores like gathering eggs and helping clean up after supper, but nothing like they'd done in the old place.

Father had more free time, too. As he got the place in order, he had less repairs. With all the birds around the place, he soon took to bird hunting. The meat was a nice change from fish, and the hunt provided great joys for Father.

With the electric lights, no one had to go bed right after supper. Instead they got out their musical instruments or played games. Hannah loved the card game called Auction 45s and she played it with great ferocity. She delighted in strategizing and forcing her opponent into a shutout. She even beat Father much of the time.

Mother seldom joined the games. She often spent the time stitching or knitting, which she enjoyed. Sometimes she read aloud to the family. As an educated woman, she made sure to expose the children to good literature.

She also made sure catechism and prayer were regular aspects of life. The painting of the Sacred Heart of Jesus hung on the kitchen wall next to the crucifix and she prayed there daily. She made sure all the children knew their prayers and said them every night before getting into bed. On Sunday evenings, as well as every day in Lent and holy days of obligation, the whole family sat together and prayed the rosary through to the end.

On Saturdays the children played outside. They made toy sailboats and raced them in the pond. The pond served as a great place to build and float a raft, too. Other days the children watched and chased the ducks and geese that lazed in the ponds by the hundreds. Sometimes they gathered goose eggs for breakfast. Birds of all kinds abounded in all directions of the lighthouse grounds and the youngsters spent plenty of time watching the birds and dreaming about flying the skies with them.

In the spring and summer, the children took their pails and went berry picking. The nearby bogs and fields overflowed with partridge berries and bakeapple berries. They ate their fill of berries while picking and came home with stained faces. But that didn't stop them from bringing plenty for mother so she could bake them in a tasty pie or turn them into jam.

Chapter 6

Risks

"The capelin are rolling," Father said at breakfast one morning.

"What is capelin rolling?" Gus asked.

"You know capelin. The little salted fish we eat," Mother answered.

"Yeah, the ones we bite the head off of." Leonard mimed an exaggerated chomp on a fish.

"When they have a run, it's called rolling," Father continued. "The come in by the millions to spawn. The beach is full of 'em flapping around laying eggs. That brings in the cod, too—they eat the capelin easily while they're all bunched together. Fishermen will be inshore, having an easier time."

"Let's go look at them after breakfast," Leonard said.

"Do more than look," Mother instructed. "You children take the wheelbarrow and fill it up. When you get back, spread the fish on the garden. That soil needs some fertilizer. Whoever was here last must not have put any fish on it."

"The old man I replaced didn't have a family." Father pushed his plate back and stood up. "I don't think he kept much of a garden."

"I can tell." Mother kissed Father goodbye then

turned back to the children. "I want fish over every inch of that garden. We'll see about refilling the capelin bin after that."

They finished breakfast and morning chores in a hurry, eager to get to the beach and see the capelin roll. Hannah took Freddie ahead, leaving the others to bring pails, nets, and wheelbarrow.

Women and children from town crowded the beach, filling their own buckets and carts with the rolling fish. Hannah led Freddie to a spot no one had claimed yet.

"Here, Freddie, I caught one for you." She held one of the small fish out to her brother.

Freddie recoiled. "Ew, it's wiggling. I don't want to touch it."

"Nonsense, Freddie. He's dancing for you. Look." Hannah giggled as she gave the fish a quick kiss. "You kiss it, too. It's good luck."

"Yucky. I don't wanna. Don't do that, Hannah."

Hannah took advantage of the moment and quickly kissed her little brother, making fish lips as she surprised him. "See, it's okay." Hannah smiled.

Freddie paused a moment, then grabbed the fish and kissed it. The fish wriggled out of his hands and dropped into the water. Freddie let out a big laugh. "This is fun. I like catching capelin."

Soon their siblings joined them. The children went to the other side of the sand bar, and at the harbor's edge netted capelin all day long, scooping and netting barrelful after barrelful. Occasionally a fish flopped up someone's pants leg, bringing shrieks of surprise. Laughter and delight resulted whenever one of them fell in the water.

Once the garden had been covered with the fertilizing fish, the children filled a large bin. Mother salted them generously and set the bin aside. In time, the salt dried and preserved the capelin.

Frequently, when Hannah's stomach grumbled and she asked Mother for a snack, Mother said, "Go to the capelin bin and eat that fish, chile. It's good for you."

Hannah relished the salty treat and bit into the whole fish. It disappeared in only a bite or two, head, tail, guts, and all.

~#~

One fall evening a knock on the door surprised the family. Father opened it to find his old friend Bob Tobin. The two men knew each other from back in the days when they both served as crew on a cod fishing ship called a banker. They had as strong a bond as any two friends could have.

Though he was Father's special friend, the whole family loved Bob. When he and Father got together, they'd spin some of the biggest yarns possible. Everyone circled around them and laughed themselves silly as they were sucked into some big giant fib of a story with a funny ending.

Tonight the two men swapped stories about the good old days over a bottle of rum.

After several stories, Father said, "Do you remember the time we had that Yank and his son go fishing with us on that little motor boat?"

"Yes, indeed, b'y. G'wan, tell the kids now."

Father began, "This Yank comes by one day as Bob and I were cleaning fish and asked if he could watch. He told us he never went cod fishing, but his grandpa was an old cod fisherman back in the day."

"Yes, b'y. That's right."

"So we did the polite thing and invited him to come join us fishing the next day. The Yank was thrilled and brought his son with him. It was a great day for fishing. The skies were blue with nary a cloud. We took my boat out into the open ocean, far from shore, to a great fishing place."

"Best kind, b'y."

Father went on, "So there we were, jigging away off the boat and nothing come to bite. So I tell me first mate, ol' Bob here, 'Reel your lines in, we gotta move!' Now the Yank, he's tripping all over his fishing line that's laid out on the deck beneath his feet, so he decides instead to lay his line down toward the back of the boat. But he don't pay attention to what he's doing. His fishing line winds up over the side, in the water by the engine, and when Bob here starts the motor, the line wraps around the propeller and seizes the engine up. Bob says to me, 'Lard tunderin' Jayzus, what's wrong?'

"I tell Bob, 'The Yank here done wrapped his line around the propeller and I can't reach it to untangle it. We're goners for sure. We're gonna wash out to sea and be lost forever.'

"Now, no way I could let that happen. So I tossed the Yank over the side into the frigid arctic water, and I told him, 'Free that line up or die, Yank.' He worked like a madman and sure enough cleared that line right up, no problem."

"No sooner did the Yank free up the propeller, when the largest cod I ever did see jumped right up and swallowed that Yank whole. It was some monster!"

Bob shouted, "Yes, by gum!"

Father continued, "I wasted no time. I grabbed my oar and swung with all my might across that cod's head and stunned him right good. We pulled that fish on board quick as a wink. The Yank's son, he was watching all this, and he shouts, 'Where's Pa? Where's my pa?'

"But when I saw the size of the fish that swallowed that Yank, I knew right off that we'd been fishing the wrong way. I grabbed the oar, stunned the Yank's son, and tossed him overboard, too. Sure enough, we caught another giant cod! Those two cod were the biggest fish we ever caught in all our lives."

Everyone roared with laughter.

"Aye, 'tis a good story. I best be on my way now, though."

"Where you headed, Bob?" Father asked.

"I tell ya, I'm going seal hunting. Went once before; gonna try it again."

Leonard perked up. "How do you do that?"

"Ice panning."

"What's that?"

"You ain't told your kids about ice panning, Joe? Shame." Bob turned to Leonard. "It's like this. Up north, near the pole, huge swaths of ocean turn to ice. Some ice fields are many kilometers long. Others are hundreds of meters, or dozens of meters, or even only a few meters. These ice fields are flat as a frypan, so they're called pans."

"How do they get so flat?" Hannah wanted to know.

"That's a great mystery. But it's a good thing, because then we can walk on them. When the vessel gets as far as it can, the hunters jump ship and walk the ice in search of seals. When we get to the end of one floe, or ice pan, we jump onto the next one. They rock like a cradle; got to be sure-footed to jump ice pans. If you fall off, you freeze to death."

"It's a dangerous occupation," Mother said.

"Most everything has risks, one sort or 'nother. Just gotta take care, is all."

~#~

Hannah's first year at the lighthouse saw a cold winter with an unusual amount of snow. She and her siblings had no complaints. They went sledding on the hills of the downs, or built snowmen and made snow angels. Father was able to purchase ice skates for all of them with his new salary, so they often went ice skating. They remembered Bob's tale of ice panning, and the older children had to give it a try. Leonard and Bridie were especially skilled at the exercise.

When the snow grew deep, Father drove the children to school in the sleigh—when he could. Hannah liked it best when his duties made that impossible.

One week the weather was so bad they were unable to get to school for a couple of days. On the third day, the snow stopped and the sun came out, but Father was busy. After being stuck inside for two days, the children were extra restless. Mother finally said they could play outside.

"Bundle up well. Take Freddie, too. He's getting old enough to play with you all. Hannah, keep a close eye on him."

"I will." She gave her little brother a squeeze.

Hannah made sure to include Freddie in each

activity, teaching him how to pack snow for snowballs and forts and how to sweep his arms and legs to make an angel.

"Bridie, come on. Let's do some ice panning!" shouted Leonard.

Hannah grabbed Freddie's hand and pulled him along to watch.

Leonard and Bridie jumped high and hard onto the frozen pond, which caused the flat ice to break into pieces.

"I'm going to race you and win this time," said Bridie.

The two of them took off across the pond: balance and jump, balance and jump, from ice pan to ice pan.

Hannah clapped and rooted for Bridie, but said, "I have to watch Freddie, otherwise I'd beat you both."

Suddenly, before Hannah could stop him, Freddie raced onto the ice at the edge of the pond and shouted, "Hannah, look at me! I can do it, too!"

"You come back here this instant, Freddie!"

Freddie ignored her and ran to the edge of the ice. He gave a leap onto a nearby ice pan. Hannah raced after him.

Freddie's ice pan wobbled beneath him.

"Leonard, quick, come help! Freddie shouldn't be on the ice!" But Leonard and Bridie were across the pond.

Hannah ran as fast as she could, but before she could reach him, little Freddie fell into the icy water and shrieked for help. He haplessly flailed his arms about, trying to get back up on the ice, howling in fear the whole time.

Leonard and Hannah reached him at the same

time. Leonard spread himself flat on his stomach and reached over the edge.

"Freddie, quick, give me your hand." He heaved with all his might and pulled Freddie onto the ice next to him. Frigid water soaked Freddie from head to toe.

Somehow Hannah, Leonard, and Bridie managed to get him back to shore. They raced Freddie back to the house, screaming for help all the way.

Mother came running and took Freddie. She carried the boy into the house, calling out instructions through sobs. "Madge, bring blankets! Leonard, help me take these wet clothes off him. Monica, more blankets!"

Hannah stood to the side, sobbing. Even through her tears she could see that Freddie's face and hands were blue.

Mother cried, "Freddie, sweetheart, wake up, wake up!"

No response.

Once he was undressed, Mother climbed under the blankets with him and began briskly rubbing his skin all over to warm him. "My baby, my baby. Wake up, my sweet baby."

After a long time she stopped rubbing and tucked the blankets close around him.

"We must pray for him. Pray, children."

Leonard and Madge moved kitchen chairs to the parlour and made a circle around Mother and Freddie on the couch. Mother continued to minister to Freddie throughout the night. She exhorted the children to continue praying until the wee hours of the morning; yet Freddy lay still.

Hannah continued to cry. She had not stopped crying since Freddie fell. She could stand it no longer and had to ask. "Is he going to be okay, Mother? I'm so sorry. I'm so sorry. He jumped on the ice so quickly, I never had a chance to stop him." Hannah couldn't stop sobbing.

Leonard chimed in, "She's right, Mother. It wasn't Hannah's fault."

"There is no one here to blame, child. We just need to pray."

Louise stayed by Freddie's side for close to a week while Freddie went in and out of fever. She continued to beg him to wake up, and the children to pray.

On the fifth day, Freddie moved a little. Slowly, over several more days, he regained his strength and became more animated.

When he finally woke up fully, he said, "Don't be mad at Hannah, Mother. It was my fault."

Once another week had passed, Mother said they no longer needed to worry about Freddie; he would recover. Life slowly returned to normal.

Chapter 7

The Storm

The family returned home from church just as a strong gust of wind blew up.

"Oh, my hat!" Madge reached for it but missed.

Leonard was quicker. "Here you go, sis. That was a close one."

Hannah was glad she didn't have to wear a hat—yet. Next year, when she turned thirteen, Mother would insist she dress more ladylike.

"There's no such thing as a nice winter here," Grandma Murphy grumbled. As they all settled into the parlour, Grandma picked up her rant. Hannah tried to tune her out but she spoke in a loud voice.

"As far back as I can remember, every winter was damp and chilled you to the bone. And the fog never leaves. I spent my childhood in Argentia, not far from here. You know they say Argentia is the foggiest place in North America. I remember counting the mauzy days one year and we had fog more than 200 days."

"Yes, Mother Murphy, we heard about the year you counted 200 mauzy days." Mother said. "We live in the Northern Maritime; we have to live with the weather the Good Lord gives us, and that includes all the fog and snow here."

"It's time for the Nor'easters. That wind can get

over a hundred kilometers per hour. I've seen it many times." Grandma continued on about the weather.

I'll get my drawing pencils, Hannah thought. *Maybe there'll be a boat or a bird to sketch. At least I'll be away from Grandma's techy comments.*

She bundled up and took the lighthouse path down the hill to her favorite drawing spot at the edge of the cliff.

No boats. No birds. Only a dark, gray sky over a dark, gray sea. Nothing worth sketching. But maybe something would show up if she waited a bit. Hannah sat twiddling her pencil while her thoughts wandered.

Suddenly she shivered and realized she was cold. Had she dozed off? Snowflakes were falling, mixed with sleet. When did that start? The wind had picked up too, and it had a bite.

Hannah stood and gathered her drawing materials. An abrupt gust almost blew her down. *The cliff—* Being so close to the edge of the cliff sent a shiver of fear down her spine. She needed to get away from there, and back to the house.

She stood only a few meters from the lifeline rope running along the path between the lighthouse and the residence. Head down, she fought the gale, making a beeline to the rope as quickly as possible.

Hannah clutched her pad and pencils in one hand and held tightly to the rope with the other, sliding it along as she walked. The wind intensified rapidly as Hannah made her way up the path toward the house. Sleet stung her face and made it hard to see. Wet, slippery ice now covered the ground and her feet slid as she moved forward.

"Oh!" A sudden, intense gust slammed her full force and knocked her off her feet. Hannah lost her grip on her materials—and the rope.

Thud! She hit the icy ground. The impact knocked the breath from her lungs and left her stunned.

Sliding—

The icy path had no traction. There was nothing to stop her descent. Hannah became aware of the crashing waves battering the rocks fifty meters below.

She shrieked with fear and wildly waved her hands in the air hoping to grasp something, but they grabbed only air. She slipped closer to the cliff's edge.

"Help me!"

Suddenly her shoulder slammed into the wooden post that held the lifeline rope. Her body began to slide around it. Hannah reached out and wrapped her arms around the post. She held on for dear life, not moving a muscle lest it make her lose her grip and begin slipping again.

What can I do?

If she lost hold of the post she'd be lost. Nothing else stood between her and the cliff's edge.

Hannah planned her next moves. Exactly where and how to put her hands and knees and arms and feet.

I can—

She managed to keep her hold as she rolled over onto her stomach. Hugging the post, she got to her knees. She kept one arm around the post and slid the other up the post until she could grab the rope and grip it tight. Then she slid the other hand up to the rope.

Don't stand. She might get blown over again. Instead she inched forward up the hill on her knees. She kept a death grip on the rope. It took every ounce of will to force herself on, and every bit of strength to do it.

Hannah concentrated on the ground before her. After what seemed like hours, she looked up to gauge her progress. Not even halfway.

It's too far. I'll never make it.

Then a strong arm encircled her tightly.

"Keep hold of the rope," Father shouted over the howl of the wind as he pulled her up. Hannah almost fainted with relief.

But they weren't safe yet.

Father held Hannah in front of him and helped her along, keeping hold of the rope with his other hand. Hannah continued to grip the lifeline with both hands.

At the end of the path, Father helped Hannah unclench her fingers. She collapsed against the doorframe. The door opened and she fell into Mother's arms.

Mother hugged her tight, then led her to a kitchen chair. "My dear child! I don't know what I'd do if something happened to you. Praise God you're safe."

Hannah couldn't catch her breath. Despite now being in the warm house, she began to shiver uncontrollably.

"The girl's in shock." Father's voice seemed to come through a tunnel.

Mother appeared to be a shadow in a dim place. "Monica, get a blanket. Quickly. I'll put on some tea."

As the warm tea spread into Hannah's body, she was able to stop shivering and breathe easy. Things came into focus. "I'm all right, thanks to Father."

Mother hugged her tightly.

"I have to go back. I turned off the lamp and foghorn this morn. Got to turn them back on."

Everyone froze for a moment. Father going back into that storm Hannah had barely escaped... and it raged even worse now. Hannah shivered again.

"Lard tunderin' Jayzus, wife!" Father exclaimed. "I'll be fine. You just have some hot soup ready when I get back."

He turned to walk out the door. It didn't open. The force of the wind outside blew so intensely against it that even when Father leaned his full weight against the door, he couldn't push it open.

"Leonard, come help me." Before pushing on the door again, Father said, "It'll take fifteen minutes for me to turn everything on and get back. You stand here and listen close; I'll need your help to open the door when I get back. When you hear me knock, push hard as you can. Louise, you help."

On Father's signal he and Lennie heaved their weight against the door and forced it ajar, inch by inch, against the heavy wind.

The storm howled into the room as the door opened wider. Gusts blew papers into a swirl. When the door gaped wide enough, Father disappeared through it. Immediately the door slammed back with a fury, throwing Leonard to his back on the floor. Bridie hurried to help him up.

Hannah had been watching them so intently that everything else faded. Now a cacophony filled her ears: howling wind, sleet lashing the windows, waves crashing ashore, and, above all, the creaking of the house as its frame shifted and the ghostly groan of the cables that kept it from blowing away.

Could Father make it to the lighthouse and back safely?

The family waited silently, watching the clock. Even Grandma Murphy had no comments.

Fifteen minutes passed, then twenty. Then thirty. Leonard stood by the door, head cocked toward it, listening. Hannah strained to hear a knock.

Nothing.

BLEAT!

Father had made it to the foghorn.

"That took half an hour. It'll be that long again before he's back," Leonard said. He sat down in the chair closest to the door.

Twenty minutes later Monica exclaimed, "The light came on." Hannah breathed a sigh of relief.

"Might be an hour before he gets back, then, judging by how long he's been gone," Madge murmured.

An hour passed, then another.

BANG!

Something slammed against the door. Gussie ran to help Leonard open the door.

"No," Mother said. "That's not him. That had a metallic sound—I think it was the big kettle from the barn." Under her breath she added, "Lord, please watch over my Joe."

Hannah begged God to keep Father safe.

Twenty minutes later the lights went out, plunging the house into an eerie gray. Mother found candles while Madge and Monica lit the oil lamps.

Mother said, "He won't come now. Father's a smart man; he knows to wait in the lighthouse until the storm dies down." The worry in her eyes belied her words.

Besides, she continued to pray to the Sacred Heart of Jesus.

The day stretched into evening. If Father had been safely with them, the house would have been filled with games and laughter. Instead, everyone sat still and silent, fear etched on each face. Only Angie seemed unaware of the danger, running around and playing with her doll.

The house grew darker, and colder. One by one they moved their chairs closer to the potbellied stove in the kitchen.

Bedtime passed. Mother put Angela to bed. The rest of the family sat still where they were and waited. Gus and Freddie eventually fell asleep in their chairs. Mother and Madge carried them to bed.

~#~

Hannah woke. She'd fallen asleep, just like the little boys. But she was too big to be carried to bed, and remained in her chair. The clock read four a.m. Mother sat reading her Bible by lamplight. Everyone else dozed in their chairs.

Mother looked up. "The storm is breaking."

That's what woke Hannah: the silence. Relative silence, at least. Wind still blew, but it no longer howled. The surf was barely audible, and the cables groaned at a normal level.

BANG, BANG, BANG!

There was no mistaking the sound this time. Someone pounded on the door. The noise woke the other children.

The whole family jumped up and raced to the entrance. Leonard got there first. He threw the door open with ease.

There on the threshold stood Father, smiling. He stepped into the house and called out, "Woman, where's my soup?"

Mother threw her arms around him and he embraced her. They clung together for a full minute. The rest of them surrounded the couple until Father gave each one a bear hug. He even went and gave Grandma Murphy a short embrace while Mother dipped up his soup.

Then the family gathered around as he ate and told his story of the many hours away.

"I expected the wind from the fact we could hardly open the door, but it was even more fierce than I imagined. I grabbed the life rope first thing. Sleet stung my face and eyes, and I couldn't see more than a meter ahead.

"When I started walking, I realized I was wading through about ten centimeters of water. It flowed back and forth, to and from the sea." He looked at Leonard. "Do you know what that means?"

Leonard shook his head, but Grandma spoke up from her rocker. "Lops."

"That's right," Father said. "The storm caused giant waves to blow over the cliff. Those are lops. They came down on the land just outside this house, only meters from the door. That's when I knew how truly terrible the storm was."

He paused and took a few sips of soup before continuing.

"I'm ashamed to say that for a moment, I thought about turning right around. Not lighting the lamp this one time."

"Why didn't you?" Madge asked. "I sure would have."

Hannah doubted lazy Madge would have gone out in the first place, but she didn't say so.

"Well, I'll tell you," Father said. "First of all, I took on this job, and gave my word. I can't go back on my word.

"Besides that, I thought of Bob, and John and old Tom and all our other friends and relatives. Not only them, but all the people we don't know who might've been sailing the seas at that very moment. They depended on me for the horn and the light. It might save a ship. Maybe even all the lives onboard. So you see, I had to go on.

"It took all my strength to hang onto the rope and walk against the furious storm. Normally I get to the lighthouse in less than a minute. It took I don't know how long this time."

"Half an hour," Monica said.

Father gave her a questioning look.

"That's how long it was before the horn sounded."

"Aye, well, I knew it took a good while. I was glad the doors on the horn-house and lighthouse are leeward so I could open them. Got them turned on with no trouble.

"When I came downstairs in the lighthouse, I could tell the storm had grown even worse. There was no way I was going to make it back. So I did the only sensible thing. I sat me down on the steps and waited.

"Was mighty sorry I couldn't let all of you know I was safe and sound. Knew you'd be worried for a bit, but I also knew you'd figure out that I wouldn't risk it." He winked at Mother.

"And now my soup's finished, I'm ready for a bit of shut-eye."

"I think we can all do with a good rest," Mother said, and everyone agreed.

Hannah had no more than settled into bed when the storm picked up again. The terrifying sounds returned. The old wooden house creaked again under the force of the gale. Hail and sleet slapped against it, and the roaring surf relentlessly slammed the cliff. The cables twanged louder than before. Hannah spent a fitful night.

She stayed in bed later than usual the next morning. With such a storm, the children wouldn't be going to school. When she couldn't wait any longer, she ran to the bathroom, more thankful than ever for the indoor facilities. Then she quickly readied for the day and went downstairs. The family's voices drifted up the stairwell, Father's among them. Hearing him made Hannah feel safe.

"Do you have to go to the lighthouse today?" she asked as soon as she saw him.

"No. I made sure the tanks were full, so they'll last a few days. We'll keep an eye on the light, and an ear on the horn, but the storm should be over before they run out."

Relief flooded Hannah.

"What I'm worried about is the animals," Father continued. "No rope to the barn; and even if there was, don't know that I'd risk it. They'll have to live in dirty stalls without feed nor water, but it can't be helped. They should be okay, long as the barn holds together."

With no work or school, the family spent the day in the kitchen. Mother led them in the rosary and read from the Bible, and knitted. The children played cards and games and drew.

When Hannah got tired of that, she begged Father, "Tell us a story. Please?" The family had heard all his tales, but enjoyed listening to them again. Father was a wonderful storyteller.

"What do you want to hear about?"

Everyone shouted out their favorite. Father chose Hannah's, as she was the one who asked for a story.

"Poor Uncle Ned, you remember him? He spends hours staring at dust bits floating in the sunlight and sings the same song over and over again. He collects clothespins; says they protect him against evil spirits.

"People think he was born crazy, but it ain't so. When we were kids, he was right as rain. We played together all the time. He changed the day the fairies touched him, when he was just nine years old.

"Those nasty fairies! They mean you all kinds of harm and play all kinds of tricks and pranks. I've seen them myself, but always from a distance and only at twilight.

"People say they come in all shapes and sizes, but every one I've seen looked the same. Like little old men, but no bigger than Angie there. They always wore an orange neckerchief, a pointy orange cap, and a long orange coat that reaches all the way to their ankles.

"Fairies live in places out of your reach, off the normal path. Some live at the edge of the forest. Others live in holes below a cliff's edge."

This was a new fact Hannah hadn't heard before. *Good thing Father didn't tell this when we first moved here. Being such a little girl then, I'd have been terrified all the time, living so near the cliff.*

Father had continued, "Always be on your toes around the cliff or close to the woods—otherwise, they'll use their magic to lure you away.

"If you get too close to them, you can hear their fairy music. If you ever hear it, better run before the music can hypnotize you. It'll make you lose track of time and place, and then you'll get lost.

"Best thing you can do to stay safe from the fairies is to always keep a fairy charm on you. A good charm is a small piece of bread in your pocket. If you find out too late, and they got you under their spell, turn your clothes inside out to break the spell.

"Nothing grows on fairy ground. If you see a clearing, look for grass. If there's no grass, fairies are nearby. Sometimes you can help yourself by making a fairy ring. Find thirteen stones the size of your fist and lay them out in a circle. Sit in the middle of it, and the fairies can't get you.

"Fairies love freckles. If you ever go out with a freckle-faced kid, rub his head and say a prayer that the fairies won't get either of you. That's for sure.

"I hear tell, if they get mad at you, they'll hit you with a fairy blast. All sorts of crazy things like fish bones, balls of wool, or even sticks, will spout out from the wound.

"So poor Uncle Ned, when he was nine, he didn't know how to protect himself and he was walking close to a cliff's edge."

Hannah glanced at Leonard, who grinned at her and shook his head. He'd caught it, too. Always before when Father told this story, poor Uncle Ned had wandered too near the edge of the woods.

"The music hypnotized him, sure enough, and he paid no heed when a fairy swooped in on a horse and snatched him away, right quick. He was missing for three days. We found him at the bottom of the cliff with his head banged up."

Not in the road near the woods.

"From that day onward, he was never the same. He was touched by the fairies, you see; and once the fairies touch you, you spend the rest of your days living like they do. Like Uncle Ned does.

"Don't ever let your guard down! Don't go in the woods, and stay far away from the edge of the cliff."

"I'll never go there," Gus said.

"Me, either," Freddie replied.

Hannah suddenly knew why her father told that story.

~#~

The family spent the next two days the same way, occupying themselves as they could in the dim light of oil lamps and candles. Sheets of ice and snow covered the windows, blocking out any natural light that might have pierced the tempest.

The storm raged for three days. On the third afternoon, the sounds outside suddenly stopped. The noise had agitated Hannah, but now, after three days of wishing for it to quit, the silence felt wrong somehow.

Father got ready to go out. "Gotta check the lighthouse and other buildings."

When he tried to go outside, Hannah had a weird sense of reliving a memory. Father pushed on the door but it didn't open. He pushed harder, with his entire body, and it still didn't budge. As before, he called Leonard to help; but this time, even the two of them together couldn't open the door.

"Must be wedged shut with snow, and iced over. The storm has iced us in," Father said. He walked to the big kitchen window and tried to open it, but found the same problem.

"Maybe upstairs will work. Or at least let me get a look outside."

Hannah and Leonard followed him upstairs.

Layers of snow completely darkened all the upstairs windows except one. A bit of light shone through a single window in the back of the house that faced away from the sea.

With much tugging, Father got the window open. He tried to push the snow away, but found it frozen over.

"Son, bring up the hatchet by the woodpile, the biggest pot lid we have, and an empty barrel. I'm going to have to dig myself out."

"I'll get the lid," Hannah volunteered.

She got back before Leonard. He returned with a hatchet, a pail, and a kettle.

"No barrels in the house," he explained.

"This'll do." With the hatchet, Father began to beat the icy snow into chunks. He used the pot lid as a shovel, and dumped the snow into a pail. When the pail was full, Hannah carried it to the sink and dumped it out, while Father continued with the kettle. By the time she got back, he'd filled the kettle.

Progress was steady but slow. When Father tired, Leonard relieved him for a bit. Hannah continued to dump the pail and kettle. In a half hour, they cleared enough ice from the window that Father could crawl outside.

"Lard tunderin' Jayzus," he muttered.

Leonard and Hannah scrambled out after Father. If Mother had allowed Hannah to use that language, she would have repeated Father's words.

The view contained nothing for the eyes to see except an expanse of white in every direction. Enough snow had drifted against the house to cover it completely. No one could see any evidence to suggest a house lay beneath that snow; it looked like a big snowy hill. Other out-of-place snow hills showed where the barn and other outbuildings stood.

"It looks like a foreign land," Hannah said. She shivered; she hadn't put on a coat.

"You two go back inside," Father said. He gathered his tools. "I'm going to cut the snow from the kitchen door."

Hannah crawled back inside. Leonard, also coatless, followed her.

Two hours later, Father sat in the kitchen, warmed up once again with Mother's soup.

"Now I've cleared the doorway," he said, "everyone can go out for a bit of fresh air."

"I'm not going outside in this weather."

"You don't have to, Ma. You can keep Angie in here, but I need Louise and the rest of the kids to help clear the snow from the barn and lighthouse."

They all bundled up and went with Father.

"Tool shed first," he said. "Leonard, you take first turn with the hatchet."

The other children played while Leonard, Father, Mother, and Madge hacked into the tool shed. Pickaxes and shovels made the work of getting into the buildings easier.

Before the day finished, they cleared the important paths and buildings. The barn had held.

"You and the girls tend the stock," Father said. "I'll take the boys with me to the lighthouse."

So Mother checked the animals over while Monica and Bridie mucked out the stalls. Hannah and Madge put out water, hay, and feed. The animals seemed well but hungry and thirsty.

The snow chopping and other work tired everyone. After the urgent outside chores had been tended to, they went inside for warm soup and an early bed.

Chapter 8

Castaways

Just as Hannah began to drift into sleep, a pounding on the kitchen door startled her. She sat up and listened. Bridie did the same.

When the pounding repeated, Hannah jumped up and dressed quickly. She ran downstairs, getting to the kitchen just in time to see a group of men traipse in through the door Father held open.

"Praise God," one or two exclaimed, while another shouted, "Our salvation," and yet another called out, "We're saved!"

Hannah counted eleven men, from Leonard's age to Grandma's. They straggled in one by one.

"Welcome. Have a seat, wherever you can find one," Father said as he lit an oil lamp. The men took seats around the table.

Good thing we're a big family. Just enough chairs for them.

Mother spoke from behind her. "Hannah, put on some tea. I'll make coffee. These poor souls need to warm up."

Hannah jumped to obey. She laughed when Father asked them how they came there and they all started talking at once.

A tall, older man with a commanding presence and

heavy beard held up a hand and the men immediately stopped talking.

The man smiled warmly. "I'm Captain Bob Noseworthy of the banker *John Leary*, and these men are my crew."

Hannah and Mother took around cups of coffee and tea as the captain told his story. This gave Hannah a chance to look them over more closely. They appeared tired, hungry, and worn out. Captain Noseworthy's muscular build gave evidence of years of hard work at sea. The youngest sailor seemed not much older than she. The cute boy cast several glances her way.

The captain explained that his ship, based out of Placentia, was a cod-fishing vessel that fished offshore on the grand banks. They made month-long fishing expeditions far out at sea several times each cod-fishing season.

"We were one day out when we started taking a beating from the big storm that just passed. It looked to be a long one, and seemed too big a risk to ride out at sea. I decided to return to Placentia Harbor and sit out the storm there."

The whole family had come down while the captain spoke. Grandma took one look and headed back up the stairs. The rest of them stood around the kitchen and at the parlour door, listening intently to the exciting tale. Little Gussie came to Hannah and asked her to lift him up so he could see the captain's face. The young sailor continued to eye her.

"It took longer than expected to return," Captain Noseworthy continued. "About 500 meters out, a lop hit us. The seas were too heavy for the ship to right herself. We capsized and wallowed in the raging waters until she washed ashore on the rocks and sand at the base of a cliff 600 meters south of here. The vessel was solidly grounded there for the length of the storm.

"Our hull stayed intact. With the storm raging as it did, we thought it best to remain inside the vessel, where we would be dry and warm. We had plenty of supplies to last. We couldn't cook with the vessel on its side, but at least we had shelter from the weather."

"Must have been interesting," Father commented.

The captain nodded. "Yes, but when the storm ended, we emerged from the hatch, said a prayer of thanks, and assessed our situation. We clearly weren't going to get the vessel to port, grounded the way she was. We were relieved to see the glow of your lighthouse and hear the foghorn. So we headed this way. Took two hours to make the 600 meters through the high snowdrifts."

"Oh, my," Mother exclaimed.

"Now I ask you for help. If you can get us to Placentia, we can make our way home from there. I'll send a salvage operator to rescue the remnants of my ship."

"Of course we'll do what we can," Father answered. "We'll take a look at the road tomorrow. It may be washed out—even if not, it may be a few days before it's passable, what with the snow blocking it. Until then, you and your men are welcome here."

"We thank you most kindly."

The men continued to visit, but Hannah couldn't listen anymore. She and the other girls went to gather all the blankets and sheets they could find, for the men to make sleeping pallets on the floor.

"Will we have enough food?" Monica asked Mother when they were out of earshot.

"Surely. We've plenty to last many days, and the government will resupply us once they know how we used up the stores."

Hannah listened to the sailors' banter as she and Bridie handed out blankets.

"Watch your language, now, lads," Captain Noseworthy said. "Be on your best behavior. There's many children about."

Hannah made sure to get bedding to the cute young sailor before Bridie could.

"Hi. I'm Andy Ryan," he said with a smile. "Thanks for helping us out."

She returned his smile. "My name is Hannah. Pleased to meet you."

Andy spread his blanket on the kitchen floor and fell asleep immediately.

"I'm sorry, that's all we have," Mother said when the last blanket and sheet had been distributed.

"We're most grateful," the captain answered. "We can share. Even if we had none, we're safe and warm. That's enough, praise God."

"Tomorrow we can bring in some hay for you to lie on," Father said. "Then there'll be enough bedding to cover everyone."

"Off to bed, children." Mother said. "Good night, everyone."

~#~

When Hannah went downstairs the next morning, the fishermen were already up. Some sat around the table while others relaxed in the parlour. Mother and Madge worked busily in the kitchen. The aroma of bread baking told Hannah they'd been at it a while already. But something seemed strange.

"You're mixing bread now?"

Mother always mixed bread in the evening, let it rise overnight, and baked it in the morning.

"With so many people, we'll eat all of what's baking by lunch. This batch will be for supper. As long as the sailors are here, we'll mix twice as much in the evening. For now, Madge is making porridge, and I want you to break two dozen eggs. I'll fry them with some fatback. When you've finished that, bring up a dozen apples from the cellar."

The morning passed in a flurry of work preparing breakfast for 23 people. When everything was done, Mother fixed a tray and handed it to her. "Take this tray up to Grandma."

Hannah balanced the tray carefully and knocked on Grandma Murphy's bedroom door.

"Come in."

"Mother made you a tray. Why are you eating up here?"

"I don't want anything to do with those rough men. I'll stay right here until they're gone." Grandma continued complaining about the sailors while she organized the tray to her liking. Hannah couldn't leave; it would be disrespectful to walk out while Grandma talked to her. She fidgeted from foot to foot, willing the old woman to hurry and put food in her mouth. When Grandma said grace, Hannah took the opportunity to slip from the room.

Downstairs, the sailors sat around the table

having breakfast. The young one, Andy, looked around and smiled when he saw Hannah. She couldn't help smiling back. She joined her siblings standing in the parlour doorway, listening to the men make plans to unload what they could of the ship's supplies.

When the men finished eating, Hannah helped clear the table and wash the dishes for the family to eat from. After they ate, Hannah again helped clean up. Then she had her regular chore of milking the two cows.

As she walked to the barn with the milk bucket, she passed some fishermen returning from the ship. They carried boxes and crates and barrels. Most of these they stacked neatly near the kitchen door. A few they took inside.

When Hannah took the milk in to the kitchen, Captain Noseworthy stood near an empty crate on the table, saying something to Father and Mother about tokens of appreciation. Around the crate sat several foodstuffs: sugar, cheese, ham, oranges and lemons, dates, and a bottle of rum. Some small boxes, not much larger than an envelope and about an inch thick, were stacked to one side.

When the captain noticed Hannah, he handed her one of the small boxes. "For you, my dear girl." Each of the children received one of the boxes. Hannah opened hers. Six little chocolates lay nestled inside.

"Thank you, Captain," Hannah exclaimed, and her siblings joined in with a chorus of thanks.

Hannah reached for a chocolate.

"Best wait until after lunch," Mother said.

Hannah closed the box. She looked at Leonard. "I'm going to hide it where you'll never find it," she teased. Father told the sailors about Lennie eating Hannah's orange when they were little.

After a hearty laugh, the captain reached for one of the oranges and gave it to Hannah. "For the one you missed out on," he said. "Maybe you should hide it with the chocolates." Everyone laughed again.

"Off with you children now," Mother said. "Have a play outside before lunch."

It seemed only a few minutes before she called the girls back inside. "I know it's early, but we need to start lunch. It takes longer to cook for so many." She started to give instructions on what each of them should do.

"Ahem." One of the fishermen, an olive-skinned man with a mustache, stood in the door.

"What can I get for you?" Mother asked.

"Naught, thank you. I'd like to offer my services. Name's Cookie. I'm the ship's cook. Feel strange if I'm out of a kitchen for too long. Be obliged if you'd let me help."

Mother and Cookie talked about food and cooking. Evidently satisfied with his ability, Mother put him to work.

Several hours were taken cooking lunch, serving the sailors, cleaning up after them, eating with the family, and cleaning up again. Then Hannah had a little time to play before starting the process over for supper.

A few of the younger fishermen, including Andy, were hardly more than children themselves. They trooped out with Hannah and her siblings and helped them build snow forts. Andy seemed always near Hannah. When the snowball fight started, he saved her from many hits by stepping in front of a snowball meant for her.

All too soon Mother called the girls in to begin the long process of supper. When it was ready, Cookie wouldn't let her call the sailors to table.

"No, Miz Greene. Our bunch can wait, and I'll serve them. You all sit now."

So the family ate first. Cookie insisted on helping wash the dishes. Then he ushered them into the parlour and wouldn't let any of them help him serve and clean up after the sailors.

Hannah took Grandma Murphy's tray up while the men ate. Their laughter drifted up the stairs. She hated missing the jokes. Maybe Leonard would tell them to her later.

"We're going to have some songs after supper," Hannah told Grandma. The old woman loved to sing. "Don't you want to come down for that?"

"No. So many strange people make me jittery. You make sure you conduct yourself like a young lady around those gatching nokes..." She carried on about how Hannah should act. Hannah tried not to be insulted. She knew how to behave, and the men weren't bragging fools.

When Grandma finally finished eating, Hannah took the tray downstairs as quickly as possible. A few of the sailors held instruments—accordions, fiddles, and harmonicas. Father had his bodhrán and Gussie stood tuning his guitar. Leonard and Bridie sat at the table making ugly sticks with the broom and mop.

Someone started playing and singing *The Deaf Woman's Courtship* and everyone joined in.

Old woman! Old woman!
I have come to see you.

Speak a little louder, sir-
I'm very hard of hearing,
Old woman! Old woman!
I have come to marry you.
Well bless my heart and bless my soul,
I do believe I hear you.

Song after song followed, until Mother sent Hannah and her siblings to bed.

~#~

For five days the family enjoyed their guests. Since Cookie took on much of the kitchen work, Hannah and her siblings still had plenty of time to play, often with the young sailors.

Despite the cold, they spent a few hours outdoors each day. Sometimes they ice skated on the frozen pond, or cut holes in the ice to fish. Sledding and snowball fights became common. One young fisherman mentioned ice panning once, but stopped when Bridie gave an emphatic, "No! No way."

Whatever the activity, Andy always managed to partner with Hannah. She never refused. His easy manner and quick laugh made him fun to be around.

Indoors, games of some sort were always afoot. Captain Noseworthy seemed to enjoy cards as much as Hannah, and she taught him Auction 45s. Andy already knew how to play it, and Hannah took special pleasure in beating him. When he lost, his brows drew together with a huff and his mouth set in a thin, straight line. But he kept asking her to play again, even though she won most of the time.

Those not playing took turns telling jokes and tall tales. The roar of laughter filled the house all day long. But they worked, too. Father never lacked for help with repairs around the house or property. Frequently sailors took over chores for the children. Andy went with Hannah to milk the cows every morning and every evening.

He was a handsome boy, and funny and kind. His attention sometimes made Hannah blush. Though he always acted properly, his attention flustered her. He seemed interested in more than a casual friendship.

What if he wanted to someday date her? She couldn't imagine being a fisherman's wife. When Father fished for a living life was hard, especially for Mother. They were always poor. Hannah didn't want to go back to that kind of life.

~#~

Every morning, Father and Captain Noseworthy went to check the road into town after Father completed his lighthouse duties. On the fifth day they said they found the road passable. The crew prepared to leave, as Father would take them to town in the wagon right after lunch.

By now everyone ate together, though still in two shifts. For this last meal before the sailors left, Hannah wanted to be there for the whole thing.

"May I take Grandma's tray up early, so I can be down here for lunch?" she asked.

Mother considered. "Yes. If she complains, tell her I'll make sure she has an extra good tea this afternoon."

So Hannah prepared an early lunch for Grandma

and carried it up. As Mother predicted, Grandma grumbled and fussed as she ate.

Hannah interrupted her suddenly. "Grandma, I need your advice about a boy."

"What boy?" Grandma quickly responded.

"One of the sailors, Andy Ryan. He's fifteen. He follows me everywhere. I don't know what to do."

Instead of making a snide remark as Hannah expected, Grandma seemed interested in her situation. "Go on, chile. Tell me all about him."

"He's from Placentia. His father took sick two years ago, so Andy had to leave school and fish for a living."

Grandma shook her head. "Fishing is hard times, Hannah. That boy will probably be poor the rest of his life."

"I think he likes me. He's always talking about my red hair. He even does my chores. I...I admit I like the attention." Surely Grandma would scold her now.

But she didn't. She merely asked, "What do you think of him?"

"He's sweet. He makes me laugh, even when I'm annoyed with him following me around all the time. I'm surprised he didn't follow me up here to help you."

Grandma actually laughed. "There's nothing wrong with enjoying his company. When I was young the boys flocked around me like flies to honey. It's fun to be young and free."

"We have fun times. And he's easy to talk to—we talk about everything. But I don't think I could ever fall for him. I don't want to be a fishermen's wife. I don't want to be poor again."

Grandma laughed again and reached over to pat

her arm. "Who's talking about being a fisherman's wife? You're too young yet. He's too young himself, and bound to know it. You're jumping the gun, chile. Have fun; just don't lead him on."

"Thank you, Grandma. I'm going to follow your advice."

"Go on, then. I'm finished."

Hannah considered Grandma Murphy's words as she carried the tray downstairs and to the kitchen. If Andy knew she was too young to get serious about a boy, as Grandma said, she didn't have anything to worry about.

At lunch he sat beside her, as usual. She found it hard to concentrate on the conversation around the table with him staring at her all the time.

After lunch each sailor said goodbye to each family member. Andy came to Hannah last. He leaned to her ear and whispered, "Someday, Hannah, I will make you my wife."

Chapter 9

The Assistant

Hannah heard talk of a Depression, but the fact that it had been four years since a good fishing year appeared to affect Point Verde more. Her own life seemed unaffected by either since Father had a government job with a regular salary. In fact, the family had never been this prosperous before.

Father paid back his old debts to the fish merchants. The government kept them supplied with plenty of food. Mother had the money to buy new fabric; and since she excelled as a seamstress, the family wore new clothes for the first time in their lives.

The new clothing brought Hannah thrills for a while. She felt pretty and proud going out in a dress made for her from new store-bought fabric. Her school friends exclaimed with excitement over it. But when she wore her second new dress in less than a year, she sensed envy. She understood; they still wore hand-me-downs and flour-sack dresses. She found it hard to watch friends suffer when her life had bounty.

Her friends envied more than her new dresses; they also resented her full lunch pail. At lunch the girls stared her down with forlorn faces. Some of them often had only a turnip or potato to eat, while Hannah enjoyed a bologna sandwich, and more.

Hannah couldn't bear the hunger in their eyes any longer. At lunch, she sat with her friend Winnie, who was also her cousin. "Here Winnie, take half my sandwich. I have too much."

"Are you sure? Mother says I shouldn't take charity, but I'm real hungry."

"Don't be silly. I have plenty of carrots in my lunch box. Besides, we've always shared. It wasn't charity before. Why should now be any different?"

Each day that week Hannah tried to sit with a different girl to share her lunch with. On Friday when she got home and made a beeline for the pantry again, Mother stopped her.

"Snacking again? You're so hungry lately. Don't you have enough in your lunch pail?"

"I've been sharing my lunch with friends."

"Good grief, Hannah. Why?" asked Mother.

"We have so much, and my friends at school have so little. They're hungry all the time. I can't stand to eat so much in front of them."

"I know it's hard and you love your friends, but I make your lunch so you can grow healthy and strong. That won't happen if you give it all away. I wish we could feed the whole town, but we can't. You must promise me you won't give your food away anymore!"

Hannah's heart sunk. She couldn't disobey Mother. "I promise."

"Good. Now it's time to do your chores and homework. Run along."

What would she do tomorrow at lunchtime?

Next day as they walked to school, Hannah talked it over with Leonard. He'd been encountering the same problem. They devised a plan.

On the way to school they hid their lunch pails at a little clearing known as Hockie's. At lunchtime, they walked back to Hockie's and ate lunch without the staring eyes of the other children.

It didn't take long for their classmates to guess what Hannah and Leonard were doing. This made them more resentful than ever, and they took it out with the most insulting comment: "Hey, Hannah, you got the smell of the government coming off you!"

The remark tore through Hannah's heart like an arrow. The other children had never teased her before. They'd always been friends. She couldn't hide her tear-filled face.

But the remark changed something inside her. She still felt sorry for the other kids, but now she felt angry and determined as well. She'd never become a fisherman's wife. She'd never be poor again.

~#~

That evening, someone knocked at the door. Monica ran to answer, Hannah and Leonard close behind her.

"Andy! What are you doing here?" Leonard asked.

"I'm after some fun. Thought we might have a game of Auction 45s." He looked at Hannah as he spoke.

Remembering his last words, her face grew warm and she turned away quickly. "You all go ahead. I have to milk the cows." She hurried to the kitchen for the milk pails.

Andy followed her. "I'll keep you company. Plenty of time for a game later." On the walk to the barn he chatted about odd jobs he'd been doing since his ship got grounded. He didn't mention anything about that comment he'd made before.

Maybe he forgot, or changed his mind. Surely he's figured out I'm much too young for such talk.

"How are the other fellows?" she asked. They settled into comfortable conversation.

Back at the house, instead of going to the parlour where the other kids played cards, Andy said, "I'd rather walk along the cliff than play a game. Want to come along? Nice day today, and you never know when the next Nor'easter will hit and keep everyone cooped up."

By the time they returned, Mother had supper ready. She hadn't called Hannah to help.

"Care to join us for a bit of cabbage hash?" Father asked.

Andy did, and after supper stayed for a round of Auction 45s. He didn't leave until bedtime. He never strayed from Hannah's side the whole time.

~#~

The supply boat came the next morning. As soon as Father winched the first crate up the cliff, the boys lugged it to the house and Mother and the girls began putting away foodstuffs and dry goods.

It took the entire weekend to put all the supplies away. Mother made simple meals on those days, leaving more time to deal with the boxes and barrels.

"Saved the best for last." Father came in with the last crate.

"What is it?" Gus asked.

Instead of answering, Father opened it. He lifted out a big wooden box.

"A radio!" Leonard exclaimed.

"A marine radio," Father said. "Now when a ship is in distress, it can radio us."

Mother humphed. "And just what are we supposed to do about it?"

"Mayhap I can guide them to safety. Or, with this radio, I can call other ships in the area to assist. Or with the telephone—"

"Telephone!"

"What telephone?"

"Are we getting a telephone?"

Everyone spoke at once.

Father laughed at them. "Yes. The government's putting in a telephone next week."

"But we have a radio right now," Madge said. "Can we play it?"

"Someone's coming with the telephone installer to teach me how to talk to ships with it, but maybe I can figure out how to listen to broadcasts." Everyone stood around watching Father study the little booklet that came with the radio, looking from it to the radio and back. Hannah and her siblings jostled for position to read over his shoulder. She never got to stay there long enough to read anything.

Finally Father said, "Let's give 'er a try." He turned some dials and knobs. A prickly sound came from the radio. "That's static. Means there's no station there." He turned a knob some more.

"*...now and at the hour of our death. Amen.*

"*Glory be to the Father, the Son, and the Holy Spirit...*"

Mother and Grandma Murphy immediately pulled out their rosaries and began reciting with the smooth, deep voice on the radio. The rest of the family joined in.

Even as she said the words, Hannah wished for music instead. She loved the rosary, but they said it all the time. A radio should be for something extraordinary.

When the rosary was finished, classical music came on. Listening to it relaxed Hannah—but she remained alert enough to beat Bridie at cards before bedtime. Tired from the day of unpacking supplies and relaxed by the music, Hannah slept well that night.

She woke early, feeling refreshed. Bridie still lay curled in bed, and the silence in the house meant none of the other children had risen. Hannah dressed quietly so she wouldn't disturb Bridie, then walked softly down the stairs.

"...are good girls. You don't need to worry about them," Mother said.

Hannah stopped. Did Mother mean Hannah and her sisters? Why was Father worried? She stood silently and listened.

"It ain't them I'm worried about," Father said. "It's this Billy fella. A randy nineteen-year-old living in a houseful of girls is a waiting problem."

Who was Billy? Why would he be living in the house?

Mother asked that too, and added, "No way to put him in the barn or the lighthouse, then?" Her voice asked but her tone answered her own questions.

Father replied anyway. "You know we can't. No heat anywhere but this house. No, we'll have to move Lennie in with Gus and Freddie, and give his room to this guy. Don't know what I'm going to do with him, anyway. Don't need no more help, what with Leonard getting so big and strong."

He sighed heavily. "Wouldn't be so bad, maybe, but for what the letter said about him being sent out here to get him away from town."

"I thought it said they were sending him because he liked to be outdoors and didn't want to work in his family's store."

"Aye, but read between the lines, wife. He could go on any banker and fish cod to be outdoors. They're trying to get him away from other bad'n arders."

"I'm sure they wouldn't send him here if he was that bad. They know we have daughters in the house."

"Lard tunderin' Jayzus, woman. They don't care none about that. I'm telling you, keep an eye on this Billy when I ain't around."

Footsteps at the top of the stairs meant someone else coming down. Hannah walked into the kitchen so she wouldn't be caught eavesdropping.

"Who's Billy?" she asked.

Mother and Father startled. Father's face wore the furrowed brow it used to, back when he worried about catching enough fish to feed the family.

Before they could question her, Madge came in. "Who? What Billy?"

"Lighthouse Commission's sending an assistant lightkeeper," Father answered. "Young man named Billy Corbin. You girls won't be needing to have anything to do with him."

How silly. Like we can avoid somebody living in this house with us. Hannah didn't say anything, though, or they'd know she'd been listening longer.

"When's he coming?" Madge asked.

"Your father's going to pick him up at the train station after he's finished at the lighthouse."

"Can I go?" Hannah hadn't been anywhere but home and school in ever so long. They didn't even get to church as often, living so far from town and with snow often blocking the land bridge.

"Go where?" Leonard came into the kitchen stretching. The other girls entered with him.

Mother quickly filled him in.

"I want to go. He'd probably like to have a boy closer to his age to talk to."

"I asked first," Hannah protested.

"Okay, you can both go." Father said in a resigned voice.

When Bridie and Monica and Madge asked to ride along, Father gave a firm no.

"Gotta take the sleigh and there's only room for four. Besides, we don't need to overwhelm him with a bunch of girls first thing."

~#~

They arrived at the depot just as the train stopped and passengers got off. Hannah knew which boy was Billy immediately, though she couldn't have said how. Father seemed to know it too; he waved at the young man, who quickly came over.

Still a teenager but already a man. A very handsome man. Clean, not scruffy like the fishermen and boys around here. Nice clothes. So many thoughts tumbled around Hannah's mind she almost missed his greeting and introduction.

An accent! I didn't know townies talked so differently.

Father and Leonard seemed to take to Billy right away. The ride back to the lighthouse went quickly with conversation about Billy's life, his new job, and the lighthouse. He spoke respectfully but confidently. Father's face relaxed more and more as they drove. Leonard and Billy chatted and joked as if they'd known each other a long time. They seemed destined to become good friends.

Back home, Hannah's sisters surrounded Billy immediately. Each spoke over the other, trying to be first to introduce herself, and continued with animated conversation that verged on flirtation.

Father frowned. "Come on, Billy. Let's go get you lined up at the lighthouse." He gave the girls a stern look, and they closed their mouths without asking to go along.

Father kept Billy at the lighthouse and foghorn all day. He even took a lunch for the two of them out to the lighthouse. But even in his absence, the newcomer created an air of excitement among the girls. Though the rest of the day progressed as usual, Hannah and her sisters worked and played with more energy.

"You won't bring him to the house again any faster with all that scurrying," Grandma Murphy commented.

"Bring who?" Madge asked with feigned innocence.

Grandma Murphy snickered, and teased them all day about gatchin after the new fella.

At one point Monica muttered, "Tetchy snaz."

Hannah gasped. "If Mother heard you calling Grandma names—"

"You keep your long tongue in your head, Johanna Greene. Besides, you know she's a cranky busybody as well as I do."

Father brought Billy to the house just in time for supper. The family always enjoyed lively meals, with lots of conversation and joking. Billy fit right in, with a quick wit and easy manner—not to mention stories they hadn't all heard a hundred times already.

After supper he proved to be a complete hand at cards. He beat Hannah more than she beat him. No one else came close. Leonard whittled instead of playing and the other girls were too busy making moon eyes at Billy to pay attention to the game. Grandma Murphy had gone to bed, and Father and Mother sat talking at the kitchen table.

When Hannah went to get a drink, she heard Father say, "I don't care. First chance I get, I'm building a cabin and out he goes. Too bad winter will prevent me for a few months yet."

At bedtime, Hannah, Monica, and Bridie all climbed into Madge's big bed to gossip about Billy. They all talked so fast, Hannah couldn't keep up with who said what.

"He's so cute."

"I love his accent."

"That's because he's from St John's."

"A city boy. He's some different from the boys around here."

"He could take me away to a life in the city. Just think, movies and dances and—"

"Don't you get any ideas. I'm the oldest—he wouldn't want to go with a kid."

"I think he's rich. His family owns a business in the city."

"Who cares about money? I like the way he makes me laugh."

"I wonder what it would be like to kiss him." They all gasped, then giggled.

"Shh! He's right across the hall—he could hear you."

"You could be Mrs. Corbin."

"Or I could."

Chapter 10
The Esmerelda

Eventually Billy's newness faded and life settled back into a quiet routine. The girls still liked him, but didn't try to capture him anymore. He spent most of his time off with Leonard. Though Billy had five years over Leonard, the two young men had much in common. They often went fishing together, or bird hunting.

More and more often, when Hannah sought Leonard out for some activity, she found him and Billy hiding around some corner. The odor gave them away.

"If Father catches you smoking, he'll tan your hide."

Billy looked at her sharply, then asked Leonard, "She got a long tongue?"

"Nah, she can keep a secret. You won't tell, will you, sis?"

She ignored the question. "I see that bottle in your pocket, too, Billy."

"I'd offer you some, but I don't think you'd like it."

"She wouldn't take it, anyway."

"Never you mind, Leonard. You should stop that right now."

"Don't worry. I'll make sure he doesn't have too much," Billy said.

"Oh, you're some influence," Hannah scoffed. "I can't figure what to do with you." She walked off.

She snuck back a few minutes later and spied. The boys kept smoking. Lennie had several drinks from the bottle, but didn't show signs of getting corned. He mostly seemed to be asking Billy questions about his parent's store and ideas to generate more profit.

Figures. Always wheeling and dealing, every chance he gets. Lennie's as determined as me not to be poor. Bet he owns a store someday.

She left when Billy started telling Lennie about the girls.

~#~

One November evening in 1929, Father and Billy reported a small but unusual wave when they performed the evening tasks.

Later, the family gathered around the radio laughing at Amos 'n Andy, a new show broadcast from America, when a news bulletin broke in. They listened aghast as the announcer said that a powerful earthquake had occurred just off the Grand Banks of Newfoundland. The tremors from the quake created a giant tsunami that came in the form of three tidal waves. Those waves struck the Burin Peninsula—just across Placentia Bay—with huge force. The tsunami devastated the coastal villages, destroying hundreds of homes and fishing rooms. It swept several schooners and boats out to sea. Twenty-eight people were killed.

Mother told them to pray for the people who died. As Hannah recited her prayers, she pondered the fact that the radio, which usually brought much fun and joy into the house, could also bring such horror.

~#~

A few days later Hannah sat in her favorite spot at the cliff with pencils and pastels, sketching. Billy walked along the cliff a little way off, having a smoke.

Suddenly he stopped, staring down with surprise on his face. After a minute he ran off around a bend and out of sight.

A couple of hours passed and Hannah gathered her things to go inside. Billy returned, moving quickly, and hurried into the house. Moments later, he came back out with Leonard.

Billy pulled Leonard around the side of the house to a place they often smoked and drank. But he didn't pull out a bottle or pack of cigarettes. Instead he talked to Leonard in an urgent manner. The two engaged in a lively conversation.

Hannah sat too far away to hear them, but those boys were up to something. When they went back inside, she left her spot and took her things in. Billy and Leonard went about their normal business. If she hadn't seen them outside, she wouldn't have known anything was afoot. The rest of the family didn't seem to realize anything odd, but Hannah noticed the way they kept glancing at each other with a knowing look.

They're definitely up to something. Something big.

The next morning Leonard slipped out of the house early, while Father and Billy tended the lighthouse. He loaded a supply of wood and nails and some tools in the back of the wagon. He tried to sneak back in without anyone seeing him. Hannah didn't let on that she saw him. Lennie ate breakfast with no comment about the wagon of wood and tools.

When Billy completed his duties and returned to the house, Lennie said nonchalantly, "Hey, Billy, want to go bird hunting?"

"Sure."

Those liars! Hannah raced out to the wagon and waited for them to show up.

"Where are you two going?"

"Bird hunting," Billy said. Lennie didn't look at her.

"Since when do you need a wagon of lumber and tools, but no guns, to go bird hunting?"

"Hup!" Billy shook the reins and drove the wagon away quickly before Lennie could answer. No way Hannah could catch a loping horse.

Just wait'll they get back. I'll find out.

They didn't return in time for lunch. They weren't back for Billy to help at the lighthouse. At supper they didn't appear to table.

"Should I worry?" Mother asked. Her face and voice proved she already did.

"Ah, those boys can take care of themselves," Father replied.

Grandma Murphy added her opinion. "Up to no good, I bet."

Finally, an hour or so after supper, they burst through the door with cat grins and a bag full of something.

Before Father could speak, Leonard said, "You're going to be happy about this. I have something for you.

Something for all of you. But first you have to promise not to tell."

"Not to tell who?" Father asked.

"Anybody. Only this family can know, nobody else."

Mother spoke, her voice like velvet. "You know I can't do that, Lennie, until I know why. You must promise you won't ask me to keep a secret of anything illegal or immoral."

"I promise. I'd never ask you to keep a secret like that. So, will you?"

Lennie must be really excited. Usually a comment like that would insult him.

Father and Mother looked at each other. "Okay," Father said. "So what is it?"

Billy reached into the bag and handed Leonard a bolt of fabric, which Lennie gave to mother. Billy continued to pull things out of the bag and Lennie passed them out. Rum for Father, tea for Grandma Murphy, drawing paper for Hannah, books for the older girls and gum and candies for the little boys and Angie.

"Where did you boys get this stuff?" Father demanded.

"The steamship *Esmerelda*," Billy answered.

Father looked hard at him. "I heard that ship was washed to sea in the tsunami. It was docked at Port Au Bras waiting to unload when the waves hit."

"Yes, it's one counted as lost to sea," Lennie said.

Billy explained. "This afternoon I was walking along the cliff and saw smoke. It looked like it was coming from a grounded vessel about half a mile down the coast. I ran down there. It was that steamship, the *Esmeralda*. She lay on her side, broken up. Every time a wave hit the open cargo hold on the top deck, a huge cloud heaved from her smokestack. That's what I first thought was smoke. So I climbed over the hull—"

"Knowing it could be on fire?" Monica cried.

"By now it didn't look so much like smoke so that didn't worry me. I was more afeared of falling and getting stuck and drowning. Every time a wave hit, she shifted and seemed to drop a little more."

"Oh, Billy!" Hannah gasped.

Billy ignored her and continued his story. "I was too curious to let that stop me. When I got to the hold, I saw what the smoke was. The smokestack was broken, and part of it landed near some bags of flour that had split. Every time the boat heaved under a wave, the gust of air blew flour out the broken smokestack. Poof—poof—poof!"

The entire family laughed at Billy's antics.

"Since she hadn't been unloaded yet, she's still full of supplies. Molasses, salt pork, salt beef, all kinds of dry goods, cigarettes, rum, flour." Billy looked at Father. "You know salvage is legal. Whoever finds it can keep it."

"Aye, it is. As lighthouse keepers we have to watch for scaly rogues that set up imitation lighthouse lights to lure ships aground, just so they can take the salvage."

"I'd never do that. The *Esmerelda's* a real salvage. And her cargo means riches. But I have to make sure nobody else finds her before I get her unloaded. Word gets out, it's all over. So I dumped all the flour into the sea. Took a couple hours, but no more smoke to attract attention."

A sound from Mother told how she felt about that

waste. Billy didn't pay any more attention to her than he did Hannah.

"I secured the rest of the cargo best I could. But then I needed help. Too much for me to handle by myself—someone's bound to come across her before I can unload everything. So I come for Lennie."

Lennie took over the story. "He came in last evening all in a dither and pulled me outside. Said he knew how we could make a fortune, if I swore not to tell a soul. We could be fifty-fifty partners."

He looked at Mother and softened his voice. "We're not gonna rip anybody off. We figure we can sell the stuff at bargain prices. We'll still make money and they'll get supplies cheap. Good for everybody."

"I've always known you're destined to be a businessman," Mother said.

"So the next day we loaded up some tools and supplies and went to work. I know a spot in the cliffs where everything would be sheltered, so we cut some branches from the tuckamore woods to hide it. Then we started unloading."

"Didn't get half of it unloaded, what with having to camouflage the cave first," Billy said. "Plus we had to keep watch all the time, make sure nobody saw us."

"Sorry we're late," Lennie added. "Just never thought about the time until it got too dark to see."

Hannah looked at Father to see how he'd react. For a few moments he stared at the floor, his lips pressed tightly together.

Finally he said, "You've done nothing wrong. We're glad you two thought fast and acted quickly. I have another worry. The ship herself."

Hannah didn't know what he meant, but he explained.

"I'm thinking of what Billy said about how she shifts and sways. She must lay in a strong current, and she's not solidly grounded. That means danger. The surf will break her up. Mark my words. Sooner or later, she'll sink or float out to sea. And when it happens, it'll be sudden. If you happen to be on her, you'll be lost with her."

"I'll watch out for him," Billy said, at the same time Lennie said, "We'll be careful—"

"Makes no difference," Father replied. "You won't know when it's going to happen. I can't tell Billy what to do, but you don't go on that ship again."

Leonard started to interrupt but Father held his hand up.

"Don't go on the ship—until I can look her over, see if she looks safe enough." He looked hard at Lennie. "You hear?"

Leonard mumbled something.

"Give me your word," Father insisted.

Hannah knew he'd keep his promise to stay off the ship until Father looked at it.

~#~

The next morning Father came in before the children left for school.

"I went to the *Esmerelda* with Billy when we finished at the lighthouse," he said. "She bobbed heavily, and Billy said she'd definitely shifted. I warned him against boarding on her again, but he's his own man and reckless. You're not to set foot on her, and that's final."

Father's tone brooked no argument. Lennie didn't even try, though he plainly wanted to. All the way to school, and home again, he was gloomily silent. Hannah gave up trying to talk to him.

~#~

Mother waited supper fifteen minutes before Billy came in that evening. As he ate he told the family how much he'd unloaded. Leonard appeared unhappier than ever, until Billy said, "And don't worry, Lennie. Even though I'm doing more work now, you'll sell more because everybody knows you. We'll still be equal partners, okay?"

So that's why he was so upset. Not so much about not going on the ship; he could see it was dangerous. He just didn't want to miss his share of the profit.

The next evening Billy said he was almost finished. "If I'd had another hour of light, I could've got the rest. But I'll get it in the morning. We can take an inventory after you get home from school."

"And finish your chores and homework," Mother added.

~#~

Hannah could hardly keep up with Leonard the next afternoon. She trotted beside him, leaving the other children behind.

"Can I help you do the inventory?" she asked.

"We'll see. Of all the days to have extra homework."

Hannah, usually the last one to finish her homework, was done before Lennie. She went to milk the cows, and when she got back to the house with the milk, he was putting his book and papers away.

"I'll bring in the wood for you," she offered.

"Thanks, sis." He still had to clean out the horse stalls. By the time he finished, it was nearly suppertime.

"You might as well wait," Mother said. "By the time you got there, you'd have to turn right around and come home. There wouldn't be time to do anything. You'll get an earlier start tomorrow, I'm sure."

So Lennie went with the other children to wash up, complaining all the while about his homework. Again, Billy didn't come in time for supper.

"In my day we didn't wait for the help," Grandma Murphy complained.

"Neither are we," Father answered firmly. "Billy knows when supper is. If he's not here on time he can eat a cold plate later."

Hannah had a hard time swallowing. Her stomach didn't want food, but she forced herself to eat. She wouldn't get a plate later and would be hungry once Billy came in and relieved her worry.

The family finished supper, and Billy hadn't shown up. The wind picked up while Hannah washed dishes, and still no Billy.

An hour after dark, Father said, "Come on, Lennie. Let's go check on him."

Mother put Angie and Freddie to bed. Gus insisted on waiting up with Mother and the girls. Madge offered to play cards, but Hannah couldn't concentrate. They all sat anxiously, listening to the wind and staring out the windows for any sign of a wagon in the moonlight.

Hannah didn't know how long they were gone. She dozed off once or twice, and Gus had fallen asleep in his chair.

When Father and Leonard returned, the blast of wind through the kitchen door blew her drowsiness away. Billy was not with them. Leonard went to his room without a word. Hannah stayed to listen to Father tell Mother what happened.

"I knew the *Esmerelda* would be gone; the tides were high today. Sure enough, she's disappeared. Not a sign of her anywhere. Leonard checked their shelter; Billy wasn't there. We went up and down the coast, searching and calling. Too much wind to hear anything, and then clouds came in and covered the moon, so we couldn't see anything, either. We'll try again in the morning."

Mother pulled out her rosary and prayed as Father went to the marine radio and contacted the Placentia Harbormaster. Hannah went upstairs when he started to explain the situation. She didn't want to hear it again.

~#~

"Billy! Biiillllyyyy!"

His name echoed through the air as the whole family searched for Billy. They walked the cliff and rode the wagon searching the beach and the rocks for any sign of him or the *Esmerelda*. Hannah wept as she walked the cliff, calling out Billy's name while she dreaded the worst.

Boats in the area responded to the Harbormaster's call for aid, and a flotilla of local fishermen sailed the bay, combing the coastline for any trace of the missing man. Leonard rode to Point Verde Village to spread the news to the locals, who joined the search.

Mother didn't cook that day; bread and butter, apples, and dried, salted capelin were available for anyone who felt like eating. Instead of playing games or listening to the radio in the evening, the family repeated the rosary, praying for Billy's eternal soul.

The next day mirrored the previous one. When the family returned home that night, Father said, "It's no use searching anymore. We have to face the fact that Billy is lost at sea."

Hannah and her sisters cried themselves to sleep.

In the morning, a photo of a young Billy hung next to the Sacred Heart of Jesus. Hannah stared at it.

"I found it in his things when I gathered them for his family," Mother said. "Whenever you pray or recite the rosary, pray for Billy's soul."

Left: Joan

Below: The saltbox house built by Joe Greene ("Father"). Standing in front l-r: Joe Greene left of window; his brother and nephew; his mother Mary ("Grandma") holding Joan's sister Mary as a baby; his wife Louise ("Mother").

Margaret (Maggie)
Flynn Greene
"Grandmother"

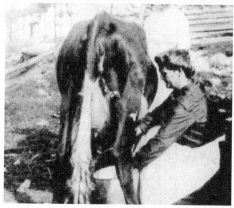

Above:
Cemetery Hill

Right:
Joan

Below:
Sacred Heart Catholic
Church, Our Lady of Angels
Parish, Placentia

Above: Codfish drying on a flake

Below: The lighthouse at Point Verde

Above: Joe and Louise
"Father and Mother"

Left:
Joan

Next page:

Top: Joan

Center left:
Joan's sister
Monica

Center right:
Joan's brother
Leonard

Bottom: The town
of Placentia

Leonard

Chapter 11

Grandma Murphy

After a few weeks life began to return to normal. Father said there would be no more assistant lighthouse keepers.

One day Hannah asked Leonard, "What about the cargo? Are you going to sell it?"

"I can't yet. Besides, I don't want to make money from something that..." He didn't finish. Hannah let it drop.

But the next week she asked again, and received the same response.

"If you don't have the heart to sell it, you can give it away to needy people. Right now everything's just sitting there spoiling or rotting away."

Leonard shook his head silently.

He gave the same answer the next week.

"Lennie, all that work Billy did will be wasted if you don't do something with the things he moved."

After a minute Lennie said, "You're right. I won't let his work be for nothing. But I'm not charging for food. Maybe I'll take a trade, or they can pay a little later, when things pick up or there's a good year for cod."

"I'm proud of you, son." Mother spoke from across the room.

Hannah went with Leonard to keep him company on his first trip to Point Verde with goods to sell.

True to his word, he never asked payment for food. Still, everyone offered something. Whether it was a few pennies or a trade, Lennie always took less than they offered. Hannah wanted to give him a hug every time.

For dry goods he asked only a token payment. "I know you don't need charity" he always added, "but everyone can use a little credit these days. Pay when you can."

Those words never failed to bring a shine to the customers' eyes.

When Lennie sold rum and cigarettes, though, everything changed. "Nobody needs these," he told Hannah. "Anybody who can afford to have such luxuries should pay for them."

He sold those for a strong price and only for cash. "Someday I'm going to own a store," he said. "I think it's my calling."

"You're sure good enough at selling."

~#~

The gravelly squawk of crows set Hannah's teeth on edge as she walked home from school with Bridie and her brothers. She'd never seen so many crows. Where did they all come from? Last week she thought the trees couldn't hold any more of the raucous birds, but it seemed twice as many filled the branches now.

Gus spit at them, having recently learned how to hock up a nasty wad and deliver it with accuracy.

At supper Madge complained about them too.

"They're eating everything in the garden. We won't have a vegetable left if they keep this up."

"They're bad all over," Lennie said. "Everywhere I go, people talk about how the blasted crows have descended on Newfoundland like a plague. Some places, they wipe out an entire field's crop overnight. Next night, they wipe out another."

"There'll be a lot of hungry people in coming days if that's so," Mother commented.

"Can we eat crows, like we do ducks?" Hannah asked. "Maybe Father can hunt them instead."

"Don't you try to feed me crow." Grandma Murphy's voice grated just like a caw.

"I wouldn't want to eat one either," Mother answered. "They're filthy birds."

"But they can still be thinned out," Father said. "Even if we don't eat them, think I'll go bird hunting tomorrow."

Later the family gathered around the radio to listen to *Radio Train*. Hannah especially enjoyed the program. In each episode, a train traveled to a new exotic location and the conductor told about the land, people, and culture of the place.

Father turned the knob a few minutes before the program began to catch a bit of news.

"*...severity of the problem, the legislature has announced a bounty on the pests.*"

"Shh! I want to hear this." Everyone fell silent at Father's command.

"*...twenty-five cents for every crow's beak. Bring them to the local postmaster or constable to receive immediate payment.*"

"Hear that, Leonard?" Father said. "We can hunt

all the crows we want. Just keep the beaks." The two went off to talk about bird hunting.

Hannah couldn't remember ever hearing Father so exuberant. *He must love bird hunting more than I thought.*

After that Father's shots could be heard for hours on end, every day. He had to be a great shot; if Hannah counted thirty shots, he was sure to come back with at least two dozen beaks.

"What do you do with the birds?" she asked him the first day he came back with a pail full of beaks but no crows.

He set the pail next to the barn door. "Leave them for the wild animals."

The next morning when Hannah went to milk the cow, the pail sat in the same place, still full of nasty beaks. The stench of old blood rose from the pail.

"Eww," she muttered to herself, holding her nose as she walked past.

Each day the pail contained more beaks. Each day the fetor grew worse. Finally, on Saturday, Father took the pail to town to get paid.

About time he got rid of that mess, Hannah thought. But as soon as he returned, Father went hunting, and the process began again.

~#~

A few days later Hannah sat in the kitchen peeling potatoes. Gussie came in from outside, bringing a chill into the room with him.

"Where have you been?" Hannah asked as she moved her chair closer to the stove.

"Practicing."

"Practicing what? Your guitar?"

"Nope." He paused a minute and then asked, "Hey Hannah, what's that new hairdo you're wearing called?"

"They're called spit curls." She shivered. "When did it get so cold?"

"When the iceberg got here."

What on earth was he talking about?

"Well," he continued, "I don't think you can call them spit curls unless they're spit on." No sooner had the words come out of his mouth than Gussie made a gross hawking noise and puckered his lips. Before Hannah realized what he was up to, Gussie delivered the grossest collection of nastiness—right into her hair.

Hannah dropped her paring knife and jumped up. "I'm going to get you for that, Gus Greene!" She chased him around the table.

Mother came in and Gussie ran into her. "What's going on here?" she asked.

"He spit in my hair," Hannah cried.

Mother's nose wrinkled when she looked at Hannah's hair. "Go wash it out, Hannah," she said. "And you, young man, don't let me catch you doing that again or I'll take a switch to you."

Her wet hair made Hannah colder than before. The weather had been pleasant so far this spring. The sun shone brightly, and a cold front had not come through.

"Why is it so cold?" she asked again, to no one in particular.

"I told you, because of the iceberg," Gus answered.

"We don't have any icebergs around here."

"Yeah, we do." Gus argued with her for a minute, then went to the kitchen door and threw it open. "Look!"

Hannah could not believe her eyes. There in the bay, not fifty meters away, sat a humongous mountain of ice, hugging the shore's edge and peeking above the cliff.

She stared in awe. The enormous berg filled the doorframe and completely blocked any view of the bay. Many times larger than the house, the iceberg ranged in color from brilliant white to sky blue.

The giant floe rocked slowly with the waves as it ground against the rocky shore. It threw off a cold wave on what should have been a warm spring morning. Hannah had an urge to say her rosary in praise of such magnificence.

She'd heard of such things happening but never dreamed she'd see one. In the spring, glaciers up north calved into icebergs that slowly floated south. They traveled a great distance over a long time. Frequently, the currents would bring them past a landmass where they'd become lodged, sometimes for a number of days. When that happened, the temperature dropped many degrees in the immediate area close to the iceberg.

Suddenly she heard that disgusting hawking sound again. She shrieked and ducked, to no avail.

~#~

One night in the fall of 1930, the family spent a typical quiet evening at home. Louise darned socks and mended. Joe sat in his easy chair listening to a musical variety show on live radio from St. John's. Gussie sat on the floor in front of the radio strumming his guitar, trying to harmonize with the songs that played. Hannah and a few siblings gathered around the table playing a game.

"Hannah," Grandma Murphy called from the top of the stairs. "Bring me up a cup of tea, chile."

"Guess I'm out of this game," Hannah said as she rose. The idea of asking someone else to do it flitted through her mind, but didn't settle. Mother would scold her for being disrespectful—besides, none of the other children wanted to drop the game.

While the water heated Hannah pulled out the tray with short legs, made to fit over a person's legs as they sat up in bed. She set a cup and saucer, sugar, milk, and a spoon on the tray. She filled the tea ball with dried leaves and dropped it gently in the teapot, then poured the hot water over it. The cozy over the pot would keep it warm. She carried the tray carefully up the stairs. Grandma's door stood slightly ajar so Hannah tapped lightly on the frame with her foot.

"Come in, chile."

Pushing the door fully open with her elbow, Hannah entered and set the tray on Grandma's lap.

"May I bring you anything else, Grandma?" she asked politely.

Instead of her usual harrumph, Grandma gestured to the foot of her bed. "Set a spell with your old Grandma, chile. I need someone to talk to."

Surprised, Hannah obeyed. Grandma Murphy's requests for company came rarely—usually when she had extra complaints to make.

But she listened to me about Andy Ryan without any scolding, and even advised me to have fun. I don't have anything to ask about tonight, though.

It turned out that she didn't need to ask a question. Grandma seemed to want an audience as she remembered the old days. Between sips of tea, she told Hannah about her childhood days, being courted, her handsome husband, and raising children. Many of the stories were new to Hannah and she listened eagerly.

Grandma Murphy talked on and on. She didn't seem like the same grandmother—no complaints or scolding, only nostalgic anecdotes from her past. Hannah had never thought about the old woman as a girl or a young lady in love, or even a mother trying to raise a family. A warmth toward Grandma surged through Hannah as she realized how much her elder had lived through.

Hannah didn't make a sound, lest she disturb Grandma out of her reverie and the stories ended. When Grandma sipped the last of the tea from her cup, Hannah jumped up and refilled it from the teapot without being asked.

After a while Grandma grew silent. When she didn't begin talking for a minute, Hannah stood and reached for the tray.

"Get my hairbrush, chile," Grandma said.

Grandma cherished the antique pearl-handled hairbrush as a memento of her own grandmother, from whom she'd received it as a gift. Hannah had never seen a lovelier hairbrush, but seldom got to enjoy it. Grandma usually told her not to meddle with things that didn't belong to her.

Hannah held the brush out to Grandma, but she didn't take it. Instead she closed her hand around Hannah's and patted it gently.

"I want you to have this, chile," she said.

Hannah's eyes opened wide as her jaw dropped open. "But it's yours—"

"Now it's yours. I'm giving it to you, just like my grandma gave it to me. Now turn the light out and shut the door. I'm tired."

As Hannah closed the door, she heard Grandma mutter, "I've got to get out of here. It's a prison to me."

That night Hannah lay awake a long time, going over all of Grandma's stories in her mind and remembering the warmth of the older woman's hand over her own when giving her the brush.

Chapter 12

The Funeral

Shouts and running footsteps. Hannah came awake slowly while her brain tried to sort the sounds of her dream from those in the house.

Cries and more hurrying footsteps.

Real sounds. Real cries.

Hannah threw the covers back and scurried toward the commotion. It came from Grandma Murphy's room.

Half the family stood there with shocked and solemn expressions. Father kneeled at his mother's bed with his face buried in her outstretched and unmoving hand, sobbing loudly. Hannah had never heard her father cry before.

She stepped forward and sat at the foot of the bed, in the exact spot she'd used the night before, and reached for Grandma's free hand. Instead of the warmth of the previous evening, the flesh felt cold as ice. That's when Hannah's mind understood that Grandma had truly died in the night, and was no more. She wept at the great, sad hole left in her heart.

After a few minutes Mother pulled Hannah up and hugged her. "We must prepare for the funeral," she said into Hannah's hair. "Do you feel able to help?"

It would be the last thing Hannah could do for Grandma. "Yes," she whispered.

"Good. Sponge off her good dress and make sure it's pressed neatly."

While Hannah made sure the dress looked as nice as possible, Mother and Madge washed Grandma's body. Then they dressed her. Monica found some makeup and applied just enough to cover the deathly pallor. Hannah used the pearl-handled hairbrush for the first time to brush out Grandma's hair.

When she was ready, Father and Leonard carried Grandma downstairs and placed her on the sofa in the parlour. Father crossed her arms neatly over her chest, and Mother wound Grandma's rosary into her fingers.

"Leonard, go to town and tell everyone to come to the wake tonight," Father said. So Lennie biked to town to inform Grandma's many relatives and friends of her passing.

The older girls began to prepare food for the wake.

Father called the priest at Sacred Heart Church to make arrangements, then went to the barn to make a pine box.

"Gus and Freddie, I need you to do Hannah's chores so she can help me," Mother said as she went to the kitchen.

So while Gus went to milk the cow and Freddie gathered the eggs, Hannah got out a cast-iron pot.

"We must drive death from the house," Mother explained. "We'll start with rosemary, as much as you can carry."

They worked together to chop the rosemary and put it in the pot. Hannah brought more spices—summer savory, sweet marjoram, and lemon balm—which they added.

"Now bring me some dried lavender and rose," Mother instructed. Hannah did. When all the herbs and spices were mixed together Mother pushed them to the sides of the pot. Then she reached into the stove with a pair of tongs and pulled out a smoldering piece of coal, which she put in the middle of the pot.

"Sprinkle a good amount of spices on the coal," she said to Hannah. When the herbs became hot, they released their aromas.

Mother set the pot on the back of the stove. "Several times a day we'll sprinkle more of the spice mixture on the coal. When this coal goes out, we'll put it back in the fire and replace it with a hot one."

When Mother wasn't looking, Hannah put in extra rose petals. Grandma loved roses. Then she and Mother helped the other girls prepare lots of food. Mother even set the little boys to slicing meat and bread and bringing vegetables from the cellar to peel.

Soon the first relatives showed up, followed by more and more. Father had some of the men help him carry the coffin to the house. They placed two kitchen chairs in the corner of the parlor and placed the pine box on the chairs, then gently lifted Grandma's body into it. Hannah brought a quilt and laid it over her.

She stood staring at the body. She'd never seen a dead person before. Even with the makeup, it didn't look like Grandma. Hannah's stomach became queasy from the swirling odor of burning herbs mixed with that of the body. The smell made her suddenly think of the sulfur of hell.

Grandma wouldn't be there! Is she in heaven yet?

Everything she'd heard about death and heaven and souls crowded into her mind and began to roll around.

At the same time she replayed Grandma's last words: "I've got to get out of here. It's a prison to me."

Oh! Grandma's prison was her body. She knew she was going to die! That's why she called me into her room and told me all the stories.

Agitated, Hannah raced to the picture of the Sacred Heart, blessed herself, and prayed. Her faith swelled into her heart, bringing peace with it.

After her prayer she looked around. The house had filled with many people of all ages, there to pay respects to Grandma Murphy and comfort the family. Everyone brought food; many also carried beer or rum. Some brought musical instruments.

At first, the musicians played hymns; then, slow and sad musical ballads filled the house as people compared stories about the deceased. The afternoon wore on, and the beer and rum took effect. Friends and family who had not seen each other in a while visited and laughed. The noises got louder, and the music got faster. By evening, the event no longer seemed like a wake for the dead but more like a kitchen party.

Then the musicians started playing a song new to Hannah, called *Paddy McGee's Mare*. People even started dancing to it. She suddenly realized the song used names of her friends and relatives. The crowd sang along and laughed with glee whenever the names came up, so she paid close attention to the lyrics.

This mare was bred in Canada, she was of a noble fame,
And by her famous conduct, a racer she became.

*She next was brought to Newfoundland, to the
Reids she did belong,
And there she won the races on Quidi Vidi Pond.*

The song told of an adventure the mare had, and
at the end sang of Hannah's father:

*And Joe Greene is watching over her with a
double barrel gun,
And every crow that he shoots down you'll hear
an awful shrill,
For every crow that Joe Greene shoots, he gets
twenty-five cents a bill.*

*And now my song is ended, I haven't delayed you
long.
And if you want to know the man who made up
this song,
My name is Anthony Tobin and in Ship Cove I
belong.*

The song aroused Hannah's curiosity. She'd ask
Father to tell her the whole story after Grandmother's
funeral.

While the kitchen party raged on, incense and
candles burned quietly in the next room, where
Grandma Murphy lay. A few old women, lifelong friends
of hers, sat in the fancy parlour chairs around her body,
weeping softly. Hannah did her best to stay in the
kitchen with the noisy festivities and avoid the room
where quiet order and death reigned.

~#~

When Hannah came downstairs the next morning, Leonard and Father were nailing the pine box closed. They loaded the box onto the horse-drawn wagon outside and covered it with a linen cloth. The family took seats in the wagon for the slow ride into Placentia.

As they made their way through Point Verde and then Placentia, relatives and friends came out of their homes and followed along. The procession grew larger with each part of town they passed. By the time they got to the edge of the village, a dozen wagons made their way first to the church service and then up Cemetery Hill for the burial.

The hill had a beautiful view of the town and bay. It belonged to no one. For as long as people lived in Placentia, almost 300 years, this place had become the chosen final resting place for all the deceased. The hill had no organization. A family picked a spot and, over the years, placed more relatives adjacent to the first spot, so eventually whole sections had families grouped together, buried alongside one another. Gravestones spanning centuries stood all along the hill. Some graves looked well cared for while others were dilapidated and falling down. The lots of the Greene family were neat and clean.

The priest gave a sad but quick funeral service and soon they lowered Grandma Murphy into the ground next to her deceased husband and three of her children who had died years ago. The people said their goodbyes and slowly went down the hill to their homes.

~#~

A few days later Father walked in from his work at the lighthouse to have a cup of coffee. Hannah grabbed her chance.

"Father, I loved that song about Paddy McGee's Mare. I never heard it before. Will you tell me the story?" said Hannah

"You remember Paddy McGee from Placentia, don't you? He loved horses—especially fast ones—and horseracing. He used to buy retired racehorses, and he'd challenge men to races. To up the ante, he'd sell tickets to the races and arrange betting and sell food and beer."

Bridie and the little boys came to sit by Hannah and listen.

"Paddy had one mare that was his favorite. He bought her on the mainland of Canada and took her to Quidi Vidi Pond near St. John's, where he won several races. By the time he got the mare to Placentia, everyone knew she was the fastest in the Avalon Peninsula. That includes Placentia, about twenty kilometers to our west, and the village of Angel's Cove, the same distance east of here."

Monica and Leonard joined the family at the table. Everyone loved to listen when Father told stories.

"Not long ago, on a cold and snowy evening, a young lad in Angel's Cove named Coffey had an accident and cut his leg real bad. His father knew if something didn't happen fast the boy would lose his leg, so he phoned up the only doctor around, who lived in Placentia, and told him it was an emergency."

Father took a couple of sips of coffee before continuing. "Since time was dear, the doc ran to Paddy McGee's and begged for the fast mare to reach the poor boy before it was too late. McGee agreed, and they hitched the mare to a sled because snow completely covered the roads. They raced off to Angel's Cove as fast as the horse could go."

Hannah leaned forward.

"They did make it in time to save the boy and his leg; but the speedy trip took its toll on the poor mare. She was cowed out. Despite that, after treating the boy, the doctor insisted he needed to get back to Placentia that night. As the only doctor, he could be needed any time. He convinced Paddy and they headed out. By Patrick's Cove the mare was faltering so they stopped for the night."

Mother set a cup of tea in front of Hannah. She and Madge had made tea for everyone.

"The next day, they hitched up the sled, but the mare hadn't recovered so they made slow progress. The ice on Point Verde Pond looked firm, so they thought to cut across it to save time. Just before they got to the other side, the horse, sled, and passengers plunged right through the ice into the cold water below."

Bridie and Hannah gasped together.

"You know the pond ain't deep, so nothing got broke or lost. But it took some time and work to get the horse and sled back on land. Some fellas had been passing by and saw 'em, and came to lend a hand. Still, the effort proved too much for the poor mare, and the minute she hit dry ground she collapsed and couldn't get back up."

Hannah's heart squeezed for the poor animal, so sorely used.

"The men rigged up a stretcher plank and rolled the mare on it with the idea of using fresh horses to haul her to our barn, where she could warm up. But the mare died before they got here.

"Paddy said, 'I don't want a dead horse. I ain't gonna drag her all the way to town.'

"I told him she couldn't come here. 'It's your horse,' I said. 'You deal with it.'

"Before we had a proper fight, the doc broke in and said, 'Leave her here. It's far enough from any house. Nobody'll notice the smell.'"

Hannah's stomach turned at the remembrance of the stench of death.

"So we left the horse where she lay. Turned out to be a good thing for me. Crows from all around came to feed off her carcass. I sat nearby with my shotgun and picked off crows by the hundreds, one by one. With the government paying a bounty of twenty-five cents a beak, I made a lot of money off that bait."

Joe finished his cup of coffee. "The story became the gossip of all the pubs around. It got taller and taller, as these things do. Before long, my friend Andy Tobin wrote the song you heard. And now I've got work to do."

~#~

A couple of Saturdays following Grandma Murphy's funeral the door opened as the family finished breakfast. In strode Mary and her boyfriend Jack, whom the family had recently become acquainted with.

"Lard tunderin' Jayzus. If it isn't me firstborn come to give her papa a big hug and kiss," Father said.

Mary embraced Father first, then greeted the rest of the family, who all crowded around the couple.

Under her breath, Mother said, "Oh, dear." Although she smiled, it didn't reach her eyes. Before Hannah could ask why, Mother spoke up loudly.

"Sit down, you two, and don't hold back. I know you didn't come here to idle around on a beautiful Saturday morning. Out with it and be easy on me. I don't think I can handle big news if you don't spill it right out."

So that's it. Mother figures they have news, and she don't think she'll like it.

Monica put the kettle on while everyone else settled around the table again.

As soon as the sound of chairs scraping the floor stopped, Mary did as Mother asked.

"A new magistrate is taking over in Placentia and Mrs. O'Reilly is moving away. I don't have a job in Placentia anymore." She paused. "She's offered to keep me on and let me live with them at the new post in Gander. But the trains don't go there, and that means I wouldn't get to see Jack much. I don't want to be separated from him anymore. It's time we got married."

"Well, you are a bit young yet, but we've seen it coming," Father said. "You're welcome to the family, b'y." He clapped Jack on the shoulder.

"Thank you, Mr. Greene."

"No more 'mister.' You call us Father and Mother, now."

"Yes, indeed. A wedding is good news." Mother said those words but her smile still didn't reach her eyes. Hannah knew why when she asked, "Will you be taking a house in Placentia? Or will you be all the way over in St. John's?"

Mary glanced at Jack before answering. "That's

the thing. We don't want to be separated anymore. Jack's job as conductor takes him away for days at a time, no matter where we settle here." She squared her shoulders and Hannah could tell she reached for Jack's hand under the table.

She continued, "Jack found an opportunity where he can work at railroad headquarters full time as a supervisor. He won't have to travel at all. But it's not in Placentia or St. John's."

The more Mary spoke the more Mother's face faltered.

"His family in New York City has connections. They got him a firm offer to work."

"It's really a good opportunity," Jack said. "I'll be able to support Mary and the family we'll have"—he blushed when said that—"in a way I never could here on The Rock."

Everyone clamored with questions. Hannah couldn't keep the answers straight with the right questions in all the confusion. They got quiet when Mother sighed.

"It appears the fates are lined up against me. You two have been smitten with the idea of moving to America for months."

"Well, at least you get to plan a wedding party," Father soothed.

"I'm sorry, but...no," Mary said. "We don't have time to plan a wedding. The job is open now, and the railroad can't hold it. The trains have to keep going. If Jack wants the position, he has to take it now."

"Now? How soon is now?"

"Day after tomorrow. The steamship leaves for New York Monday."

"How can you be married so soon?" Mother's face suddenly went dark. "No! You can't go off with any man you're not—"

Jack protested but Mary spoke over him. "Of course not, Mother! What do you take us for?"

"I'm sorry. I'm just so surprised. How will you manage so quickly?"

"Mr. O'Reilly helped us get a marriage license yesterday. I also went to Sacred Heart and spoke to Father Kelly last evening. He said he can marry us today, whenever we can get there."

"A wedding today?" Hannah could scarcely believe her ears. It seemed like something from a dream. Excitement ran through her so that she had to dance around the table. "A wedding today!"

As the realization took hold, everyone broke out into celebratory congratulations, hugging Jack and Mary all over again. But Father walked to Mother instead. He pulled her up and squeezed her tight for a long time.

Then Mother broke away. "Monica, put a pot to boil. Leonard, go down to the root cellar and bring up lots of salt beef, potatoes, and vegetables. We have a celebration dinner to make, and it's going to be a big scoff! Bridie, you help. Hannah and Madge, get the young ones cleaned up and dressed, then yourselves. Come on, girls—no time to lose. I'm going to my room to get right pretty for my daughter's wedding. I want her to be proud and happy on this day. Move it!"

But when Hannah passed by Mother's room a little later, Mother sat on her bed, weeping.

Chapter 13

The Mysterious American

Andy frequently visited over the next year, seeking out Hannah's company. She maintained a friendly relationship with him, often walking with him through the meadows or along the cliffs on pleasant days. Hannah enjoyed the fresh air, but she made sure Andy kept a proper distance.

A few weeks before Christmas, they walked along the cliff's edge on a windy day, watching the water lap against the shore. Hannah suddenly stopped.

"Look, Andy." She pointed to a grounded boat. "It's not a dory or fishing boat."

"It's a lifeboat. Let's go!" Andy clambered down the rocky cliff. Hannah followed close behind him.

"There's somebody in it," Hannah said. "Is he... dead?"

"Don't know yet." A few more strides and they reached the boat. The lone occupant, a boy about Andy's age, lay still and pale in the bottom.

Andy jumped in and gently shook the boy. "He's alive, but not for long if we don't warm him up. He's cold as an iceberg, out here in the wind."

"I'll get Father."

Hannah ran up the rocks, yelling for Father. She

got halfway up before Father's face peered over the edge.

"Help!" She pointed to the boat. Father's eyes grew wide and he rushed down.

With Father's arms under the boy's shoulders and Hannah and Andy each supporting one of his legs, they got him up to the house. As soon as they opened the door, Father began shouting instructions. "Louise, get his wet clothes off. Madge and Bridie, get a towel and some blankets. Monica, put some tea on to boil."

They lay the boy on the sofa in the parlour. Mother undressed him and dried him off, then covered him with several blankets. Father called the doctor in Placentia.

Hannah and Andy fielded excited questions about how and where they found the boy. Everyone speculated about who the lad was and how he ended up on their coast.

"I bet he survived a shipwreck."

"More likely he's a runaway cabin boy."

"No—a stowaway criminal!"

"From America."

"Or England."

"Maybe he's somebody famous..."

"All right, children, calm down now," Mother chided. "There's no point in guessing. We'll just have to wait until he wakes up and tells us."

"Doc's on his way," Father said when he hung up the phone. "It'll take him some time to get here."

Hannah and Bridie helped Monica get supper while Mother sat with the boy and prayed for him. By the time the family finished eating supper, they'd asked and wondered until the thrill evaporated. Everyone went about their usual activities. Andy stuck by Hannah.

The doctor arrived soon. Hannah and Andy followed him and Father into the parlour. The boy seemed to be waking. He moaned some, and his body twitched.

The doctor looked him over. "I don't see anything particularly wrong with the lad except this fever, no doubt from being exposed in that open boat. He does have some bruises and scars that don't seem normal, but they're not fresh."

From where she stood, Hannah could see the crisscross of scars from a lashing across the stranger's back.

"Any idea how long it'll be before he wakes up?" Father asked.

"No; at this point I can't even say for sure that he will wake up, much less how long it might take. All you can do is to keep him comfortable."

He took a bottle from his black bag. "Give him some of this medicine every few hours to fight the fever, and swab him with wet linen to keep him cool. I'll come back around in a day or two. Call me if something happens before then."

"Mind if I ride with you back to town?" Andy asked him.

Once they left Mother said, "It's time for everyone to get ready for bed. We'll take turns sitting with the boy, youngest to oldest."

"Even me?" Freddie asked.

"No, not you. Or Gus either. Hannah first, then Lennie, and so on. Get ready for bed first so you don't wake anyone up later."

Hannah changed into her nightgown and brushed her teeth, then settled into a parlour chair Mother had pulled near the sofa. Now she had time to take stock of the boy without everyone seeing her stare. He had good-looking features with clear skin and blond hair. He appeared reasonably strong and healthy, though skinny. He did have several small round scars on his arms. Hannah felt sure they were burns.

His wet clothes still lay in a pile at the foot of the sofa. Hannah carried them to the bathroom sink to be washed. They'd been patched and mended several times, but still appeared threadbare and poor.

Despite the medicine and Hannah's wet cloth on his forehead, the lad seemed to grow more feverish. His moaning became louder and more frequent, and in addition to the twitching his body occasionally convulsed. Still, he never opened his eyes or spoke while Hannah sat with him.

The next morning, as soon as Hannah reached school her friends surrounded her. Word about the mysterious boy had already spread through the village. The kids threw out questions faster than Hannah could answer them—not that she had many answers.

Several times during lessons, her mind drifted back to the unknown lad. Perhaps he'd be awake when she got home, and ready to tell his story. She and her siblings rushed home after school to find out.

They found him worse instead of better. Still unconscious, his fever now burned even hotter and he often shouted with delirium.

"Everybody in town knew about him, but nobody had any idea who he could be," Hannah told her parents.

"No, even headquarters doesn't know," Father

replied. "I radioed in, but there's been no report of a ship going down, or anything that would've required use of a lifeboat. And the boat has no markings, so no way to tell where it came from."

Hannah found it hard to concentrate on her homework with the mystery demanding attention. The other children finished and went to play games or listen to the radio while she struggled on. She couldn't even help Mother and her sisters prepare supper. As they got ready to serve, Hannah slapped her books closed.

Good enough. She didn't say it aloud—Mother would insist on better.

After supper the doctor called. Father reported the change in the patient's behavior. Hannah couldn't hear the doctor's side of the conversation, but Father's expression said it wasn't good news.

When he hung up, Father confirmed her suspicion. "Doc got called out to some emergency down Jerseyside way. Won't get this direction again for a few days." He paused. "Said to keep doing what we're doing, but he don't hold out much hope."

Mother didn't reply but began reciting the rosary.

That night Mother sent all the children to bed. "It's not healthy for growing bodies to miss too much sleep," she said. "I'll sit with the boy tonight."

As Hannah went upstairs she heard Father say, "I'll spell you some, Louise."

The next morning Mother asked Hannah if she'd like to stay home. "I need some help, and I know you don't mind missing school as much as your sisters."

"I can't help it. School's so boring." *And all that homework for nothing.*

Hannah sat by the lad's side while Mother tended

to other duties. As the morning went on, his fever lessened more and his thrashing stopped. He no longer shouted or even moaned.

A little before lunch, he suddenly opened his eyes. "Who are you? Where am I?"

A smile so big she couldn't stop it spread on Hannah's face. "I'm Hannah. You're at Point Verde lighthouse. We found you in a lifeboat day before yesterday, almost dead."

"Can I have a drink? I'm real thirsty." His voice was so raspy Hannah couldn't tell if it truly had an accent or she only imagined it.

"I'll get you some broth. That'll help get your strength back." She hurried to the kitchen. Mother sat outside the door plucking a chicken.

"He's awake," Hannah said. "He wanted water but I'll give him broth from the soup."

"That's my girl. I'll be there soon as I finish this and get cleaned up."

Hannah spooned broth into the boy's mouth. All the questions she wanted to ask would have to wait. No use asking them now—he couldn't answer while swallowing.

When she'd fed him the last drop, she couldn't wait any longer. "What's your name?"

He stared at her for a minute and finally said, "I'm tired." He laid his head back down and closed his eyes. When Mother came in, he was asleep.

"I'll have a nap, too," Mother said. "After being awake all night, I can use a bit of rest."

Hannah had never been in such a quiet house. The radio might disturb the patient, so she got her sketch pad and drew.

A couple of hours later, Mother came downstairs. "Any news?" she asked.

"No, he's been asleep."

The boy woke just then. Mother said, "Well, hello, young man. I'm Louise Greene. What's your name?"

"Tommy—" he stopped abruptly.

"What's your last name, Tommy?"

Tommy stared at her for a few seconds then exclaimed, "I don't remember!"

"Do you know where you come from?" Hannah asked.

"No." Tommy replied almost before she finished asking the question.

"Okay, Tommy," Mother said. "Do you want some more broth?"

"Yes, please."

The other children arrived home from school while Hannah fed him. They crowded around and peppered him with questions, but all to no avail. No matter what they asked, his answer remained the same: "I don't remember." The Greenes did learn one thing about him—he was most likely American. Hannah had been right about his accent. Otherwise, he remained a mystery.

Tommy became more animated as the evening progressed. At supper he sat up and fed himself, though he wasn't strong enough to walk to the table yet. When Lennie and Bridie brought a deck of cards to him after supper, he said, "I'm not up to it. But soon. Do you play black jack? And dominoes—you got dominoes?"

They talked about games, which led to all sorts of other things. Tommy made good conversation about everything, except himself. The more Hannah listened to him, the more suspicious she became. How could he remember the rules of games and all the kinds of fish but not his name or his family?

I don't believe him. He's either hiding or in trouble. Maybe both. She remembered the scars. *Aye, both.*

When the family retired for the night, Tommy had enough strength that with Leonard's help, he made his way up the stairs to the now-empty room that used to be Grandma Murphy's.

~#~

Each day Tommy became stronger than the last as he spent many hours resting and recuperating. True to his word, he soon joined the kitchen games. Mostly, the family played the card game of Auction 45s.

"What kind of game is that?" Tommy asked about it.

"It's a game from Ireland," Hannah answered. "We usually play the partner version, but you can play one-on-one as well. Everybody gets five cards. Some cards are stronger than others, especially the trump cards. In each round everyone plays a card, and the person who lays the strongest card wins that trick, which is worth five points. The team that reaches 120 points first wins."

Tommy said, "I thought trump cards were only in bridge."

Hannah responded, "No, several games have trump cards."

"Teach me the rest of the rules, please. I want to learn to play."

"Before each round begins, the teams bid, and the

highest bidder gets to say which suit is trump. They better make sure they win enough tricks to reach the score they bid, or they go in the hole."

Several of them went through a round slowly, explaining the bidding, trumps, and tricks along the way. Then Tommy said he was ready to play.

And play he did. Hannah had met her match in Auction 45s. Though competitive, everyone played all in good fun.

As the days passed Tommy became a lively conversationalist. He told tall tales and jokes to rival Father's. A bright lad, he could add something to almost every subject—other than himself. He also played a darn good harmonica, which brought new fun when he tuned in with Gussie for some lively songs. Tommy even taught them a few new ones.

One Saturday evening Andy stopped in for a visit. Lennie introduced Andy to the boy he'd helped save. Hannah expected such a connection to start a friendship, but instead the two boys treated one another with cold politeness.

Andy had arrived after supper, just in time for a game of Auction 45s. The family partnered up the way they usually did. Tommy, Andy, and Hannah ended up on opposing teams. As the game progressed, the competition grew more intense. In fact, Andy and Tommy seemed fairly cutthroat. The boys moved fast and each time one of them won a round, took a trick, or put someone in the hole, he looked at Hannah, puffed out his chests, and heckled the opponent. The boys concentrated so hard on beating each other that they didn't pay enough attention to the other teams. Hannah and Mother won the game.

After cards, the family had a break from games and sat talking around the kitchen table. Andy stepped up his conversation with livelier stories than usual. Each time Tommy told a story or joke, Andy tried to best it. Then Tommy came up with an even better one. Always they looked at Hannah as they did, as though she was the only one present.

For once, Hannah breathed a sigh of relief at Mother's announcement of bedtime and Andy's subsequent departure. One at a time she could handle Andy or Tommy, but together they tried her patience.

~#~

What will happen to Tommy? Hannah wondered as she organized the closet under the stairs one day.

He gained strength every day, and started helping with chores. But no matter how well he got, he had nowhere to go. He still claimed not to remember anything about his past or family. There were no nearby facilities for boys like him. He didn't have a penny to his name, or any possessions—not even an extra set of clothing. Lennie gave him some outgrown clothes to replace the scraps he'd arrived in. As likeable as he was, Tommy remained a mystery.

Footsteps sounded in the parlour. Hannah turned to go see who was there when Father's voice stopped her.

"I brought you in here to have a man-to-man talk," he said. "You know we all like you and enjoy having you with the family."

He's talking to Tommy.

"But we can't keep you here indefinitely. It

wouldn't be right. Now don't worry—I'm not kicking you out right now. But when spring comes, you'll need to move on."

"Where?" Tommy asked. "I don't have anywhere to go."

Surely Father won't throw him out to fend for himself!

But Father said, "There's some options. For one thing, there's an orphanage in St. John's. You say you don't remember how old you are, but I guess you're plenty young enough for that. You can't be more than thirteen or fourteen. Fifteen at the most."

"I don't think I'd like that." Tommy's voice had a higher pitch than usual.

I'd be scared too. There's all kinds of stories about the awful things that happen in those places.

"Then you might think about hiring on as an apprenticeship somewhere."

"What kind of apprentice? I don't know how to do anything."

"They'd teach you—that's the point of an apprenticeship. They'd give you room and board while you learn the trade."

"Maybe." Tommy sounded doubtful.

"Of course, you washed up in a lifeboat," Father continued. "That indicates you probably came off a ship. You could hire on as a deckhand—ships are always looking for crew—and you might find some of it coming to you naturally, from before." He paused. "Anyway, you don't have to decide this minute. Like I said, you got until spring. Just be thinking on it so you'll be ready and know where you want to go when the time comes."

Just a couple months before he has to face the world

alone, Hannah thought. *He'll be all by himself, with no one to help him or even encourage him. I'm going to be extra nice to him while he's here.*

~#~

Hannah found herself more attached to Tommy each day. The American boy often made her laugh, and always made her feel special. The two spent more and more time together when Hannah wasn't at school.

Toward the end of winter, Andy stopped by.

"Where have you been, Andy? We haven't seen you in ever so long," Hannah said.

"And I can't stay now, but I brought you some seal flippers. I've been up north, seal hunting." He pointed to a pail beside the kitchen door. "Take a look in that pail, Tommy. I bet you've never seen anything like that."

Tommy looked. "I've never had seal. It looks kind of slimy, but I'll try it."

"You haven't? It's a delicacy," Hannah said.

At the same time Andy taunted, "I bet your stomach couldn't handle it."

"It will when I make it," Hannah retorted. "Tommy will love my cooking."

She turned to Tommy. "I'll make you a delicious dish of seal flipper with brown gravy."

When Andy left, Hannah set about making the dish. Since this was a special snack for Tommy and not a family meal, she prepared only one flipper. Tommy watched her.

Hannah laid the flipper out on the cutting board. It looked like a little webbed bear claw no bigger than a child's hand. She removed the outer skin, cut off the end at the outer joint, and discarded the small, fingertip-like appendages. The lower knuckles remained attached to the palm.

Hannah trimmed the flipper to remove the thick blubber, then placed it into a cast-iron skillet along with tiny cubes of salt pork. A pungent smell of oily fish wafted from the pan as Hannah added spices and onions to the mix. She cooked the dish slowly until the meat fell from the bone and the cartilage melted into a gelatin that coated the cooked meat. Then she added some flour to make a dark gravy.

"It's ready. Sit down." She dished the fishy mixture into a bowl with pride and anticipation. Tommy had to be impressed with her cooking.

When she set the bowl in front of Tommy, he didn't seem eager to try it. His nose crinkled as if he'd never smelled fish and his lips pressed together.

"I know it looks like slimy mud and smells like rotten fish, but flipper is really delicious," Hannah encouraged him. "Go on, try it."

Tommy picked up his fork and poked at the meat a few times before putting a bite in his mouth. Now his entire face crinkled, not just his nose.

"Don't you like it?"

Hannah wasn't sure if his answer was a moan of pleasure or groan of disgust. He swallowed, glanced at her and gave a tight smile, then forked another bite.

BLARF!

The food spewed out with the force of a tidal wave, accompanied by loud retching.

Hannah froze in mortification, then burst into tears. How could she have made him so sick?

"I'm sorry," she hiccoughed between wracking sobs. "I didn't mean to—"

Tommy had rushed to the sink and washed his face and mouth. Now he turned back and wrapped his arms around her.

"Don't cry. It wasn't your fault. I'm sorry! I didn't mean to...it must be because I'm American."

"An American? Americans can't eat seal?" she cried. Then suddenly that struck her as funny and she laughed so hard she couldn't stop.

He laughed with her, and they both laughed until Hannah could hardly catch her breath.

Tommy gasped, "I haven't laughed like that since before my mama died!"

Hannah stopped dead. "I knew it! I knew you remembered things you weren't telling. Now stop this malarkey and tell me the truth from the beginning."

Tommy stepped back and looked away from her. "My name is Tommy Baldwin, and I'm from Boston. My father was a longshoreman on the docks there." He paused and his face drew in as it had with the flipper.

"He was a drunk. Always drunk, and usually a mean, nasty drunk. When my mama was hit by a car and died, he went on a drinking binge. Never stopped, even when he lost his job. I had to quit school to work—selling newspapers, odd jobs, anything I could find—just to buy food. But he usually stole my money to buy another bottle."

He stopped. Hannah couldn't think of anything to say, so she waited silently for Tommy to continue. He stared at the wall.

"The more he drank, the meaner he got. He'd whip me with his leather belt, then he turned it around and whipped me with the buckle. He crushed out his cigarettes on my arms."

Another pause. He continued to stare off into the distance. "One night I fought back. There was an empty whiskey bottle on the table, and I grabbed it and whacked him over the head with it. Hard. He fell to the floor, bleeding all over the place."

Tommy looked Hannah in the eyes. "I didn't mean to hit him so hard! I tried to wake him up, but I couldn't. Then I wasn't sure I wanted to. If he woke up, he'd beat me worse."

He looked back at the wall. "I was terrified. So I ran away. Somehow I ended up at the docks. The steamship *Nova Scotia* was there. I knew she'd break anchor in the morning, bound for St. John's. So I snuck onboard and hid in the cargo hold.

"After a couple weeks, some crewmen came down to get some supplies and they started talking about a stowaway. How the captain wanted them to search the ship. I didn't know what would happen. Would the Captain beat me, or shanghai me into slavery? Or take me back to Boston to face either a murder charge or a father livid with rage and bent on revenge?"

"Oh, Tommy."

"So I snuck around behind them, climbed on deck, jumped in a lifeboat and cut it loose." He laughed bitterly. "I regretted it soon enough. I didn't have any provisions, not even fresh water to drink. I got colder and hungrier and thirstier until I passed out. Next thing I knew, I woke up on your sofa."

"You're lucky we found you when we did." Fear of what might have been made Hannah's voice sterner than she intended. "Even one more day, you probably wouldn't have made it."

"I'm really sorry for lying to you. I was afraid if the truth came out, someone would force me back to Boston. I have to stay away from there."

"I understand," said Hannah. "This is a secret you need to keep. I promise, I won't tell anyone. But Tommy, you can't risk another slip like you said earlier."

"I know. I just have to hold out a few more weeks, until spring. I have to leave then anyway."

"What will you do? Where will you go?"

"St. John's. I figure I can be just another Yank in the crowds there."

~#~

Spring arrived gently, with each day growing warmer. Hannah sat at the cliff's edge one sunny day sketching and talking with Tommy, who sat nearby, when Father approached.

"Tommy, what do you think?" he asked.

Hannah knew immediately what he meant. So did Tommy—he answered, "I want to go to St. John's."

"St. John's, eh. What will you do there? Do you have a job lined up?"

"Not yet. But I'm sure I'll find something there."

"Why don't you let me wire ahead to some folks, see what I can find for you in the way of an apprenticeship? That would be a stable position."

"No, thank you. I'd rather find my own way."

"I can't just turn you lose all alone, with no prospects. How about—"

"I really want to do it on my own," Tommy

interrupted. "I promise if I can't find something on my own right away, I'll call you and let you help. Okay?"

Father thought a moment then said, "I admire your spunk and independence, anyway. Okay, I'll agree on the condition that you give me your word you'll call if you haven't gotten a job and a place to stay within one week. Do you?"

"Yes, I promise."

It was a sad evening, knowing Tommy would be heading out in the morning and no longer around for fun and games. The whole family would miss him, Hannah knew—but no one as much as she.

The next morning Hannah rode with Father to take Tommy to the train station. As Father bought a ticket to St. John's, Tommy asked Hannah, "Can I write to you?"

"Oh, yes! Please do. And I'll answer every one."

Father walked up as the train conductor called "All aboard!" He gave Tommy a few dollars to get started with and wished him well.

Tommy jumped on the train and disappeared.

Chapter 14

My Name Is Not Johanna

Hannah answered a knock on the door.

"Mrs. Murphy," she said in surprise at seeing her school teacher. "Won't you come in? I'll get Mother."

"Actually, I came to see you. It's such a nice day; why don't we walk?"

"Me? Okay." Hannah stepped out and they headed to the cliff and Hannah's favorite walking path.

"I'll get right to it," Mrs. Murphy said. "Your grades have been suffering for quite some time. You're a smart girl. What's going on? Why don't you put more effort into your schoolwork?"

"It seems so pointless," Hannah answered. "Everybody around here seems stuck here forever. Why bother to learn history or geography? What good is it if all you're going to do in life is jig codfish in a dory or make fish day after day?"

"Education and knowledge open doors, Hannah."

"I don't see any doors around here. I'm fourteen, and still doing the same things I did at nine." Hannah's voice caught and she took a breath. "It seems like there should be something more, but I don't know what it is."

"You know, I think you need a change. Have you ever thought about following your sister Mary's path? The day she moved in with your grandmother in Placentia to attend the convent school was a good moment in her life. It might be good for you to make new friends and experience life in a bigger town. If you want, I can help you transfer there."

"Would you?" Hannah cried. "Thank you, Mrs. Murphy. I do want to."

Soon after, Hannah threw open the kitchen door and raced in, breathless. She stopped next to Mother, who stood at the stove preparing supper, to catch her breath.

"Goodness, Hannah, what's wrong? You look like you've run a mile."

"Nothing's wrong, Mother. Something's right. I had a talk with Mrs. Murphy about my bad grades. She had a wonderful idea to help me to improve. I told her how I've been feeling, and she suggested a change in my life that will solve everything."

"A change? What kind of change?"

"Can I go live with Grandmother Maggie and attend the convent school in town, like Mary did? Please, Mother."

Mother didn't say anything, so Hannah continued, "You know Grandmother has been lonely since Mary moved away to New York. I can stay in Mary's old room and keep Grandmother company. Besides, she's getting old and could use help around the house. And, the school and church are close to her house."

Hannah had to take a breath but then hurried on. "I know I'd get better grades there. And I'll come home on the weekends. Please, Mother, let me do this. I do need a change."

Mother smiled. "Let me talk to your Grandmother

and see what she thinks. If she agrees, then I'll talk to your father about it."

Hannah hugged her mother and laughed and danced around the kitchen. Of course Grandmother would say yes; and if Grandmother, Mother, and Hannah all thought it a good idea, Father would go along too. She might as well begin packing.

After Mass at Sacred Heart Church on Sunday, Mother and Hannah walked with Grandmother Maggie to her home while the rest of the family followed Father on his regular Sunday visit to his brother's house.

"We have a favor to ask of you," Mother said.

"I'll sure do whatever I can," replied Grandmother.

"Hannah needs to change schools. She's not doing well in the Point Verde school. Her teacher suggested she might thrive and do better in the convent school. We hope she can enroll there and live with you during the week, as Mary did. She would come home to us on the weekends."

"Please say yes, Grandmother! I love you and I want to live with you," Hannah chimed in.

Grandmother smiled. "Yes, chile, come live with me. The house has been some lonely since Mary left. You would bring blessings and joy to me."

Hannah threw her arms around Grandmother and smothered her cheek with kisses.

Grandmother promised to work with Mrs. Murphy to make the arrangements with the convent school for Hannah's enrollment. Then she said, "All the weekend travel back and forth is going to be a lot for the horse and buggy."

"Joe and I have talked about the time it'll take

away from the weekend," Mother replied. "It's an easy sacrifice if it helps Hannah as much as it did Mary."

Grandmother said, "You know what Joe needs? An automobile. That horse and buggy is old-fashioned and too much trouble. A lighthouse keeper needs a car in case of an emergency; and now with your daughter here at my house, he absolutely must have one."

"We've saved a little. Joe's salary has been good for us. I wonder if we could manage it," Mother mused, almost to herself.

"You go home and tell Joe it's time the family had a car," Grandmother insisted.

Father agreed immediately. Hannah had the feeling he'd already been thinking about it.

The very next Saturday, he took Hannah with him on the morning train to St. John's, where he bought a brand-new Ford. He'd never driven before, but after he paid for the car, he and Hannah got in for him to drive home.

Hannah laughed hysterically at her Father's antics in trying to keep the car running. Somehow, every time he handled the clutch, the car stalled. As the day progressed, she found less humor in the situation and instead wondered if they'd ever get home. The journey should have taken less than five hours, according to the salesman. It took them eight.

~#~

Placentia! Though Hannah had been there practically every Sunday of her whole life, pulling into the town to live brought an excitement all its own. The town had so much more to offer and so many more people to meet and befriend than little Point Verde.

It had a lot of history, too. In her "useless" school lessons, Hannah had learned that the peninsula had been used by the Portuguese, the French, the Spanish, and the English since the 1550s. It was considered a perfect safe haven for fishermen and their boats. It had even been the capital once. Only St. John's was more important. Anything could happen in a place like Placentia.

Hannah carried her suitcase into her new room at Grandmother's house. *My own room.* She'd never had a room to herself. It seemed to symbolize freedom.

Grandmother was well off and had always spoiled Hannah and her siblings when they visited. Now there were no siblings to share the attention. Hannah felt sure of living in luxury.

She was proved right when Grandmother insisted she needed new dresses. "Those were fine for the country or Point Verde," Grandmother said, "but here in Placentia the standards are different. We must be ladies."

That meant more rules, but Hannah was glad to learn the etiquette Grandmother wanted to teach her. It represented the first step in preparing to meet the world.

~#~

Hannah woke to the aroma of coffee. She dressed and groomed carefully for her first day at the convent school. When she got to the kitchen, she found Grandmother buttering toast.

"Good morning, Grandmother," she said brightly.

"Good morning to you, too. Would you like some jam on your toast?"

After that Grandmother chattered on about her own schooldays. Hannah enjoyed the new stories. The time with Grandmother made the morning special.

She left in plenty of time to take in the sights on her short walk to school. The sun shone gloriously and the fresh sea air energized her as she passed the little well-kept bungalows where all her new neighbors lived. The scents of fishing and the sea were familiar but the sights and sounds were new.

Hammers banged where men worked on a building in the distance. Voices and shouts seemed to come from all directions. Some of the shops that lined the waterfront served customers. Even a pub looked open, but of course Hannah would never look inside a pub any more than she'd go to the Anglican church.

Several other pedestrians walked along the street and Hannah blended in with them, passing a couple of restaurants and the only hotel in town. Several men stood outside the doctor's office talking in low tones. One of them was saying, "Blood was everywhere... There was nothing I could do."

Across the street stood a warehouse with large open doors facing the street. A sudden acrid odor hit the air from that direction. Hannah flinched. The odor came from many nearby barrels marked cod liver oil, stacked up inside the building. Encircling the warehouse stood a pier occupied by a half dozen women at work making fish on wooden flakes. Hannah picked up her pace. She came to Placentia to escape the fishing life.

Closer to the school, children her age stood staring

into the windows of Monkarsh's Dry Goods Store. Some of them were friends from church, so Hannah joined the group. The window display offered many different items, including a woman's corset, a harmonica, and some bolts of cloth. But the children looked beyond that. A few meters past the display stood a service counter with an array of penny candy, a cash register, and a funny-looking man standing behind the counter. He wore a mustache, a bow tie, a red vest, a straw hat, and a huge smile. Hannah knew Mr. Monkarsh well. He made friends with every kid in town, acting like everyone's uncle. She thought him one of the nicest people she'd ever met.

Our Lady of Angel's Presentation Convent School was old—the oldest building in town, if you didn't count the French fort up on the hill. The Congregation of the Sisters of the Presentation of the Blessed Virgin Mary managed the school and taught the classes. They lived upstairs above the schoolrooms.

The nuns all wore full, long, black and white habits, including heavily starched white headpieces and neckerchiefs, that covered them from head to foot. They looked very uncomfortable.

Hannah reported to the classroom of Sister Georgine, an older nun. As she stepped in the door, someone whispered, "Watch out. Sister Georgine is the strictest nun here." One look at her and Hannah knew the sister wouldn't tolerate any deviation from required behavior.

"Class will come to order," Sister Georgine said. Immediately every mouth closed and silence reigned. She pulled out a sheet of paper and began calling roll.

The girls responded "Present, Sister," when their name was called.

After several names, she called, "Johanna Greene."

No one answered.

"Johanna Greene."

Still no one answered.

"Johanna Greene." The nun's voice was hard.

When there was still no reply, Sister Georgine moved on to the next name. At the end, she looked over the class, eyeing each student in turn. Finally her gaze landed on Hannah.

"You, young lady, stand up."

"Yes, Sister." Hannah stood.

"What is your name?"

"Hannah Greene, Sister."

"Why didn't you respond when I called your name?"

"You did not call my name, Sister."

"I certainly did call Johanna Greene."

"That is not my name, Sister."

"You are being insolent; Johanna Greene is your name. It is the only name unchecked in my roll call roster."

"No, Sister; my name is Hannah Greene."

"Come here."

Hannah walked to the front of the class.

"Step closer."

Hannah stepped closer.

Sister Georgine said again, her voice almost a shriek, "Step closer."

Hannah stepped closer. She now stood only a few centimeters away from the woman. Why did the nun insist on her being so close?

"Step even closer!"

Hannah moved so close her eyes crossed to see the sister properly.

Sister Georgine pointed at her neck and said, "Young lady, do you see these wrinkles?"

Would she get in trouble for saying the nun had wrinkles? Nevertheless, Hannah had to tell the truth. Nerves made her stutter. "Y-Y-Y-Yes, Sister."

"They prove..." Sister Georgine paused a few seconds, and then continued, emphasizing each word with pauses, "that...I...was...not...born...yesterday!"

The classroom burst into a cacophony of giggles which stopped immediately when Sister Georgine whipped around and glared at the students.

She turned back to Hannah and snapped, "I saw your baptismal certificate when your grandmother enrolled you. It clearly says your name is Johanna Greene. You were insolent when you refused to respond after I called your name."

"No, Sister," Hannah pleaded. "I've never been called Johanna or answered to that name. I've always been Hannah."

The sister did not reply to that but said, "Go stand in the front corner over there. You will remain there all day as punishment for your behavior. You will also stay after school is out, when I will mete out an additional punishment as I see fit."

Hannah tearfully obeyed. She stood in the corner quietly crying for an hour. Then Sister Georgine turned one desk at the back of the room toward the rear wall, and told her to sit there.

Such humiliation would be hard to endure

anytime, but on her first day! How could this be happening?

This is worse than Point Verde school! I'm leaving here as soon as ever I can!

The next day when Sister Georgine called "Johanna Greene," Hannah didn't answer.

But when the nun stared at her with daggers in her eyes and said "Johanna Greene" again with a cutting voice, Hannah gave in.

"Present, Sister."

At break some of the girls came to make friends. When one of them called her Johanna, Hannah spoke quickly. "I have to let the sisters call me that, but I hate that name. Please call me Hannah."

They seemed to try, but after a few days one of her new friends, Annette, said, "Hannah, Johanna! This is crazy. I want to be nice to you, but in school all we hear is Johanna, Johanna, Johanna. It's hard to remember to call you Hannah."

"But I hate the name Johanna. It's so old fashioned. I feel like some kind of biblical old maid," answered Hannah. "I can't believe my parents gave me that name. Leon Coffey is starting to call me Johanna Hosanna. It's driving me crazy."

"When I catch myself saying Johanna, I cut it off and it comes out JoAnn. Maybe it would be easier if you shorten it so we can call you JoAnn."

"Gosh, no! That Leon would turn it into something like JoAnn Bedpan. That would be worse. But..." Hannah considered. "I do like the idea of shortening the name, but I'm not crazy about JoAnn. It's still too close to Johanna."

"What about Joan?" Annette asked. "Like the movie star, Joan Crawford."

"Oh, I love her. She's so glamorous," Hannah answered.

"Joan Greene. It sounds good. Should we start calling you that now?" Annette asked.

"Yes. From now on I am Joan Greene!"

She now had three names. Sister Georgine and the other nuns insisted on calling her Johanna. Everyone else in town called her Joan. To her immediate family and oldest friends, she remained Hannah.

Hannah, now Joan, gained a reputation as being a bit of a rebel because of her answering back to Sister Georgine on the first day, and then changing her name. As with all independent thinkers, this made her a popular leader among her classmates.

Chapter 15

Grandmother

Living in Placentia, Hannah was now closer to Andy, who also lived in the town. When he discovered where she lived, he dropped by Grandmother's often.

By now Hannah enjoyed having the attention of a young man—Andy was already eighteen. But she still would not let the friendship develop into anything more. She determined to never endure the financial struggle of a fisherman's life.

"Hannah, I mean Joan, let's go dancing," Andy pleaded.

"I'm only fourteen. You should date girls your age, not me. I think you should ask Mary Mulroney," Joan responded.

"I like you, not Mary. She's not my type. You and me have fun together."

"We have fun because we're friends. Do you want to ruin that by getting serious? I certainly don't. So let's just play a game of cards with Grandmother."

Hannah repeated this for several weeks.

One evening Andy kept on. "Come on, Joan. I bet if you gave me just half a chance, you'd love me as I do you."

Hannah swallowed back tears of frustration. "I don't want to be mean, but I will never fall in love with a fisherman. I don't want to live that hard life. Now don't mention it anymore or we can't even be friends. And I do like you for a friend."

"Okay, but you'll see things my way someday. I'm not going to give up on you. I even brought you a gift." Andy handed her a package wrapped in ribbon.

Joan's heart skipped a beat. The package was a small cloth satchel. She had an idea of its contents. "You shouldn't do things like this. How do you expect me to behave?"

She opened the satchel to find an assortment of watercolor paints and brushes. She had admired it one day in the window at Monkarsh's. Andy must have been spying on her.

"How can I refuse this? I love drawing and painting." She gave him a little punch to his shoulder in a gesture meant to show both her frustration and her affection.

"Don't refuse it. Call your grandmother in and show her your paints, and then let's ask her to play a game of cards." He added, "Someday, I'll find a way to make a better living, and it won't be as a fisherman. I promise you."

"I look forward to that day, Andy. Grandmother! Come look at what Andy brought me, and after that we can play some cards."

~#~

"Can I walk you home, Joan?"
"Joan, let's get a milkshake."
"Will you see a show with me, Joan?"
"Hey Joan, let's go dancing!"

"Joan, do you want to go for a walk?"

Joan never lacked for attention from the boys in town. She always had somewhere to go and someone to go there with. Placentia offered many more activities than she'd dreamed of back home. Many of them took place at the Star of the Sea Hall.

"Wow, this is almost bigger than the whole of Point Verde!" Joan had exclaimed the first time Grandmother took her to the huge hall.

At least a couple hundred people of all ages milled about, with plenty of room for another hundred. Off to one side, a scattering of tables and chairs sat in front of a built-in concessions stand, which sold burgers and chips, milkshakes, popcorn, and beer and rum. The other side of the hall held pool tables, dart boards, and a jukebox. A stage up front hosted a band playing the latest tunes, and couples danced in the large open area.

"Is there always a band?"

"Most evenings, yes" Grandmother answered. "Tonight they'll stop early for the show."

A traveling band would be performing a classical concert this evening. Grandmother loved classical music, so she braved the night air to attend.

"Any kind of vaudeville troop or stage show can perform here," Grandmother added.

"Is it expensive?" Joan hadn't seen Grandmother pay, but maybe she purchased tickets ahead of time.

"Expensive? No, my dear; it's free. This is a place for the community to come together. You pay for your food and drink—no alcohol for the youngsters—but it's cheap. There's a ticket charge for some shows, too, but the Star is open to anyone, anytime."

After that Joan frequented the Star. Sometimes

she went by herself, but usually she went with friends—often a boy. Her classmate Rupert Walsh regularly asked her to see a movie or share a soda or milkshake.

"Hey Mary," Rupert called to the short-order cook as he and Joan entered after a walk along the waterfront. "Can I get a batch of chips and dressing with gravy, and a Coke with two straws, please?"

"Are you here with a girl, Rupert?" Mary's voice came back loud and clear though she remained hidden in the kitchen.

"Yeah, Joan Greene and I are having a day out. We're sitting over by the pool tables."

"I'll bring them out. Go have a seat—and tell Joan I said hi."

As they waited, Joan waved to a classmate, Jim, playing pool with another fellow she didn't recognize. She found herself comparing them and Rupert with the boys back in Point Verde. The town boys dressed better, and in much newer clothes. They didn't appear as...rough, either.

"Is that a new pair of shoes, Rupert? My, aren't you a lucky boy," she said.

"Mom bought them for me. I'm still breaking them in."

"Not too many kids with new shoes these days. It's nice to see."

"It's a benefit of being an only child with a dad that works for the government. My parents aren't as hard up as most folks."

Joan thought, *When the time comes, it's definitely a town boy for me. I don't want a life of hard work that won't even clothe the family decently. Fishermen—and their families—have too many challenges. They even seem to age faster, getting beat by the sun and wind all the time.*

Mary brought out the snack and soda and set the dishes between them. As she stood chatting, Joan noticed the strange boy staring at their plate. When Mary left, the two boys sauntered over.

"Hey, Rupert and Joan," Jim said. "This is my cousin Dennis. He's a Yank, come to visit. He's never heard of fries with dressing and gravy. Is it okay if he tries a taste?"

Rupert raised his eyebrows to Joan, who smiled. "Sure, help yourself."

Dennis asked, "What is that brown lumpy stuff on top of the fries?"

"That, my son, is bread crumb dressing and beef gravy! It's a taste of heaven," replied Rupert.

"Back home we serve French fries with ketchup."

Rupert laughed. "I've only seen ketchup in a restaurant once in my whole life; and compared to dressing and gravy, ketchup is no way to treat fried potatoes. That's for sure."

Dennis agreed the dressing-and-gravy fries were delicious. He and Jim went to place their own order.

Rupert said, "Joan, there's a dance next Sunday night. Will you go with me?"

Joan quickly took a long drink, giving her time to think. She swallowed and said, "Ask me again on Sunday."

Rupert looked confused, but agreed.

~#~

As soon as Father pulled up to the house Friday

after school, Joan jumped out and ran in the house. She hugged Mother and all her siblings, then pulled Leonard aside.

"Lennie, you have to teach me to dance. This weekend."

"What's the hurry, sis? You're not dating already, are you?"

"All the kids go to the dances. I'm the only one that doesn't know how."

"Aw, come on; you've been dancing your whole life."

"Not real dancing, just silly kid playing. I'd be too embarrassed to try to dance if you don't teach me. I'll be stuck at home while everyone else has a good time." Joan pursed her lips in an exaggerated pout.

"Okay, I'll teach you. Come on—"

"Not here," she exclaimed. "It has to be somewhere nobody will see me making a fool of myself."

"Where, then?"

"I have an idea. Ask Father to borrow the car."

With permission secured, Joan directed him far from the lighthouse, through the downs, and to Cemetery Hill.

"You're kidding," Leonard muttered, but he didn't leave. There, under the trees and over the graves of their ancestors, Joan learned to dance.

Patient Leonard never complained when she stepped on his toes. It soon became evident that she'd need many more lessons. Rupert would have to find someone else to go with this Sunday.

"Lennie, please teach me every weekend. I have to learn enough to dance a lot, or everyone will call me a wallflower."

So each weekend they found time to sneak off to Cemetery Hill. After several sessions Lennie declared her proficient enough to attend a dance.

"I'll escort you," he said. "That way you'll be more comfortable since you've practiced with me, and I can keep an eye out for you."

"More like you know all the girls in town will be there and you want to go flirt with them," Joan teased. "I've heard them talk about what a wooer you are." Indeed, he had quite a reputation as both a handsome charmer and a hustler, always busy with some scheme that put another dollar in his pocket.

Joan had plenty of fun, too. During the week, she often went to Star of the Sea Hall with friends for a soda or milkshake and to enjoy the games and shows. She loved the shops and wandered along the sidewalk admiring the nice things in the window. Sometimes Andy or another boy borrowed a car and took her riding along the coastal roads to go bird watching or have a picnic. Now she added dancing to her list of social activities.

These diversions filled her afternoons and evenings. During the weekdays, school and homework were necessary evils to be endured. She'd never liked it and Sister Georgine made it almost unbearable.

In the morning and at night, Joan visited with Grandmother and attended to her needs. Grandmother became frailer as the weeks passed. Joan had been living with her a year when her health started to deteriorate more rapidly.

"I do my best, but with school and homework I can't take care of Grandmother all the time. Not to mention all the cooking and cleaning and everything else, too," she told her parents one weekend. "I need help. Madge and Monica are out of school now; why can't one of them come stay with Grandmother also? Maybe between the two of us we can manage."

"Sounds like you need more help than that," Father said. "Especially since we can't expect your grandmother to support more than one of you. That means whoever goes will need to get a job to help with expenses."

"Maybe Madge and Monica can both go," Mother suggested. "If they took jobs with different hours, one of the three could be with Mother all the time."

When Father drove Joan back to town on Sunday evening, her two sisters went with them. "You've had a room to yourself, and now we all have to share not only the room but the bed, too," Monica said when she saw the guest room. "You won't mind?"

"It'll be like the old days. Remember when we used to stay up till all hours talking and telling stories under the covers?"

Joan filled her sisters in on Grandmother's schedule and needs—when she liked to eat and nap and so forth.

"We need a schedule," Madge said. "But we can't very well make one until Monica and I have jobs and know when we'll be working. We'll do that tomorrow while you're at school, Hannah. I mean, Joan. Come home right after school, and then we'll sort out the rest."

When Joan arrived the next afternoon, Madge told her, "We both got jobs at Monkarsh's. He's kind enough to let us work different hours as long as we need to."

They needed to for about a year. Then one night

that summer, Grandmother Flynn died quietly in her sleep.

Monica ran to Monkarsh's to phone Mother and Father while Madge and Joan began to prepare for another funeral. Joan recalled helping Mother after Grandma Murphy's death and knew what to do. Through tears she helped Madge wash Grandmother's body and dress it in her finest outfit.

Then Madge said, "You were closest to her, Joan, so you should do her makeup. You know best how it should look. I'll go start getting the house ready for visitors. Monica should be back any minute, and she can see about preparing some food."

Joan gathered the makeup, brushes, and lipstick and went back to Grandmother. Tears filled her eyes so that she couldn't see. Joan dropped the cosmetics and ran to the bathroom, sobbing. It took several minutes to gain control of herself.

When she went back to Grandmother, tears again filled her eyes. "Oh, Grandmother, how can I do this?"

Somehow saying the words to her dear grandmother helped. Joan continued talking, telling Grandmother how the day looked and what Madge and Monica were doing. Soon she picked up the makeup, and while she fixed Grandmother's face Joan told her all the secrets she'd never shared with anyone. Then, as she brushed Grandmother's hair and pinned it in place, she told her the latest gossip from town.

When Grandmother was ready, Joan bent over and hugged Grandmother tightly. "Oh Grandmother, I love you, and I'll miss you so much." Suddenly she realized the body lay cold and lifeless. She ran from the room, sobbing again.

Leonard arrived at the house before Father and Mother. "I'll make the coffin," he said. Joan went to help her sisters in the kitchen until he brought the pine box into Grandmother's bedroom.

Joan helped him place Grandmother inside it. She folded Grandmother's hands over her chest. Then they carried the casket to the parlour. No sooner had they placed it on the coffee table than people began arriving to pay respects.

Soon the house filled with people from all around. Grandmother had been an important person and well-loved not only in Placentia but also Point Verde and the surrounding area.

As mourners from town and country arrived, the difference between the two groups seemed pronounced. After living in town for two years, and seeing only her relatively prosperous family on the weekends, Joan had forgotten how ragged and weary the fishermen's families truly were. The hard life they endured wore them down too soon.

It didn't decrease their large hearts, though. Warmth and love filled their stories of Grandmother. The party that soon resulted did justice to the dear woman. Still, Joan retired early and cried herself to sleep.

The next morning she remained in her room as long as possible. Breakfast held no appeal, so she tarried until the bang of Lennie's hammer sealing the lid on the coffin signaled time to head to the church.

When Joan entered the parlour, the six men meant to bear the coffin to the church two blocks away stood at the door with the box on their shoulders. The narrow end of the coffin was outside the door, but the wide end wouldn't fit through the opening.

"I never made one before," Leonard said in frustration.

"Mayhap if we tilt it a bit," one man said. They tipped one side down a bit and the other side up, but the box still wouldn't go through the door.

"Everybody's at the church waiting," Madge said. "Even the priest. What can we do?"

"We'd have to turn it on its side," the man said.

"NO!" Joan shrieked. Everyone stared at her. "You will not flip Grandmother over! She'd rattle around in that big box and be splayed out or...or...bent or twisted..." She choked on her tears but swallowed and finished, "I won't have her spend eternity that way. No! I won't allow it."

Madge and Monica joined Joan's pleas, supporting her both with their words and their arms around her.

"Don't worry," Leonard soothed. "Calm down. We won't do that."

He strode to his hammer still lying next to the coffee table, picked it up, and walked to the large bay window overlooking the street. One powerful swing and shards of glass lay all over the floor and ground outside. He quickly cleared the remaining glass. As Joan and her sisters watched with gaping mouths, the pallbearers hoisted the pine box through the window to some men waiting on the other side, then ran outside to resume their duties.

"At least Grandmother will be buried properly, like a lady," Joan commented.

Monica added, "One thing's certain. Nobody'll ever forget her funeral."

Chapter 16

Monkarsh's

Life seemed empty without Grandmother. Everywhere Joan looked in the cottage, Grandmother should be but wasn't. She wasn't in the kitchen with toast and coffee in the morning. She wasn't in the parlour in the evening, waiting to hear all about Joan's day and add her wisdom and wit to the stories. She wasn't there to tell Joan to sit up straighter or have another cookie or do her homework.

Homework. Ugh.

School had been almost insufferable, but discussing the lessons with Grandmother and listening to her thoughts on education had made it bearable. Without her loving hand to guide Joan along, school and Sister Georgine became intolerable.

"I'm not going back to school," she told her parents. "Now that we're sixteen, most of my friends have to quit and get a job. That's what I'm going to do."

"We wish you'd finish school," Mother said, "but we know how you've always hated it. We won't oppose your decision."

"Where do you plan to work?" Father asked.

"Madge and Monica like it at Monkarsh's, and he likes them. Monica will probably be the manager soon. I'm sure I can get on there."

"How can you be sure he has enough business to support all three of you?"

"Oh, lots of ways." Joan counted them off on her fingers. "One, it's the only store in town. Two, it's always busy. Monica and Madge come home cowed out. Three, everybody loves Mr. Monkarsh. Four, he sells things you can't get anywhere else but St. John's. Maybe even some you can't get there. Five, he gives credit when people need it. Nobody will forget that."

Joan had to switch hands to continue keeping count on her fingers. "Six, he's a tradition. Everybody's always shopped there, since the days he sold straight onto the fisherman's boats. They aren't stopping now. Seven—"

"Okay, okay, I believe you." Father held up his hands to stop her barrage.

Father took her back to Placentia Monday morning, and she went straight to Monkarsh's Dry Goods Store.

"You think three sisters working together will work?" Mr. Monkarsh asked. He acted concerned but the twinkle in his eye gave him away. Joan laughed.

"I can use you, that's for sure. When do you want to start?" he said.

"Right now."

Joan liked the work. It sure beat sitting at a desk all day, and she enjoyed visiting with the customers. Between Mr. Monkarsh and her sisters, she learned the ropes quickly.

On Friday Joan called home. "Can I invite Mr. Monkarsh to Sunday dinner?" she asked Mother. "He's been so good to us. And then he can bring us back after, save Father the trip."

Her parents knew Mr. Monkarsh, of course—like everyone in the district, they did much shopping at his store. Mother said they'd be delighted to get to know him better, especially since he now employed three of their daughters. They planned the meal over the phone, and Joan brought provisions when Father picked up the three girls for the weekend.

Mr. Monkarsh arrived as the family got home from church on Sunday. Father showed him the lighthouse while Mother and girls scurried about the kitchen, finishing the meal they'd started the day before. Joan always had fun working with Mother in the kitchen.

After the blessing, Joan said, "Mr. Monkarsh, you said you don't come to church because you're Jewish. You're the only Jew I've ever met. Can you tell me about being Jewish?"

"Hannah, it's rude to ask such personal questions," Mother scolded.

Would Mother never learn to call her Joan?

"No, no, I don't mind at all," Mr. Monkarsh said. "I believe it's good to learn about people who are different from us. I certainly like to know more about Newfoundlanders. So I will tell you my story, if Mr. and Mrs. Greene do not object."

Father and Mother both urged him to continue.

"When I arrived in Newfoundland in 1921, fewer than fifty Jews lived on the whole island. I wouldn't be surprised if that is still the case today—I haven't seen another Jew in years."

"How did you wind up here, of all places?" asked Madge.

"I tried to get into the U.S. first, but they had a quota law. Too many Jews already immigrated to that country. Newfoundland was next choice. I've always been glad; I love this country."

"Where did you come from? And why did you leave there?" Hannah asked.

"I was born in Eastern Poland. We lived in the countryside, far from any big city. My people were suffering a great deal, at the hands of the czar and then from the Bolsheviks that took over after they killed him."

Monica piped up, "I don't understand. Why did those people cause you trouble? Just trying to survive occupies most of our thoughts around here."

"It has been the story of the Jews throughout the ages. We find and make ourselves a new home and before long, either prejudice rears its ugly head, or hunger and jealousy turn the people against us. In Poland, the government forced us off our farms and into the cities. We lost everything as they herded us into ghettos. I scraped by making and selling leather goods, like belts and wallets. We wanted to leave, but they wouldn't let us."

"That doesn't make any sense," Joan said. "If they didn't like you, it seems they'd be glad for you to leave."

"Prejudice never makes sense," Mr. Monkarsh said. "When I couldn't take it anymore, I waited for a moonless night and escaped across the border with nothing but the clothes on my back, a few coins, and a suitcase full of leather belts. I walked across Europe selling them. When I reached Liverpool, I booked passage to St. John's."

He stopped for a drink before continuing.

"I peddled those belts door to door from the suitcase, walking up and down the streets of old St.

John's. The hard work eventually paid off, as it usually does. I saved all I could until I was able to expand my wares. Then I purchased an old automobile and travelled from village to village, selling from what would fit inside. One day as I drove down Orcan Drive in Placentia, I saw a vacant store. And I've been there from that day to this."

~#~

The next morning, Mr. Monkarsh promoted Monica to floor manager.

"I do this now because I need to go out for a while. The packet boat just brought a delivery; they're unloading on the dock. Please unpack the crates and begin stocking." He disappeared out the door.

Monica immediately said, "You two take care of that delivery. It needs to be finished before Mr. Monkarsh gets back. I'll take care of the customers up front."

"You can't start ordering us around," Madge objected.

"I'm the manager, so actually I can." Monica walked off to assist a customer.

A grumbling Madge followed Joan to the back loading dock. Cool, crisp air and a refreshing breeze off the water greeted Joan when she opened the door. The blue skies and puffy clouds invited any normal human to appreciate the joys of life and put aside earthly concerns. The lapping water provided a soothing backdrop.

Accepting Mother Nature's invitation, Madge sat down on the bench and lit a cigarette.

"Madge, we need to work. You already had a coffee break."

"The day is too beautiful to think about work. Here, sit next to me and have a puff." She held the cigarette out to Joan.

Joan looked around. No one to see. She sat down and took the cigarette. "It is nice here."

After the two girls finished the shared cigarette in silence, Joan stood up. "Okay, let's get to work."

"You go ahead. I'll join you in a minute."

Joan frowned. Madge once again stooped to her old lazy tricks. She'd milk this time out of Monica's sight for all it was worth, and she'd get out of the work one way or another. Joan went to work herself, loading the crates onto a dolly to move them to the proper place in the back room, all the while muttering about Madge taking advantage.

"You know I'll be along to help you in a minute," Madge retorted.

As usual, her minute lasted forty-five. Joan wasn't yet half finished with a job that would have taken only a half hour with both of them working together.

Madge lit another cigarette and once again passed it to Joan.

No sooner had Joan taken a puff than Monica appeared. "I knew you two would be slacking off. What am I supposed to tell Mr. Monkarsh when he gets back and the job's not done?"

"It's Madge's fault; she hasn't done anything. I did all this myself."

"I suppose she forced that cigarette into your mouth, too" Monica snapped.

"Madge, tell Monica the truth, that I did all this work."

"I guess we shouldn't have taken a cigarette break, Joan. Let's get to work fast now and finish up." Madge evaded telling the truth.

"You have fifteen minutes to finish this job. I don't want to hear any more excuses." Monica headed back inside.

With Madge's grudging help, Joan got the rest of the crates moved and the two returned to the front of the store. The three sisters gave each other mean looks and snide remarks all afternoon, even after Mr. Monkarsh's return.

Shortly before closing, he came out of his office. "I don't want to know what happened today. But this can't continue. You all make up right now, or I'll fire the lot of you."

"I'm sorry," Joan said. The words broke a wall, and suddenly all three were hugging and apologizing.

They got along until the next day, when Monica again told her sisters what to do. When the scene played out again, Mr. Monkarsh intervened again. "I'm sorry, Monica, but it doesn't seem that you can manage your sisters. Today Madge is in charge."

But she was worse than Monica. The next day Joan became floor manager.

Joan tried not to make her sisters' mistake of ordering the others around, but Madge lazed around doing nothing.

"You can't get away with this," Joan finally told her. "Get to work."

"I don't have to take orders from my little sister." Madge inspected her nails.

"Why can't you girls work together calmly?" Mr. Monkarsh asked. "You always did before."

"We were equals then," Joan said. "We're not used to one of us having authority over the others."

"I can fix that. None of you are in charge anymore. I will be the only manager. Now go back to work."

~#~

"Where's my gal?"

Joan looked up at Andy's call with a frown. He strode toward her from the back of the store.

He must've just got in from fishing and docked his boat at the loading dock. Joan turned back to her customer, a handsome young man.

"They're very stylish," she said as she showed him a pair of leather boots.

Andy hung behind her like a vulture as she sold the boots, then he swooped in. "Who was that?"

"Frank Warren."

"I never heard of him. Who is he?"

"I don't know. He said his name was Frank Warren, and he bought a pair of boots. That's all I know."

"Why'd you have to spend so much time with him?"

"People don't buy things from a salesgirl who isn't friendly."

"But I want you to be my girl, not making nice with other guys."

"I keep telling you, we're only friends, and that's all we'll ever be."

"What about the garden party at Sacred Heart tomorrow night? It's the first one of the season. As my friend," he emphasized the word with only a little sarcasm, "you'll go with me, won't you?"

Joan loved garden parties. They gave her an opportunity to get dressed up in her most elegant dress and fancy Easter hat. The men wore their Sunday suits.

Sacred Heart always hosted the first garden party of the season as a fundraiser. From right after church on Sunday and into the night, there were bands, games, tasty treats, dancing, and even a horse race. Joan and Andy had a great time playing, eating, visiting with friends, and dancing until long after dark.

BOOM!

The music abruptly stopped as everyone went still and looked east, toward the sound. The sky lit up bright as noon and huge plumes of smoke snaked skyward, several blocks away.

Voices shouted.

"Dear Lord! What was that?"

"Look over there. Something's on fire."

The entire party ran toward the scene.

"Lard tunderin' Jayzus! Look at that," someone yelled.

The mangled remnants of a safe sat at the end of the landing, blasted almost beyond recognition. Pieces of shredded metal lay all bent and twisted among burned bits of paper and money strewn over an area of about forty square meters.

"Looks like someone tried to blow it open with dynamite but didn't know what they were doing. They blew the bejeesus out of it!" a ranger exclaimed. "Based on the damage, none of the money could have survived. The bungling thieves got away with nothing for all their effort."

"I found a piece of the safe door over here," shouted another, from a distance away. "Has Monkarsh's name on it. But where in God's name is the other half?"

"Monkarsh?" a familiar voice questioned. "It's mine? Oh, I hope no one is hurt."

Joan pushed her way to the front of the crowd. The front door of the shop remained properly locked and secure. Mr. Monkarsh opened up and turned on the lights. Most of the goods stood untouched, but the jewelry and watch cases had been ransacked.

Everyone stood waiting while the rangers inspected the place. Their investigation paid off as the story of the robbery unfolded easily.

The thieves picked the perfect time and target. Everyone in the area knew of the garden party. With the whole town there, the burglars were able to break into Monkarsh's without detection. Since more people had been in town, and everyone had to buy clothes and necessities for the party, the store had more cash than usual in its safe.

Apparently, two or more thieves rowed a boat underneath the store through the pylons that held it up over the water. They used an axe from below to bust a hole in the shop floor. Once they got inside, they pillaged the store and lowered Mr. Monkarsh's heavy safe into the waiting boat below. Then they rowed to the landing, where they blew the safe and its contents to smithereens.

When Joan went to work the next morning, something new had been placed in the window. Mr. Monkarsh took the remnant of the safe door with his name still printed on it and displayed it in his front window with a big sign above it: BLOWOUT

SALE TODAY. COME ON IN TO SEE OUR EXPLOSIVE DISCOUNTS. People flooded in to purchase goods and become part of the event. Mr. Monkarsh told Joan he'd never had a busier day.

Chapter 17

Frank

The young man with the stylish boots returned to Monkarsh's. He wandered around, declining assistance from both Monica and Madge, until Joan finished with her customer.

"Hello. How are the boots?"

He held up one foot. "Working out great."

"Is there something else I can help you with?"

"Yes. It would be a great help, Joan, if you accompanied me to The Star of the Sea Hall square dance tomorrow evening."

He remembered my name.

"Would it, now, Frank Warren? And how's that?"

"I'm new in town, and haven't met many people yet. You could introduce me."

"I don't know you myself."

"Sure you do; you just said my name."

"That's only a name." Joan plunged ahead. "Maybe I need to know more about you first, before I start introducing you to my friends."

His eyebrows raised. "What do you suggest?"

"Maybe a milkshake. Just the two of us, so we can talk and get to know each other."

"You are a sly one. Very well, a milkshake it is. When do you get off work?"

After making arrangement to meet at the dairy bar later, Frank left. When Joan turned around her sisters rushed over.

"Who was that you were flirting with?" Madge asked.

"I wasn't flirting."

"We have eyes, little sister," Monica said. "You couldn't be more coy." She struck a coquettish pose and batted her eyes with a smile to make her point.

"Well, I don't see what business it is of yours, but he's Frank Warren and we're going for a milkshake after work. I'll be home after that." Joan flounced away before they could ask more questions.

She tried to behave maturely with Frank that evening. After all, she hung out with different boys all the time. Why should this be any different?

No matter how often she repeated that to herself, her heart still pounded like the waves on a rocky shore every time Frank looked at her. She couldn't help her moon eyes gazing at him, but he seemed to like the attention.

"So, what do you want to know about me?" he asked after they settled at the end of the bar and gave the soda jerk their order.

Joan didn't mean to ask, but before she could stop the words they blurted out. "How old are you?"

"Twenty-three." Frank paused. "I won't return that question as I'm told it's impolite to ask ladies their age."

She was glad. He might think seventeen too young for him. She changed the subject. "Are you from around here? I've never seen you in Monkarsh's before you bought the boots."

"No, I'm from St. John's."

A big-city man. The waves crashed in her chest again.

He continued, "I came here to take a job with my uncle. He owns Placentia Bank; I'm assistant manager."

The more they talked, the more she fell. She didn't try to fight it, but let the feeling of falling in love wash over her completely.

~#~

When Joan and Frank arrived at the hall, people already packed the place. All her older siblings would be among the crowd somewhere, but she didn't see them. Her old classmates Annette and Jim stood near the door and came over.

Joan introduced Frank to them.

Annette lit up. "I know you. You're the very nice bank manager who just started working over there." She smiled prettily at Frank and batted her eyes a little.

Frank seemed a tad embarrassed by Annette's open flirtation. "Assistant manager. But I'm pleased to meet you." He quickly reached over to shake hands with Jim.

"Remember my Yank cousin Dennis that tried your fries?" Jim asked Joan. "He's back; plans to move here. I think him and Madge would get along swell. He came by himself. Is she here? Think she'd have a dance with him?"

"Sure. Go get Dennis and bring him to that table. I'll find Madge. Frank and Annette can hold the table." She slipped through the crowd and found Madge at the bar with a few friends.

"Madge, I want you to meet a poor, lonely Yank. He's desperate to buy you a beer and dance a few with you."

"An American? Good looking?"

"Yep. He's Jim O'Reilly's cousin."

"Let's go." Madge gathered her things.

One of the girls nearby said, "Hey Joan, how'd you snag a catch like Frank Warren?"

Joan's face grew warm with pride. "I believe what my father always told me: I'm as good as the best and there is none better than me. Once I let Frank know that, everything else was a piece of cake."

Back at the table, Frank, Annette, Jim, and Dennis sat in animated conversation. Sounds of people drinking, talking, and dancing filled the hall. Scents of tobacco, perfume, popcorn, and beer wafted over the table. Joan introduced Madge to Frank and then Dennis.

The musicians on stage stopped playing to announce Placentia's special square dance. Dennis looked at Madge. "What does he mean, Placentia's special square dance? I square dance back home, but this sounds like they plan something different than I'm used to."

"Don't worry, just follow what I do," Madge answered as the girls pulled their men to the dance floor. "Everyone'll be doing the same thing. They call it Placentia's dance because every town has some special moves, different from anywhere else."

"Won't there be a square dance caller to call out the moves?" asked Dennis.

"I don't know what you're talking about. What's a square dance caller?"

Before he could explain, the group lined up with some other folks along one side of a square, with an equal number of dancers on the other three sides, close to fifty in all.

The band struck up a tune similar to an Irish jig in double-time, with no instructions or calls, or even lyrics. The dancers sprang to life, clapping and stomping with the music.

Joan's side and the one opposite remained in place, while the other two moved to the center and performed a variety of steps.

"Just watch them," Madge said to Dennis. "In a minute we'll copy them."

Dennis wore an expression of panic and Joan wondered if he'd bolt. She heard him mutter, "It's so insanely fast."

After a few minutes those couples returned to the sides.

"Our turn!"

Joan tore her eyes away from Frank several times to watch Dennis. He seemed a good sport, trying his best to keep up but always a step or two behind. The musicians improvised often, playing extra measures to give him a chance to catch up. The good-natured dancers helped Dennis along, pointing or pulling him to where he needed to go.

When the dance ended Joan and her group headed back to their table, laughing. As Dennis took a big swill of beer, Madge asked, "What do you think of the Placentia Square Dance?"

"It's great fun. I've never been so out of breath. It's very different from our square dances back home."

"How so?" asked Frank.

"To start with, our squares have only eight people. If there are more people, they make more squares. And, all the dances have a square dance caller who calls out the step to do next, like 'Do a do-si-do' or 'Promenade left,' and everyone makes that move. You never know what move will be called next." Dennis took another deep breath.

"That sounds complicated, but fun," Madge commented.

"The calls of the moves are the same everywhere, so once you learn those you can dance anywhere. The moves are similar to yours but not nearly as fast. The music is a little different, too."

Joan and Frank left the table then to mill about and chat with friends. Someone grabbed her arm from behind.

"Hey, I get the next dance. Next one is mine."

Joan jerked her arm away from the repulsive ne'er-do-well Ambrose Murphy. "No, thank you," she said. She couldn't help wrinkling her nose and shuddering in disgust at the odor and filth clinging to the drunken lout as she moved closer to Frank.

Ambrose grabbed her arm again. "You think you're too good for me? Don't be lookin' down on me."

Frank stepped in front of Joan, breaking Ambrose's grip. "Leave her alone."

"Who d'ye think you are?" Ambrose hurled insults at the couple.

Suddenly Leonard, Jim, and Dennis stood there. "Come on, Ambrose," Jim said. "That's the rum talking, and you don't want to spend the night in jail again." The three men escorted Ambrose from the building.

"Are you all right?" Frank asked Joan.

"I'm okay. He's asked me to dance before, but he's never grabbed me like that." Joan shuddered again.

"And he won't anymore, if I can help it."

"My hero," Joan said coyly. "But will you always be around?"

"I could be around Tuesday evening. They're showing *The Great Ziegfeld.*"

It wasn't the answer Joan hoped for, but she'd take it.

~#~

"Joan, won't you go to the end-of-summer garden party with me?" Andy's eyes pleaded as much as his words. "They're gonna have a rowing regatta instead of a horse race this time. Bet you've never seen one."

"I'm sorry, Andy. I already told Frank I'd go with him."

"He ain't the man for you—I am! When're you gonna realize that and stop gallivanting around with him? I hardly ever see you anymore."

"And I won't see you as long as you act like that," Joan said, and walked away.

Later, walking to the party, she asked Frank, "Have you been to many regattas in St. John's?"

"Oh, sure. St. John's has a lot of regattas. It's part of our history. In fact, St. John's holds the biggest regatta in all of Newfoundland."

"I don't know the first thing about them. What are they like?"

"They use a six-man, fixed seat shell for a boat. The boats are low slung, close to the water. They're almost forty meters long, thin and light."

"But what about the race itself?"

"They have different categories of races, divided by age group and distance. People place bets, and a big rivalry exists between the teams. Don't be surprised if the fans get a little heated, especially if there's drinking."

"Oh, there'll be drinking, that's for sure," Joan said. "It wouldn't be a Placentia garden party without drinking."

"This year Freshwater is the favorite to win. Since Freshwater is so close to Placentia, you might as well call it Placentia's team."

"I have almost as many friends and family there as I do here. I'm sure everybody around here will be cheering for them."

"Freshwater's biggest rival is the town of Come By Chance. Last time they raced against each other in St. John's, things nearly came to blows. I think Freshwater is the team to beat this year. Everyone else is a long shot."

When they arrived, Joan couldn't believe the crowd. Of course everyone from the area attended, but because of the regatta, folks came from the competing town of Come By Chance and surrounding area as well. The feud caused a feisty audience, and as drinks flowed the crowd became rowdy.

Joan and Frank placed their bets on the Freshwater team just before the starting shot of the big race, the last and longest of the day. Six teams, including Come By Chance and Freshwater, started rowing. The crowd shouted and cheered.

Frank pointed out the course to Joan. They stood near the finish, on a long pier the rowers had to pass.

"Go, Freshwater, go!" Joan shouted in unison with her friends and relatives. As the boats neared the pier, Freshwater inched ahead of Come By Chance.

"Yea! Go!" The locals went wild.

Suddenly, Ambrose Murphy broke out of the crowd. He ran full throttle to the end of the pier and jumped high in the air. He plunged into the water right in front of the Freshwater boat.

"Oh my God!"

"It's a foul!"

"Scoundrel!" Shouts filled the air as Ambrose slammed hard against the boat, which tumbled over in the water, crew and all.

Come By Chance crossed the finish line.

Pandemonium broke out in the viewing area. Citizens of Come By Chance declared a win while those of Placentia and Freshwater declared forfeiture by foul. Curses filled the air and punches flew.

Joan's friends and relatives joined the spree that grew quickly into a riot. The visitors outnumbered local boys from Placentia. Leonard and Andy jumped in to assist their friends.

"Help them, Frank," Joan cried.

He didn't move. "These ruffians deserve what they get. I'm not going to get my face punched because of a stupid race. I just want my bet returned so we can go home."

"You wouldn't abandon my brother," Joan gasped. "He needs help!"

"I'm not sticking my neck out. I don't fight."

The couple continued arguing even after the constables and rangers arrived and broke up the brawl, sending everyone home. The officials declared a draw to the race. No one could find Ambrose.

Frank and Joan argued all the way to her doorstep. "I won't go out with someone who won't stand up for my family," Joan declared.

"Fine. We won't go out anymore." Frank turned and strode away.

Chapter 18

A Wedding

The following winter, shortly before Christmas, Joan and Andy visited with Annette and Jim and Madge and Dennis at Star Hall.

"I want to do something special, but I don't know what," Joan said.

"Why don't we go mummering?" Andy suggested. "I haven't done that in a long time."

"That's a great idea," Joan cried. "I've wanted to go mummering since I was a little girl, but living so far out at the lighthouse we never had a chance."

"Let's go all twelve days of Christmas," Madge added.

Dennis shook his head. "I can't believe how many new things there are up here. What on earth is mummering? It's sure not something we do in the States."

Joan answered, "It's an ancient Christmas tradition from the old country—"

"It's really an excuse for a wild party," Annette interrupted.

"Isn't everything on The Rock?" Jim commented.

"Okay, back to the explanation," Joan said. "First off, everyone dresses up in disguises and covers their face with rags. Sometimes men wear dresses, some women dress like old men, some people make costumes of crazy things. You just don't want anyone to recognize you."

Annette broke in again. "I hear they haven't gone mummering in St. John's in sixty years. A cousin told me they made a law against it there when someone got killed."

"That's only in St. John's," Andy said. "Everywhere else it's still done, especially in the small towns."

Joan continued, "After you get dressed up beyond recognition, you walk down the street to every door. The neighbor invites you in, where you break out your ugly sticks and sing and dance. I think it'll be grand fun."

"What is an ugly stick?" Dennis asked.

Jim walked over to a supply closet and pulled out a mop handle that had bottle caps, tin cans, and tiny bells attached all over it. He shook the stick and it made crazy noises.

"It's our musical instrument for when we dance," he answered.

"The neighbor is obliged to serve us food and drink until he can figure out who we are. And while he guesses, we pull pranks on him."

"What kind of pranks?"

"Oh, little stuff—nothing dangerous. Stuff like loosening the top off the salt shaker or putting a fish head in the mailbox. Once he figures out who we are, we move on to the next house," Joan concluded.

Andy added, "We drink quite a bit so by the end of the night we're fairly pickled."

Joan's enthusiasm infected the rest of the group and soon they had the plans set. When Christmas arrived, they went up and down streets of Placentia every night. Joan had never had so much fun.

On the last night, they decided to go mummering in Point Verde. Since some of them weren't from Point Verde and Joan hadn't lived there in several years, it took a long time for the folks to guess who they were. All the while, Joan ate the treats and drank the offered rum.

At midnight the mummers headed to Placentia. Andy walked Joan to the lighthouse, where she'd stay the night.

A few meters from the door, Andy turned to Joan, wrapped his arms around her, and kissed her full on the mouth. Surprised, and full of rum, Joan started to return the kiss.

Suddenly she pulled back. "No, I can't. I don't want any regrets on this special night."

"By gosh, Joan. Why won't you open up to me?"

"I will never be more than friends with you, Andy. You or any fisherman."

Shoulders slumped, he turned, then stopped short. Joan looked over. There stood Father.

"Get on home, Andy," he said, his voice hard.

Andy slunk off, leaving Joan to face her father alone.

Father marched her into the house and gave her a jawing about getting drunk and making a spectacle of herself. Finally he sent her off to bed.

I shouldn't have drank so much, that's sure. Or bazzed Andy. But I wouldn't trade the last few nights for anything.

~#~

"Married! I can't believe it." Joan hugged the glowing Bridie with glee.

"I can't believe you're getting married before me or Madge," Monica said. "We're older."

"But you two always wanted to be independent. I only ever wanted to get married," Bridie replied, looking at her ring.

"At least you don't have to change your name," Joan teased. "Marrying a relative has its benefits."

"Oh, hush. It was ages back that Ben's family was related to ours. No one alive can remember the connection, even if he is a Greene."

"Where will you live?" Madge asked.

"Believe it or not, in our old house. You know, the one Father built, that we lived in before the lighthouse. The renters are moving, so the timing was good. We'll pay rent to Father, but he's letting us have it cheap. And it's close to Ben's store in Point Verde."

"I'm glad you're marrying a storekeeper, and not a fisherman," Joan commented.

Everyone in the village received a wedding invitation by word of mouth. Those people then invited others. The family had no idea how many people would come.

The joyful event took place in Placentia. Joan, Monica, Madge, and even Angie, no longer a baby but a nine-year-old girl, were bridesmaids. They dressed in flowing, billowy, hand-made gowns embroidered with filigree of different pastel colors and wore veils whose color matched the filigree.

The men in the bridal party sported vests outfitted with flowered boutonnieres. They passed around hip flasks filled with rum as they stood on the steps of

Sacred Heart Church with the groom. The drinking had started the night before but the men seemed no worse for wear despite the booze and cigars. They made good use of the time ribbing each other and telling tall tales about the groom.

The simple, traditional Catholic wedding mass brought tears to Mother's eyes. Even Father had trouble holding back his emotions.

"I'm a blessed man," Joan heard him say several times.

After the church wedding, all two hundred in attendance walked to Star of the Sea Hall for the reception. The warm spring air made the outdoors enticing and soft sea breezes delighted the party goers. People laughed and talked while passing hip flasks all around.

Bridie kept tripping over her wedding dress on the ill-kept street filled with potholes. Before long Ben scooped her off her feet and carried her the rest of the way to the hall.

"Aww," the women all said as one.

"Nah," Ben replied. "I just want her to stop complaining." But he smiled into her eyes and kissed her tenderly.

As soon as the guests stepped into the hall, an accordion and fiddle band struck up. One by one they played all the great Newfoundland tunes. Step dancing and Irish jigs became the cornerstone of every dance on the floor.

In the midst of the dancing, neighbors set out traditional cold plates, consisting of sliced ham, turkey, tomatoes, and beets next to scoops of potato salad and coleslaw. Many different friends had prepared the abundant amount of food in advance at home, and these same friends dished out plates to guests in line until everyone ate. The bride's parents had stocked the hall with plenty of rum and beer.

Music continued to play when Bridie tossed the bouquet of flowers, while the couple cut the cake, and even as friends made toasts. The celebration went on deep into the night.

Toward the end of the evening Joan stopped dancing for a drink and to catch her breath. Monica stood off in a corner away from everyone, crying.

Those don't look like happy tears.

Joan walked over and put her arm around her sister's shoulder. "What's wrong?"

"I'm going to lose Charlie." Monica sniffed. "He told me tonight that he's moving to St. John's. The constabulary offered him a job."

"That doesn't mean you're going to lose him. Did he say he was leaving you?"

"I don't know. He said he loves me, but then he said things would be hard to work out over such a long distance. He's going to live five hours away."

Monica wiped her eyes and continued, "I'm devastated. But look at him—he's so excited and happy. I love him so much. I don't know what to do." Monica looked up. "He proposed marriage. Said that would solve the problem. But I can't say yes. You know we've only been dating a little while. It's too soon for that." Monica began sobbing again.

"You see, all is not lost," Joan said. She gave Monica a squeeze. "He really loves you. I think he'd make a great husband."

"But he'll be over there meeting other girls. I'm

certain to lose him to some high-falutin' city girl. I feel so lost." She sniffed and wiped her eyes again. "Besides, how could he tell me this on Bridie's wedding night? For the rest of my life I'll think of Bridie's wedding as the night I lost the love of my life."

Charlie walked up. "Joan, I love this girl. I want to marry her. You've known me a long time. Our families have been friends for years. You know we're a good match. With that good job in the constabulary, I can provide for her. Even a family."

Charlie turned to Monica. "Please marry me. I'm begging you. I love you."

Monica just started crying again.

Somebody has to do something. Guess it's up to me.

"Charlie, it's too sudden. Monica isn't going to make any rash decisions, especially at her sister's wedding. She needs to reflect on everything and think things over. Don't give up hope. When we get home, we'll talk about it and find a solution. Monica found a good man in you; besides, I'd hate to see her settle for a local fellow destined to be a fisherman. The life of a fisherman's wife is too hard. Don't worry; we'll find a way."

Madge walked home with Monica and Joan a little while later. The three discussed the situation late into the night, weighing all the options they could think of.

Finally Monica said, "I can't marry him yet, but I can be closer to him. Tomorrow I'll tell Mr. Monkarsh that I'm leaving, and I'll stay with our cousins in St. John's until I decide what to do."

~#~

"Got a letter from Monica," Joan said as she entered the house a few weeks later.

Madge had her hands in dishwater. "I'll read it later, but tell me what she says."

"Mostly it's about how big St. John's is and how lost she felt at first. But she got a job at a shop downtown. Says it's easy for her since she learned so much at Monkarsh's. She sees Charlie a lot. There's going to be wedding bells for those two yet."

"I'm happy for her," Madge said. "It's just too bad we won't see her much anymore. Sometimes I miss the old days when we all giggled under the covers."

"I might."

"What do you mean? Might what?"

"See her soon. Mr. Monkarsh cut my hours again. Poor man, he was almost crying, he hated so much to do it. But with this Depression dragging on..."

"We knew it was coming. I'm sure he'll cut mine next time I go in."

"Yes, and since I knew it was coming, I've been thinking about what to do."

"You could always marry Andy Ryan."

"Absolutely not. There's no way I'm going to marry a fisherman, and that's final. But you know there aren't a lot of jobs for women. And most of the ones there are don't pay much."

"That's for sure," Madge agreed.

"Of all the women we know that work, the ones who do really well have their own business," Joan said. "A woman can be a teacher, but I quit school because I hate it so much. I sure don't want to be stuck back there forever. So that's out. A woman can be a seamstress."

"But you've never liked to sew."

"Right, so that's out. A few women own shops, but I can't afford to stock one."

"What about a nurse?"

Joan shook her head. "That would take too much schooling. Besides, I don't want to be around that much sickness and blood."

"So what does that leave?" Madge asked. "I can't think of any other business for a woman."

"Beautician."

"Oh, you'd be good at that."

"I think I could be. And then I wouldn't have to depend on a man to make a living for me—especially a fisherman. It'll be up to me to make my own way, and I'm sure I can do it."

"But don't you have to go to school for that?"

"That's the downside. But it's only for six months. I can stand that. It won't be taught by Sister Georgine, anyway."

"But where is the school? I can't think—"

"St. John's. That's the other thing Monica writes. In my last letter, I asked to find out if the family thinks there's room for me there too, and she said yes."

Madge said, "Well, I'm happy for you, but I'm going to miss you. And I don't envy you telling Mother."

Chapter 19

Career Girl

Six months later, Joan returned to Placentia and Grandmother's old cottage. Beauty school diploma and beautician's license in hand, at nineteen she was ready to go into business for herself.

"No, we don't have any openings," the owner of the only hair salon in town told her.

Joan spread the word among her family and friends that she offered a travelling beautician service: she'd go to her clients' home for their convenience. Or if they preferred, she'd see them at the cottage she shared with Madge. She gained a few clients that way, but not enough.

"Don't give up," Madge said. "It always takes time for a new business to get going."

"Yes, but I need the money now. I'm going to see if Mr. Monkarsh can use me part time. That'll give me a little income till I get going, but still leave time for my clients."

Mr. Monkarsh was happy to see her, and smiled wide when she said she only wanted part-time work.

Only a few days later Mary Kemp came in the store. "Welcome home, Joan. We've missed seeing you on our monthly visit to town."

They visited while Joan helped her find all she needed. As Mary checked out, Joan said, "We close in twenty minutes. I live right around the corner. Why don't you come home with me, and I'll take care of your hair. I can cut, shampoo, dye, whatever you need."

"I wish I could, but Paddy needs to put that boat on the water before it gets dark. He wouldn't stand for any delay. I love my outport home, but it sure has its disadvantages. Not only do we have to sail to Placentia for supplies, but we have none of the other conveniences of town, like doctors and hairdressers. All we have out there are fishermen."

Mary's face brightened. "You should come to the outport, Joan. You'd make a killing. Every woman in town would line up to see you."

That would be a godsend. "You really think so?"

"Just because we live on an isolated outport doesn't mean we're cavewomen. We'd love to be able to see a real beautician. In fact, why don't you come with us home tonight? You can stay in our spare room and do hair there if you want. I'll introduce you to everyone."

Joan did some quick thinking. "How would I get back home?"

"There's always someone coming in to Placentia. Tell you what. You stay at my house for free and do my hair at no charge. If you can't find someone heading back this way for a free ride, you can pay Paddy a fee out of the big money you're going to make out there."

"I'd like to. I need to talk to Mr. Monkarsh and grab some clothes and my supplies from home. Can you wait ten minutes?"

"No more. Paddy doesn't like to be sailing after dark."

Joan asked Mr. Monkarsh for the next two days off, which he readily agreed to. Then she ran home and gathered her things, moving like a whirlwind. She explained to Madge as she packed.

"I stand to make some good money," she concluded, "and at the same time see a part of The Rock I've never been to."

Ten minutes later she stepped onto the wharf where the Kemps were preparing to set sail.

"You didn't waste any time now, did you? You're my kind of girl." Paddy Kemp smiled.

Within moments they were off.

"How far is it?" Joan asked.

"Two hours."

"I've never been to an outport before. What's it like?"

"They're just tiny villages that grew up around fishing," Paddy said. "Nothing else there—no services like electricity or telephones. No stores or doctors. Usually a pub, though, and maybe a fish merchant. We're lucky to have a school and a church for the sixty families in our outport."

Mary joined in. "Sometimes it can be very lonely. We don't hear from the rest of the world at all unless we come to town. That's a rare trip in winter, what with the sea ice. A few of our neighbors only live at the outport in summer; they own a place on the mainland where they live the rest of the year."

"We do get a packet boat twice a month," Paddy said. "They bring news, mail, supplies. When that boat rolls into port everybody rushes down to meet it."

"Seems like a hard life. Is the money that good, to make people want to stay?" Joan asked.

Paddy and Mary both laughed. "Money from fishing is never good," Mary said. "But we make do. What we lack in money, we make up for in spirit, family, and community. You'll never find a nicer bunch of folks. It may be hard but we make sure it's a full and happy life. God is good to us."

~#~

The next morning, true to her promise, Mary brought a line of women all wishing to get their hair done. Joan stayed busy, making the time pass quickly. She found a ride back to town with a fisherman who needed to get supplies.

"I never would have thought about going to the outport if Mary hadn't mentioned it," she told Madge that evening.

"And that was only one," Madge replied. "There are dozens of outports, if you can only find a way to get to them."

"Thank goodness for Monkarsh's. You know we see all the fishermen who come in for supplies from the outports. I'll make a point to tell them about my service."

"You could tell them what a nice surprise it would be for their wives," Madge suggested. "It'd be the best present they could give, and won't cost them anything but a ride and place to stay and eat for a day or two."

"True enough; whoever puts me up gets their hair done free in return. The other women will have to pay for my work, of course, but I'll be reasonable. I remember well enough what's it's like to be so poor."

"What about Mr. Monkarsh? Will he mind you being gone so much?"

"I think he'll be glad. I have a feeling he only keeps me on out of loyalty to our friendship. It'll help him not to have to pay me so much."

The next day when she talked to Mr. Monkarsh about her plan, he confirmed that. "I'm so happy my little store can help you find customers, too," he added.

Joan's parents weren't as happy to hear her plan. "We hardly see you as it is," Mother said. "Now you'll be home even less."

"I have to make my own way. At least I'm not off in the States, like Mary. Besides, I'll probably be around even more. Being away all the time, the boys forget about me. There's a dance tonight but I came here instead because I don't have a date. Don't have one for the next party, either. Reckon that'll happen a lot now."

"Your safety is what concerns me," Father said. "Out on the water so much. Things can happen—"

"Oh, Father, that's just because you've run the lighthouse so long. You hear about all the shipwrecks and such. The fishermen are really careful when I'm on board."

"Just promise me you'll never get on a boat in a storm. Or when one's on the way."

"Of course I won't. I'm not stupid." Joan acted more insulted than she felt. Parents worried. That would never change, so no use getting upset about it.

"Besides making a living, it's a chance to see more of Newfoundland," she added. "I'd never get to those places otherwise, and I like exploring new areas. Plus I meet a lot of people."

"Still seems like a lot of danger just to cut people's hair," Father grumbled.

"But it's so much more than that," Joan cried. "The women in the outports live such isolated lives. They never know what's going on in the world. I bring them the latest news—things women want to know, not just about the price of fish like the men discuss. And I tell them stories and jokes and things. If you saw how their faces light up every time I show up, you'd know it's a lot more than just cutting hair."

She paused a moment before saying, "Besides, it's my own business. I don't like being dependent on anyone else. I intend to pursue it."

"We're not saying you can't," Mother soothed. "We're just asking you to be careful."

~#~

The life contented Joan. She worked at Monkarsh's, attended a few social events, visited her friends, and went to see her family at the lighthouse when in Placentia. At the outports she provided a real service to the women.

In places with few women, Joan had free time before catching a ride home. She often went for long walks along the shore or the beautiful woody trails. In some of the tiny communities, she could walk from one end to the other in ten minutes.

Most outports had no electricity or indoor plumbing, and using the gas lamps and outhouses brought to mind days living in the old Point Verde saltbox house. Joan enjoyed observing outport life as the villagers went about the business of cod fishing.

As Father and Mother had in her childhood, the men rowed out to the fishing grounds early in the morning while the women stayed on land and made the fish. The children worked the gardens and, if they were lucky, attended a one-room schoolhouse. Life in the outports ebbed and flowed with the seasons, predictable and comfortable though poor.

~#~

A backing wind says storms are nigh.

A cow with its tail to the east makes the weather least.

Dogs always howl more before a storm.

Pigs gather leaves and straw before a storm.

Red sky in the morning, sailors take warning.

Sea gull, sea gull, sit on the sand; it's never good weather while you're on the land.

When schools of herring race toward land, a terrible gale will soon be at hand.

When sounds travel far and wide, a stormy day will betide.

The signs were all there. Ominous storm clouds piled in the distance as Joan chatted with the women of Merasheen outport during their hair appointments. She told them about Monica's upcoming nuptials. Her sister had finally agreed to marry Charlie and the wedding would take place the next day in Placentia. Joan would be a bridesmaid, along with her other sisters.

"You're not going back tonight?" several asked through the day. "Looks like a big blow coming in."

"I want to be back in time for the wedding. I arranged for Paddy Kemp to take me back, even though

I have to pay for it instead of waiting for a free ride like I usually do."

"Reckon you better wait, Joan. When the weather turns dirt, nobody should be out to sea."

"I grew up at a lighthouse, remember? I know the danger of a storm at sea. But it's Monica's wedding. And I trust Paddy. He's one of the best seamen around. We'll leave early."

Paddy had his own worries. "Don't know we should chance it, Joan. Better stay over."

"You have to take me home; you promised."

"Now, Joan, it wouldn't be right for me to take you out in bad weather."

Joan pointed to the sea. "Look, the waters are perfectly calm."

"Calm now, but the waves could rise to ten or fifteen meters in a snap, and my boat couldn't handle that."

Joan crossed her arms. "I'll pay you extra. Double, even. I have to make it home for Monica's wedding. Please, Paddy."

He scratched his scruffy jaw thoughtfully. Looked at Mary.

"Whatever you think," she said.

Paddy slapped his knee and jumped up. "I'll do it, but we got to leave right now. Come on."

Joan grabbed her things and ran after him. A few minutes later they put to sea and headed across the water to Placentia.

The wind picked up halfway there as the squall blew in. Slow at first, it soon began to rage. The sky turned black, pierced by dazzling flashes of light when thunder boomed. Waves whipped over the sides of the boat, which shook and bounced aggressively in every direction.

Joan shrieked as the canvas cabin roof ripped entirely off the boat.

Paddy grabbed a pail and thrust it to Joan. "Start bailing," he shouted.

Joan summoned her strength to bail with one hand while holding on with the other, so she wouldn't be thrown about the boat. Paddy floundered about the rear of the boat, struggling to hold on to the throttle wire control that fed fuel to the engine.

A sudden wave caused the boat to lurch. Paddy's body pitched forward. The wire snapped off and disconnected from the engine, which immediately died.

Without a moment's hesitation Paddy grabbed his toolbox and began to sort through it. "Keep bailing, Joan," he shouted. "All is not lost yet."

The minutes ticked by and turned into hours. The tempest raged on as Paddy continued working on the engine and Joan furiously bailed water from the flailing boat, praying all the while.

"Holy Mary, Mother of God."

Joan looked up at Paddy's cry. He stared out over the side of the boat.

"What is it?" Joan yelled over the storm. She could make out a tall rocky formation in the distance but nothing to account for the horror in Paddy's eyes.

"The Sore Thumb," he shouted back. "I knew we got blown off course but had no idea we were so far south."

"What's the Sore Thumb?" Joan kept bailing as they screamed over the squall.

"Point of no return." Paddy left the engine as he

explained and scrambled to the anchor. "If we get too close, we'll crash into it. Too far out, and we'll be swept to open sea. Either way is the end of us."

Thankfully, the anchor took a tenuous hold. Still, the currents and the storm pulled furiously, yanking the boat hither and thither, inching ever closer to the Sore Thumb.

Paddy jumped back to his work. Joan never stopped bailing. The storm thundered on.

Putt...putt...

Joan's heart rose—then plunged when the engine seized.

Paddy leaned over the edge, looking. "Anchor rope wrapped around the propeller," he hollered when he stood up. "Got to free it. You take the tiller. When I say, you crank the engine and full throttle away from here." He pointed the direction to go.

Before Joan fully processed the words, he'd placed a knife between his teeth and plunged into the sea.

She stood grasping the tiller, heart pounding in her throat for Paddy as her thoughts ran amok. *What if the sea overpowers him? What if he can't cut the line free? What if he froze in the frigid water? What if—*

"Go!"

Paddy had one arm over the side of the boat. He hoisted himself over as Joan revved the engine. She pointed the boat toward Placentia and headed home while he covered himself with canvas and huddled in a freezing ball.

An hour later the storm died down. Rain still poured, but the winds slowed, and the seas calmed to a manageable level. After another hour they pulled into

Placentia Harbor. The two-hour trip had taken five. Joan and Paddy tied the boat and escaped to the cottage.

"What in the world—" Madge jumped up as Joan opened the door and they stepped inside. "Did you two sail in that storm? Father's gonna—"

"We know." Joan could hardly speak for the chattering of her teeth. "Just make some tea, will you?"

Madge hurried to comply. Joan found some towels and showed Paddy the restroom where he could dry off, then went to her room to change clothes.

When she came out, Paddy sat on the sofa wrapped in blankets and drinking hot tea. She joined him there.

"I'm so sorry, Paddy. I never should've talked you into that trip. I could've gotten us both killed!"

Paddy shook his head. "Wasn't your fault. I'm the captain; 'twas my call. We made it, eh, lassie. And my old boat is still floating."

"It may be floating but it's badly damaged. I have to pay for that."

"Maybe, but let's see what I can do."

Joan yawned. "I'm exhausted. And I have a wedding to go to tomorrow. I'm turning in."

"Go on," Madge said. "I'll get some more blankets and make up a bed for Paddy on the sofa."

The next day, everyone had a grand time at Monica's wedding, which mirrored Bridie's. Joan shared her storm adventure with all who'd listen.

"You shouldn't have risked it," Monica said. "Your safety is more important than a party, even my wedding party."

"I wasn't going to miss seeing you married to Charlie for anything."

Chapter 20

Changes

"So how is the life of a barber in St. John's these days?" Joan asked Gussie. He'd followed her example and become a barber. Though he lived in St. John's now, he was home for a visit.

"It's good," Gus answered. "I'm doing well. The shop I work in stays busy. Being downtown, we get a lot of bigwigs and famous folk coming in for a haircut."

"Like who?"

"Some big shot from Hitler's Germany came in."

"Don't be codding me, b'y."

"No, it's the God's truth I'm telling you. At first I didn't know who he was, but he started bragging right off, full of himself. Said he was the Deputy Fuhrer of Nazi Germany. That means he's the number two man in all of Germany, behind Hitler."

Joan's ears perked up. All the news these days talked about the happenings in Europe. Everyone Joan knew considered Herr Hitler a troublemaker. The radio consistently commented that Hitler could start a war. Since Great Britain administered Newfoundland, such talk made them nervous. War with England meant war with them.

"G'wan," she prodded Gus.

"Nothing much to say, just that he was a big shot.

He came in, sat down, asked for a shave and a haircut. So I did. The whole time he bragged on and on about how important he was."

Gussie paused, then repeated, "He sure got my attention when he said he was the number two man behind Hitler. All kinds of things are happening over there. Troubles are sure to come, and he'll be a big part of it."

~#~

One day early in 1940, Joan headed home to her parents' for a visit with the family. When the lighthouse came into view, her eyes and mouth opened wide.

The lighthouse buildings no longer sported the traditional red and white stripes. Instead, every structure had been painted shades of green and tan in a camouflage pattern.

Father and Mother met her on the stoop.

"What's all this?" She gestured to the buildings.

Mother hugged her as she answered. "The army painted them to match the countryside."

"Lots of things are different now, daughter," Father said. "The government thinks enemy ships and submarines are right off our shore, so they're doing everything they can to keep us hidden. The light and foghorn don't get turned on like they used to. Instead they give me a schedule with odd hours that change every day. Some days, they don't get turned on at all."

"But what about the fishermen and merchant ships? Won't they suffer without the light?"

"They're given the same schedule, and told to stay off the water otherwise."

"I had to put blackout curtains over every window," Mother added. "No interior light can be visible outside the buildings."

"Why not?"

Father answered, "If German U-boats see the light, it'll guide them to us."

"Are there really Germans that close?" Joan shuddered.

"The government says their U-boats are prowling the coast of Newfoundland intent on destroying ships taking supplies to England. I haven't seen one yet, though." Father stood straighter. "I'm officially in service to the war effort. The navy has commissioned me as an official spotter. I'm to regularly scan the sea horizon for German activity and report on any sightings by radio."

~#~

Joan witnessed many changes in the following months. The government allowed the U.S. to build a barracks at the lighthouse and a military base in Argentia, only a few kilometers from Placentia. The new base installed bowling alleys, movie theaters, restaurants, pool halls, night clubs and even a casino. Automobiles and trucks filled the streets. The town put in a bus system to help with the traffic. It seemed to Joan that Placentia became an American boomtown overnight.

The population of both Argentia and Placentia swelled as Newfoundlanders came to take advantage of the new opportunities provided. Fishermen and their families took jobs on base or in the new businesses to receive a steady income. Many lived in housing on base, but others moved to Placentia instead. Servicemen appeared everywhere with the allure of a better life in America—after the war.

Joan moved back to the lighthouse so the family could sell Grandmother's little cottage while there were plenty of buyers. She also gave up her traveling beautician business. The threat of German U-boats scared her off the water. But with the boom, Monkarsh's needed help so she worked there instead.

Several of Joan's family members took jobs on base. Angie, the youngest Greene at fifteen, wasn't old enough to work there, so she also took a job at Monkarsh's. Joan helped train her little sister, who learned fast and worked well.

"You don't need me to tell you what to do anymore," Joan said toward the end of the second day. "You've learned it all. Now just go do it."

Joan had off the next day, so she stayed home while Angie went to work.

"How did your day go?" Joan asked when Angie came home.

"Good then bad then good again."

"That sounds interesting. Tell me about it."

"Mr. Monkarsh gave me a nickname—Punk, because I'm so small. He says things like, 'Hey Punk, restock the hair combs' or 'Arrange those socks, Punk.' I love it. Mr. Monkarsh is the nicest man ever."

"He's very good to us. Then what was bad?"

Regret filled Angie's face. "I made a huge mistake. Mr. Monkarsh had to run to the bank for some change. The other girls had already gone, but he said I could handle it. It was fine at first, but then three navy boys came in."

"They didn't...trouble you, did they?" Joan asked sharply.

"Oh no, nothing like that. They went to look at the watches. They were all so cute and wearing their sailor uniforms. I couldn't concentrate on what I was doing because they were flirting with me like crazy."

"That'll always lead to trouble," Joan commented dryly.

"I got all flustered and blank in the head. One of them saw a watch he liked and wanted to try it on. They kept asking me questions and joking around. Then they said they had to get back to base and walked out. I didn't even realize one still had the watch!"

"Oh, my Lord," Joan gasped. "The watches in those cases are some expensive. You really did mess up big."

"But it worked out after all. Mr. Monkarsh walked in as the sailors left. He saw the watch case open and said, 'Hey Punk, did those boys buy a watch? There's a timepiece missing from the top shelf.'

"I said, 'Oh my gosh, they left without paying for it!' So I ran out and chased the sailors down the street, shouting for them to stop. I caught up with them and demanded the watch. The one laughed and made some flimsy excuse, but he gave it back."

"He knew there'd be heck to pay from the base commander if Mr. Monkarsh complained."

"Whatever the reason, I was so relieved. I apologized profusely to Mr. Monkarsh when I brought the watch back, but he said he knew it would never happen again and not to say another word about it. So the day ended on a good note."

"I bet you don't ever forget that lesson."

"No I won't! But Mr. Monkarsh was so nice about

it. I'll never forget that, either; and I'm going to be the best clerk he ever had."

Angie had off the next day so Joan went to work alone. Her first customer introduced himself as a doctor working at the new base hospital. "You work very efficiently and you have a pleasant manner," the doctor said as Joan finalized the sale. "Surely with your talents you've thought about a job that pays better than a store clerk."

"I had a business travelling around the outports before the war started, but it's too risky to do that now," Joan responded.

He smiled at her. "With the base growing so fast, it has a lot of openings."

"I've made inquiries, but so far nothing's called my name."

"I can arrange a position for you at the base hospital. It needs help in a big way. I think you'd do well."

"I don't have any experience in that. I wouldn't know the first thing about it—and I don't want to go back to school."

"You don't have to; there's on-the-job training. We have lots of nurses who started out with no experience. I guarantee you'll make a lot more money—and you'll have a great boss." He flashed a smile, then added, "I'm in desperate need of nurses in the infectious disease ward."

Joan couldn't help recoiling. "Infectious diseases! You mean like tuberculosis, the flu, malaria, and God knows what else? That sounds scary."

"You don't have to worry about that. We take all kinds of precautions and I'll teach you all of them. I've been doing this work for years and I've never gotten sick. Come work for me. I'll keep you safe."

"Let me think about it."

A few days later Joan passed through the entrance gate at the base. The environment seemed alien compared to the village of Placentia a few kilometers away. It reeked of the business of war. Many of the buildings dotting the landscape were off limits and cloaked in secrecy. Everything seemed organized, orderly, and efficient though work exploded everywhere with activity and traffic in every direction. The base represented the future, filled with both uncertainty and promise.

~#~

"Ye ain't squeamish, are ye?" Roslyn, the plump, young nurse assigned to show Joan the ropes, asked. "'Cause yer gonna get bled on, peed on, puked on, and worse. If that's gonna be a problem, best let me know right now and save us all some time."

"I grew up cleaning and gutting fish and chickens," Joan said. "Plus I helped raise my younger siblings and care for my two elderly grandmothers. I'm used to all the messes that can be made."

"Aye, good; that's somethin', anyway. Lucky ye got here at lunchtime. Ye can start easy, helpin' feed the ones that need it."

Roslyn stopped so abruptly Joan almost ran into her backside. Roslyn turned to look her hard in the eyes and said, "I'm gonna tell ye two important things now, so listen good. First, al'ays follow the proper protocol fer doin' things. That's what keeps us nurses safe. We get sick, who's gonna care for the fellas? So when we tell ye to wash yer hands after finishin' with one patient, and again afore dealin' with the next one, we mean it. Don't think ye can skip the second time just 'cause ye did the first one. Got it?"

"Yes, I understand. The doctor told me I'd be trained to stay safe. What's the other thing?"

"Never let these men see ye pity 'em. If ye wanna cry for 'em, ye do it after ye get home. That kind of despair robs 'em of hope. And they gots to have hope."

For many long hours each day Joan fed and cleaned ill and invalid servicemen. She held bowls when they needed to vomit and changed the bedpans when they relieved themselves. She learned to check vital signs and to dispense medication.

Following safety protocol soon became second nature to Joan. Roslyn's second rule proved more difficult. Though soldiers came and went continually, some stayed long enough for Joan to get to know well. She flirted with the servicemen in a friendly fashion to lift their spirits and keep them positive. When one of those men died, Joan mourned inside. But she kept a cheerful front and never let a soldier see her cry.

~#~

The patient pushed the bowl Joan held away. "That's all I can manage," he said. "Be sick again if I try more."

"That's fine, Harry. You had more than yesterday, and getting stronger every day. Soon enough you'll be asking me to go dancing," Joan answered in a teasing voice.

He grinned. "And what'll you say?"

"Oh, you'll have to get well and ask me, before I'll answer you. I'll see you tomorrow, okay?"

Joan carried the bowl of broth over to the cart of used dishes, then headed out of the hospital. When she reached the bus stop, she found Madge there. Madge worked in a different area of the base.

"Oh, I'm tired," Madge said as she sat down on the bench, slipped off her shoes, and started rubbing her feet.

Joan yawned. "Me, too. You know, Madge, if we got a place on base, we wouldn't have to wait for the bus or make the trip back. It's not a real long ride, but add up all the comings and goings in a week and we'd get a couple extra hours sleep."

"I've thought about it. I just don't know anyone well enough to be sure I want to room with them."

"What about me?"

"I was so busy thinking about all my coworkers I didn't think of you. But I'm game if you are."

"It's settled. Let's go in early tomorrow and make arrangements."

"Guess who I saw today?" Madge changed the subject.

Joan raised her eyebrows.

"Andy Ryan."

"Oh, how's he doing? I got so in the habit of avoiding him during the Frank Warren days that I don't see him so much."

"He's working as a carpenter. Smitten with you as ever. Wanted to know how you were and if you're seeing anybody."

"What'd you say?"

"The truth, of course. That you're too busy to have a steady relationship."

"That's the truth, for sure. But I would like to go out sometimes. Maybe I'll take him up next time he asks."

~#~

"I had a great time, Joan. How 'bout you?" Andy said one night after they'd danced until Star Hall closed at midnight.

"I sure did. Oh, look! The last bus is already there; we better run."

The pair ran the rest of the way, burning Joan's lungs and leaving her out of breath.

"You go on," she said as she gulped for air and rifled through her purse for a quarter to pay her own fare. "Here, got it." She lifted the coin from the purse but it slipped from her fingers, dropped to the ground, and rolled right under the front wheel of the bus. She bent down to retrieve it.

Andy stood on the bus step. "What are you doing, Joanie?" Exasperation filled his voice.

"My quarter fell under the bus wheel. Ask the driver to pull up a bit so I can get it."

"I'll pay your fare. C'mon, get on the bus."

"I will not leave a quarter on the ground. I work hard for my money. Ask the driver to pull forward. Just a few centimeters."

Instead, Andy repeated his previous comments.

The couple argued until the bus driver said, "Look, lady, I don't have time for this. I got a schedule to keep and we gotta get moving. If you're coming, get on now."

Joan huffed. "I want you to pull forward so I can get my quarter."

"I warned you." The driver closed the door and drove off into the night. Andy poked his head out the window and yelled at Joan for being so stubborn.

Joan scowled after him until the bus completely disappeared. Then the eerie silence and foggy darkness began to melt her anger as she stood completely alone on the dark street. All her frustration, stubbornness, and fright spilled out in the form of tears.

What in the world am I going to do now? That was the last bus. It's too far to walk to the lighthouse. Father hasn't been well so I won't call him to come get me. Can't afford the hotel. Who do I know that lives nearby?

Freddie popped to mind, but Joan pushed it aside. His tiny one-room apartment contained only a table, a pullout sofa-bed—and a wife. The two teens married only three weeks ago and moved into his Placentia apartment.

No, I can't crash in on the newlyweds. Who else?... There's got to be somebody...

Not a single other soul came to mind.

With a sigh and a sob, Joan turned and trudged to Freddie's. By the time she arrived her watch read nearly one. She pounded on the door until it opened suddenly.

"Lard tunderin' Jayzus, girl," Freddie exclaimed. "What are you doing out? Are you hurt?" He pulled her in the apartment and shut the door behind her as he spoke.

Joan answered through sniffles and gasps. "No,

but...I lost my bus fare...and stupid Andy Ryan...and the bus driver...and now I'm stuck in town...with nowhere to go. ...Can I stay here tonight? I'll sleep on the floor."

"You'll do no such thing," Lizzie's voice came from a corner of the dark room. "The floor is hard and cold. You'll just have to squeeze in the bed with Freddie and me."

"No, no, I don't want to crowd you. The floor is fine—"

"If anybody sleeps on the floor, it'll be me," Freddie interrupted.

"Nobody's sleeping on the floor." Lizzie's voice brooked no argument. "It's too cold; we don't have enough blankets for that. We can tough it out for one night, and tomorrow we'll have a good story."

Chapter 21

Illness

Over breakfast the next morning, Freddie asked Joan, "Have you talked to the folks in the past couple days?"

"No, it's been a few. Why? Is Father still having that pain in his back?"

"Yeah, he went to see the doctor again three days ago. They can't figure out what's wrong."

"I'm so glad the barracks were built out there," Lizzie said. "Every time we drop by, there's some servicemen keeping them company, playing cards or singing or swapping stories. And I know they do some of the lighthouse work; I've seen them."

"Mother's treats probably have something to do with that," Freddie said.

"How many soldiers are stationed there?" Joan coughed. "I think all that running around in the cold last night made me sick," she added.

Lennie said, "That'll teach you to stay out so late." Then he answered her question. "About fifty."

"I never understood why they put all those troops there."

"The government told Father it was top secret so he doesn't ask questions, but he thinks they're running a tracking station to try to spot any German activity."

"It's been a godsend for your folks, having them there to help out," Lizzie added.

"I'm going out there this weekend," Joan said. "I need to see Father for myself."

~#~

Joan lagged at work that day. Emotion from the previous night's fiasco still coursed through her body, and then she hadn't slept at all, crammed in bed with Lizzie and Freddie.

And now this stupid cold...

She took care not to cough on the patients. Several times Joan excused herself to avoid that.

Sure don't want these men catching whatever I have. Their poor, infected lungs couldn't handle it.

Over the next several days, instead of getting better Joan felt progressively weaker. It became harder to hide her increasingly frequent and fierce coughing fits. She caught Roslyn eyeing her several times, but always smiled and pretended nothing was wrong.

"Maybe you've been working too hard," Madge said to her that night in their room. "You'll never get well if you don't get some rest."

"You're right. Think I'll take a couple days off." Joan called Roslyn to let her know.

The next day she slept quite a bit. Between naps, she read and drew sketches.

That night she told Madge, "I'm glad I didn't work today, but I feel better now. I shouldn't have taken two days off; I'll be bored out of my skull tomorrow."

"I notice you're still coughing."

"Yeah, but not as much, I don't think."

"Why don't you go to town?" Madge suggested.

"I think I will. I can visit Annette and her sisters. Haven't seen them in quite a while."

Joan had a good time with her friends. They lifted her spirits considerably.

As Joan prepared to leave, an intense coughing fit kicked in. The pain in her ribs bowled her over. Afterward, blood spotted her handkerchief.

"Oh, no," Annette exclaimed with a step back. "I think you have consumption! Your cough sounds just like Granny's when she took sick from it five years ago. It killed her!"

Annette's sisters jumped away, covering their noses and mouths with their hands.

"I'll drive you back to the base so you can get your boss or somebody to check," Annette offered.

Joan sat in the back seat, covering her mouth and nose with a neckerchief so she wouldn't spread any germs to her friends.

This can't be happening. Not to me. I'm too young to die. But most of the servicemen she treated were also young—even younger than Joan.

The doctor examined Joan once she got to the hospital. He said, "We won't know anything until we get the test results. Until then, for your good and for the safety of everyone else, we have to assume you're infected, and act accordingly."

She knew what that meant: isolation.

Sure enough, the doctor continued, "We'll get you set up in an isolation bed, where you'll stay until further notice. No visitors; just the nurse who'll be in charge of your care. Your friend can let your family know."

The tuberculosis test came back positive.

Joan spent the first few days in bed sick with worry and fear for the health of the family and friends she'd exposed. She prayed for them over and over.

Soon she became too ill to think logically. She had constant chest pain and fever came and went. Breathing took all her concentration and effort. The hospital could do nothing other than try to keep her comfortable.

For weeks Joan remained confined to bed rest as a patient in her own ward, with no visitors. Eventually her symptoms drifted away. When she felt strong enough Joan passed the time reading and writing letters. Once the symptoms lost their intensity, the boredom became unbearable.

After two months, the doctors declared her well enough to return home to the lighthouse. Severely weakened, she spent the next months recuperating quietly in the kitchen, rocking in Grandma Murphy's old chair. She sat next to the potbelly stove and happily received visits from friends and family, which brought her spirits up.

But as Joan's health improved, Father's pain intensified. He made many trips to the Placentia doctor.

One day when he returned from such a trip, he said, "Doc thinks he might know what's wrong."

Before Joan could express relief, Father continued, "He thinks it's cancer. He's sending me to a specialist in St. John's."

The room froze. Joan's heart plunged to her stomach.

Mother collapsed onto a chair. "Cancer." She closed her eyes as she whispered the word.

"Now don't go worrying, Louise, they got to do

some tests to be sure. I'll take a train to St. Johns, and they'll tell me good news for sure."

"The train station in St. John's is nowhere near that hospital, Joe," Mother replied. "Even if it was, your back can't handle the jostling and bouncing on those wooden train seats."

"I don't think it can handle sitting up and driving for five hours either," Father said. "Don't worry; we'll figure something out. Don't have a choice."

Only five of the family remained at the lighthouse. Father's pain prevented him from driving to St. John's. Neither Mother nor Angie knew how to drive, or dared to learn on the spur. Joan remained too weak. Leonard couldn't leave, because he was now in charge of the lighthouse and had to remain on duty.

They fretted all evening about what to do, but none of them found a solution.

The next day Angie rushed in after work.

"Guess what?" she cried. "Mr. Monkarsh is going to take Father to St. John's."

"I can't ask him to do that," Father said. "You shouldn't have either, Angie. Now I'll have to tell him no. It's too much."

"But I didn't ask him; he volunteered."

"Tell us how it happened," Mother appeased. "Then we can decide what to do."

"I was sorting the new lipsticks and I got to thinking about it all, and started crying. I couldn't help it. Mr. Monkarsh saw me, and insisted on knowing why. At first I just said, because Father might have cancer. But he kept asking questions about what doctors and when he was going to the hospital and everything, until it all came out."

"So how did he volunteer? What did he say?" Lennie asked.

"He said, 'Don't fret, Punk. There's a simple solution: I'll drive your father to the city.' He said he's a good driver and hasn't had a chance to go to St. John's in a long time."

"But what about the store?" Joan asked.

"That's what I asked. And he said I could run it. I told him I wasn't sure that's a good idea—remember the watch incident? But he said, 'If you can trust me with your father, I can trust you with the store. It's all settled.' He's coming over tonight to make plans with Father."

"Mr. Monkarsh has always been so good to us girls," Joan said. "It's just like him to do this for Father."

"Yes, he's a rare man and a true friend," Father agreed. "How can I turn down such generosity?"

When Mr. Monkarsh arrived, the family could not express their thanks to him enough. Two days later, Father packed his bag and the two men headed out on the five-hour drive to St. John's.

The next day, around noon, Joan sat in the kitchen sipping a cup of tea and talking with Leonard, who was having a sandwich for lunch. Mother stood at the sink washing a few dishes and looking out the window, which faced the meadow separating the house from the army barracks.

Suddenly, Mother shrieked in terror. She turned from the sink and looked at Joan and Lennie as if she wanted to say something, but could only stutter nonsense and flap her hand. After a second, she fainted dead away.

Leonard and Joan rushed to her. Before they could

revive her, someone knocked on the front door. Leaving Leonard with Mother, Joan ran to the door and threw it open, hoping for help.

On the threshold stood a handsome Black soldier, holding a tray of pork chops.

"For the family," he said, flashing extraordinarily white teeth in a wide smile, "with compliments of the colonel."

When Lennie told Father the story later, Mother said, "He might as well have been a green Martian. I never saw a Black person before."

~#~

Father and Mr. Monkarsh arrived home three days later. Before either of them said a word, Joan saw the bad news in Mr. Monkarsh's eyes as he gave her a hug before leaving.

Father confirmed it: he had an incurable form of cancer. The specialist gave him six months to a year to live.

"Maybe a little longer, if I take it real easy."

"There's nothing at all they can do?" Mother asked through her tears.

"I got medicine for the pain. But no, they can't do anything else."

He paused a moment then said, "Now, you all stop blubbering. I don't plan to spend my last days with everybody feeling sorry and tiptoeing around. We're going to go about life as always. We didn't know when the good Lord might call one of us home before, and now we still don't know. So not another word about this."

Joan's previous work in the hospital had trained her to control her feelings, so now she hid her sorrow in Father's presence and kept her sobs deep in the pillow at night.

Father went about his daily duties manning the lighthouse and never complained about the pain he obviously suffered. The family rallied around him. Weekends often found the entire family gathered at the lighthouse. Kitchen parties became regular occurrences. Joyful noises filled the home daily.

~#~

Four months after Joan went home to recuperate, she visited the doctor.

"You can go back to work now, but not at the hospital," he said. "Your lungs are compromised; it's too great a risk."

"But that's my job. I—"

He interrupted. "You'll have to get a job somewhere else. You would not only place yourself at risk in the hospital, but you'd put the ward in a bad position if you have a relapse."

Joan sighed. Life seemed to have moved on without her, and now she was stuck with no job, no social life—even Andy had stopped calling. No doubt he found some other girl to chase. *One with lungs strong enough to dance.*

She'd waited all this time to return to the life she had before tuberculosis, only to be told she couldn't do it and that she had to find another job, another sort of work altogether.

Not Monkarsh's again. Much as she loved the man,

the store bored her after all these years. Besides, she needed more income than he could afford.

She asked her friends if they knew of any other base job opportunities. In time she learned of an opening at the PX. The PX, or Post Exchange, was like a large department store with low prices. The pay exceeded anything that she could earn at Monkarsh's, or even as a traveling hairdresser. She took the job and moved back to base.

Joan's first day on the job went smoothly. Sam Smith, the store manager, introduced her to Rose and Pat Vadors, sisters who worked there. The three girls immediately hit it off.

Rose introduced her around and explained the operation. "Our job is to do whatever it takes to keep this store running smooth. New merchandise is shipped in every day, so we're constantly stocking. Everything has to be neat and orderly. Meanwhile, customers will need our help in finding and selecting their purchases. When they're finished shopping, we walk with them to the front counter, write a receipt, and collect the money," Rose said.

"It's just like the work I had in Monkarsh's, only there's so much more inventory and variety for sale. I hope I can learn all this merchandise and the store layout fast."

"Don't you worry. These boys in uniform won't care if you're a slow worker. They come in here just to talk to a girl. Sometimes they waste a half hour of your time and only buy a pack of gum. The boss don't mind, either. He knows all these boys are heading to war and need a morale boost. Just have fun with it."

It didn't take long for Joan to recognize the truth

in Rose's words. She served all the young and handsome servicemen that came to the store. They were brave young men about to head to the war in Europe. Many of them had little life experience and were eager to socialize with a girl before heading overseas.

Still, Joan did find one big downside to the PX: the manager, Sam Smith. He turned out to be a nasty person. Every chance he could, he tortured Joan, and he always caught her completely by surprise.

"Joan, those shelves are stacked wrong. Take everything down and restock them."

"Joan, your handwriting is impossible. Rewrite all those receipts you completed today so I can read them."

"Joan, this is the third time this morning I see you coming out of the bathroom. What are you doing in there?"

"Joan, that blouse is completely inappropriate for a daytime sales clerk. Go home and change it. And I'm docking your pay for the time you're gone."

What does he have against me? She did nothing to warrant it, and she'd never met the man until she went to work for him. *Must just naturally be a brute.*

Joan put up with his antics because she needed the job. The PX offered steady work and great pay. *Maybe he'll get tired of harassing me if I just stick it out a little while.*

The man never relented. Frequently, he had her work extra hours without pay. He snuck up on her and eavesdropped. Sometimes he showed her photos of himself in a bathing suit, and made overtures to her. Once, Joan came out of the ladies' room and he stood right outside the door, staring.

When she confronted him, he lied about his

behavior. Then he called her into his office for a meeting. It began friendly, but soon he accused her of having mental problems. He reassigned her to the nastier duties of the store, like cleaning the toilets.

He thinks he can force me to quit. Well, he's got another thing coming. And one day I'll get back at him. She plotted what she would do when the time came.

Chapter 22

Vinny

Joan wasn't the only family member to work on the base. Madge still had her job as an office assistant and once again became Joan's roommate. Gussie took a job in the base barber shop.

One spring the base commander worked with Placentia City Council on a fundraiser for the annual Garden Party. The commander challenged all the barbers, both in town and on the base, to compete in a speed haircutting competition. Every soldier who volunteered to have his hair cut got a weekend pass, and whoever cut 100 soldiers' hair first would win. In addition, the commander pledged to donate $1 for each haircut to the fundraiser.

Some barbers snipped with scissors and others, like Gussie, used an electric buzz cutter. It was a close race but Gussie won. He cut 100 heads of hair in an hour and forty minutes; the second-place barber performed 98 cuts in that time.

Freddie had the most interesting job of all. He'd learned to repair things by watching his father work on the machinery at the lighthouse, and used that talent to become a machinist. Sometimes, he worked under water to spot-weld ships damaged in the war.

He donned a deep-sea diving helmet, a diving suit, and weighted boots for these tasks.

When Freddie rose to the ranks of top deep-sea diver on the base, he was asked by the navy to dive at the sites of the sunken U-boats to gather information and salvage technology from the sunken ships.

~#~

Joan found a new feature on base when she returned after her illness: the Newfoundlanders Club. The Club functioned on base as the Star Hall did in town, with food, drink, music, dancing, USO shows, and all kinds of entertainment. Servicemen and locals gathered at the Club in droves.

Now 26, Joan often headed to the Club after work. She never lacked for a dance partner, as so many soldiers knew her from the PX. The Club also had a quieter piano bar off the main hall where she'd get a drink when she needed a break from the crowd. The piano often remained silent, as the Club had no regular player. Sometimes a customer played a tune or two.

Tonight a sailor sat at the piano playing, of all things, Chopsticks. He wasn't good at it, either, but for some reason a half dozen young women surrounded him, giggling and laughing. Joan couldn't resist. She walked over to see what the fuss was about.

She didn't expect the fellow to acknowledge her, but he immediately looked up, smiled, and said, "Hi, I'm Vinny Rizzo. What's your name?"

"Joan Greene." She didn't add any more details.

Vinny appeared to be Italian. He wore a Class A sailor suit with one exception—the ugliest loud, orange tie Joan had ever seen or imagined. Despite the goofiness that gave him, he was cute and had a nice smile.

Look at all these women drooling over him. Too popular for me. After a few moments, Joan took her half-finished cocktail to a seat at the far corner of the lounge.

When his song ended, Vinny walked over and asked if he could join her. Joan nodded.

"Why'd you walk away? You could've stayed with the crowd for a few laughs."

"You looked like you had plenty of company."

"I'd rather have you join me." They chatted a while.

Joan learned a lot about Vinny. He'd just arrived on base two weeks ago. As a Seaman First Class, he usually served on the *USS Beatty*, a Gleaves-class destroyer that acted as escort for supply ships. He manned the five-inch guns. But the *Beatty* was docked to repair some minor battle damage and upgrade its defense systems, so Vinny got posted in Argentia while that happened.

"Where are you from, Vinny?" Joan asked.

"Brooklyn. My dad's a banker there."

"Is there a girl back home waiting for you?"

"Nah. I had a girl, but she broke it off as soon I as signed up. Said I was throwing my life away."

"So you're heartbroken?"

Vinny winked. "Not anymore."

Then he turned serious. "I joined up to serve my country and keep the world safe from monsters like Hitler. But I don't know what I wanna do after the war. For a living, I mean. I want to have a big family, but I'll have to support 'em somehow."

"Don't become a fisherman," Joan advised.

At Vinny's confused expression, she added, "Not enough income to support a family. Trust me. My father was a fisherman for a long time. It's a hard life for everyone, and still only poverty wages."

The couple talked until late into the night.

Joan loved dancing. Vinny bragged that he was a great dancer, but the first time they hit the floor, she laughed at his antics.

"Don't worry," she told him. "You're going to be a great dancer. I'll teach you everything you need to know."

Thereafter, Vinny seemed to always seek Joan out. As soon as she walked into the Club, he appeared at her side. She liked it that way. Soon he called every day, too. Joan felt sure he liked her as much as she liked him—a lot.

One night, they sat under the stars on a park bench. Joan rubbed her temples. "That Sam Smith gave me such a headache today."

"When my mom has a headache, my dad squeezes her head a little from front to back and then from left to right. She always says it helps. I'll do it if you want to try."

"I'll try anything."

Vinny stood and began pressing Joan's head.

"Oh, that does feel good. Harder, please."

"I can't squeeze too hard. I'm afraid I'll hurt the woman I love."

Joan's eyes popped wide open and without hesitation she threw her arms tightly around Vinny for a big hug. Then she laid her head on his chest and said, "I love you, too."

They held each other for a long time and embraced the moment. A small tear slipped down Joan's face as she hugged him even harder. Vinny blustered and hugged her back.

I'll remember this moment, and this night, forever.

Since she shared a room with her sister, Joan couldn't bring Vinnie to her room; and of course she'd never go to his barracks. They had to find private places around the base to express their love. Joan found a small courtyard at a building seldom used. There, lying on the grass, she kissed and embraced Vinny while he whispered sweet nothings to her in the late-night hours.

One evening Vinny suddenly pulled away from her and held a finger to his lips.

"Shh! Listen! Did you hear that?" he whispered.

Joan's heart pounded as they both strained their eyes to see through the dark veil of night.

"What is that?" Joan gasped. She clutched Vinny's arm and pointed. Under the bushes not four meters away, four glowing orbs floated several centimeters above the ground.

"Shh!"

The glowing orbs slowly drew closer.

Then they became four eyes fully lit by the moon. Two red foxes crept forward. They sat down under the moonlight less than a meter away, rested their heads and gazed at Joan and Vinny. They sat motionless even as Joan and Vinny burst out in laughter at the surprise.

After a few minutes, Joan kissed Vinny on the cheek. He turned to her, and they continued making out. Many nights thereafter, the foxes joined them for their evening love fest.

~#~

One evening, Joan invited Vinny to a kitchen party at her friend's house in Placentia. Several soldiers and sailors mingled with the locals. Everyone was having a high time, when suddenly someone started banging the table and hollering, "Screech-in! Screech-in!" The crowd quickly picked up the refrain.

"What's that?" Vinny asked. "I can't make out what they're saying."

"They're calling for a screech-in," Joan answered.

"I thought that's what they were saying, but what's it mean?"

"It's how folks from away can be made honorary Newfoundlanders."

"Hey, I wanna do that. What do I do?"

Joan led him to the man that started the commotion.

"Ah, our first victim, I mean friend," the man said. "So you want to be a Newfoundlander, eh?"

"Sure," Vinny replied. "What do I gotta do? Screech?"

"You don't have to, but I bet you will. All you have to do is take a drink of this here rum," he held up a bottle, "then kiss that codfish and repeat the motto, *Long may your big jib draw.* Then listen to a short story about how screech-ins got the name."

"I'm game. Pour me a shot."

The crowd grew quiet as the man poured a shot. Vinny picked it up and tipped it toward the crowd as if making a toast, then tossed it down his throat.

His eyes popped wide. "Hoo wee!" he shouted as he shook his entire body like a puppet in the wind.

The crowd roared with laughter, cheering and applauding, Joan most of all.

As soon as he stilled, the host thrust a codfish in front of Vinny's face. "Ya gotta kiss the cod."

Everyone whooped as Vinny pursed his lips and planted a bazz on the fish's lips.

"And the motto," the host prompted.

Vinny threw a panicked glance to Joan.

"Long may your big jib draw," she reminded him.

He repeated the phrase. Then Joan handed him a glass of water as everyone grew quiet again for the story:

As legend has it, in the early part of the war a few visiting American officers attended a kitchen party given in their honor at the home of a local Newfoundlander. A naval captain at the party inquired about various aspects of Newfoundland culture, including their most common alcoholic drink. The host brought out a bottle of the local rum, a low-quality beverage with high alcohol content.

The host swallowed a big shot of the stuff and offered a taste to the captain. The officer, not to be outdone, also took a big shot—and immediately screeched in horror at the harshness of the 140-proof moonshine.

An officer in another room asked one of the partygoers, "What on earth was that?"

The Newfoundlander replied, "'Tis the rum, me son."

From that day forward both sailors and locals called the drink Newfoundland Screech. Whereas before the rum was considered too low quality to serve guests, it now became part of any gathering's entertainment to offer newcomers a drink. If they accepted, and kissed a cod, they'd be considered honorary Newfoundlanders. The activity became known as a screech-in.

He concluded by clamping Vinny on the shoulder and saying, "B'y, you've been officially screeched in."

Vinny bowed to the cheers.

~#~

Joan and Vinny sat in the lounge at the Newfoundlanders' Club sharing a soda, talking and making each other laugh. Vinny's buddy Charlie rushed into the room and ran straight to Vinny, shouting.

"Big news, Vinnie! The repairs on our tub are finished. We're shipping out in two days. We're going to war."

Joan sucked in a breath of air as if she had been punched in the stomach. "Oh, no. No, no, no, no, no." She buried her face in her palms as if that would hold back the tears.

Vinny grabbed her and squeezed her tightly. "Be strong. Don't worry; I'll be back as soon as we beat those Nazis. With me and Charlie out there, we'll mop 'em up in no time. You'll see." The tone of his voice didn't quite match the words.

The two days felt like the shortest two days ever created by God. Joan spent every possible minute with him. She even talked Mother into letting Vinny stay at the lighthouse, and the two of them sat in the kitchen throughout the night, in front of the potbelly stove, holding each other and whispering about the future.

"Write me?"

"Every day, I promise."

"Wait for me?"

"I will. But what about all the fancy European girls?"

"I swear I'll be true."

~#~

Joan went out to the dock to send Vinny off. The tears wouldn't stop.

"Be strong, Joan. I'll be back." Vinny pulled himself away and boarded the ship. Joan stayed on the dock with several other Placentia girls, all looking up at the rails where their boys' faces would appear. When they did, the girls waved furiously, calling their goodbyes.

As the ship began to pull away, Vinny shouted, "Joan, I love you! Marry me!"

Her breath caught as her mind blanked from surprise. Before she gathered enough wits to reply, the ship sailed too far away for Vinny to hear her answer.

On the way home, confusion assailed her. *Why did he propose like that? I couldn't even give him an answer. Now he's gone for God knows how long.*

Joan told Mother what happened. She also told her sisters and friends. Each of them had different advice.

I promised to write, so that's what I'll do. And like Mother says, I'll be completely honest.

My dearest Vinny,

I miss you already, and you left just this morning. My love for you fills my heart.

Your proposal took me so by surprise, I couldn't

form an answer. And I can't answer yet. We've known each other such a short time, only a few months. I will give you an answer soon; but of this you can be sure—I will wait for you faithfully...

Joan prayed the letter would reach him, and soon. Thoughts of Vinny filled her days. With each passing hour, she became more certain that marriage to Vinny meant a lifetime of happiness. This wonderful man treated her like a princess. He came from a good Catholic family. His prospects for a future looked great.

Two weeks later she wrote another letter.

Vinny, my love—

I haven't received a letter from you yet, but wait anxiously. I write you every day, just as I promised, and pray you receive them.

Vinny, I love you so much. I can't imagine life without you. I accept your proposal...

With her future set, Joan went about the business of life. She didn't go to the Club much anymore, just an occasional drink with friends. Dancing would wait until her partner returned. Instead she planned her wedding and dreamed about a new life in America. To earn money for them, she continued to work at the PX, even though that horrible Sam Smith still tortured her.

When this war ends, the first thing I'm going to do is give Sam a piece of my mind.

Every day Joan walked to the post office to send her letter off to Vinny, and look for one from him.

"Nothing for you," the postmaster said.

He's writing to me. I know he is. It just takes a long time for letters to get here from...wherever he is.

"I'm sorry, I don't have anything for you."

It's been a month. Where are his letters? Maybe he's on a top-secret mission and can't write now.

"No, no mail in your box."

Two months is plenty of time for a letter. Has Vinny been hurt? Why doesn't he write?

"These just came in today." The postmaster handed her a stack of letters tied together with string.

"Oh, thank you, thank you!" Joan would have hugged the man if he hadn't been behind a counter.

She raced home and tore the letters open one by one in the order they were mailed, according to the postmark date. As expected, the military had looked at and censored every one of Vinny's letters. Entire lines had been cut out.

Enough remained for Joan to understand most of what Vinny wrote. The fifth letter expressed his joy at her acceptance of his proposal. The romantic and loving words that followed moved Joan to tears. She read the letters over and over again, until the very paper began to wear out from all the handling and the tears. Joan's heart was close to bursting with happiness.

Chapter 23
That Long Goodnight

"It's Father," Lenny told Joan on the phone. "He made it thirteen months, but he died in his sleep last night. You know the strange thing? He had a smile on his face."

As tradition allowed, the family buried him up on Cemetery Hill next to his mother and among the other members of his family resting there.

~#~

A few months later, Joan relaxed in her dorm reading Vinny's letters yet again. He wrote such sweet things. Every night she read and reread them, all the while thinking about the future and wishing the war would end.

Tonight she had a new letter to read with the others. Joan laughed aloud at some of the antics he described.

Madge rushed in the door and raced to Joan's side. She stood panting for air, a terrible look on her red face.

"What are you all worked up for? For goodness' sake, take a drink of water, catch your breath."

Madge sat on the bed next to Joan and grabbed

her hand. Tears began streaming down her face as she choked out the words.

"Vinny is gone. The *Beatty* was sunk in the Mediterranean with no survivors."

"What? I don't understand." Joan couldn't make the words make sense.

"A Nazi U-boat sunk the *Beatty* with a torpedo. There were no survivors. Vinny is dead." Madge spoke more clearly though her tears still flowed.

"You must be mistaken," Joan said. "Vinny's not dead. I've got his letters right here."

"I'm so sorry—"

"No. He can't be dead. I just got a letter from him today. He wrote about a skit he and his buddies performed on the ship, where they painted faces on their stomachs and performed Shakespeare with the painted bellies." Joan laughed but it came out deranged.

"He's dead, Joan."

Vinny's hilarious story made her laugh and in the middle of it Madge told this terrible joke about Vinny dying. Why would she do that?

"Quit saying that! He's alive. Stop joking like that."

Madge cried harder and hugged Joan.

Somehow the word *dead* kept pounding on Joan's brain. Dead...dead...dead...

"Oh, my God, no, no. He must be okay. Maybe he swam to shore. He's a good swimmer. Surely it might take a day or two after the attack before they'd find him on some beach looking for shelter."

"The day or two has passed, Joan. The ship sunk three months ago. The base only released the news today. If he survived, they would have found him by now. Joan, I'm so sorry. He is truly gone."

Dead...dead...dead...

Shrieks and wails filled the air as Joan pounded on Madge's chest. Madge embraced her and pulled her close, holding tight so she couldn't move. They collapsed on the bed and sobbed a long time.

The words woke Joan. Dead...dead...dead...

She ran to the bathroom and vomited, then crawled back in bed, sobbing.

"...call the PX," she heard Madge say. "...time off..."

At some point Leonard showed up. Joan was vaguely aware of him and Madge moving about the room. Then Madge came and sat beside her.

"Come on, Joan. I'm taking you home. You can't stay here, all alone."

Joan numbly let Madge shepherd her to Lenny's car. At home Mother helped her to the kitchen, where she sat staring at nothing.

Leonard set up a chair swing overlooking the sea. Mother bundled Joan up with warm blankets and sat with her in the fresh air.

The emptiness inside her felt unexplainable and unbearable. She cried herself to sleep at all hours of the day and night. Each time she woke up, she replayed everything in her head over and over: the courtship, the goodbye, the proposal, the letters...and then the news. That made her cry again.

Louise brought her hot tea and soup. Joan had no appetite. Friends came to visit but Joan felt too distraught to talk with them so they always left right away. No one could console her. Even her faith faltered. Vinny, the love of her life, was gone forever.

~#~

Joan endured a period of intense grief, followed by a long period of numbness. Life moved on, and before she realized it, four years had passed, with little change in her life. Time eased the pain enough that she found spots of joy amid the daily motions of living.

Most of that joy she found at the lighthouse. It acted as a beacon to the family, drawing them home to the bonds of love. Most weekends the Greene siblings gathered around Mother—now Grandma Greene—with their spouses and children. They played games and music and sang songs and gossiped as they had in the old days, while the young ones ran in and out, playing and asking for hugs and kisses.

Those days were bittersweet to Joan. The family enveloped her with love, and she loved them in return. Yet they were also a reminder of what she didn't have, what she'd lost.

Mother brought her musing back to the kitchen with a question.

"Is that boss of yours still giving you a bad time?"

"Yeah, he's evil as ever."

"Why on earth do you stay? Why don't you quit?"

"It's the best pay I can get. With the war over, the jobs have dried up." Joan sipped her hot tea.

"I see so many of our girls marrying American servicemen and moving off to America. Pretty soon there won't be any local girls left in Placentia. Why don't you find a nice boy from the base and settle down? You don't have to move; you can make a home right here."

Joan sighed. "There's plenty of servicemen, but they all remind me of Vinny. Besides, even though the war is over, many of them are destined for a new war in Asia. I couldn't stand to love and lose another man to war. And I don't want to go to Asia. Although I'd move to America. That could be exciting."

Mother's face showed her pain, making Joan regret the words. Mother lamented the loss of her oldest daughter Mary, who'd moved to New York City years ago.

"Don't fret, Mother," Joan assured. "You know I'll always love you."

Then she changed the subject. "Tell me about that new fella Angie brought home. She's serious about him, huh?"

"That girl's head over heels. Not so sure about him, though."

"What do you mean?"

"I just don't see it in his eyes. All the feelings are on her side, I believe."

"That reminds me, Andy Ryan started chasing me again. That guy never gives up."

"Does he have any more hope now than he ever did?"

Joan shook her head. "He's a good friend, but he has too many faults. You've never seen how cranky he can be. Besides, he doesn't have any ambition. I don't think he'll ever amount to much. You know I've always said my man would have to have a good living—nothing like a fisherman."

Mother stepped to the stove without commenting on that. "Jigg's Dinner is about done," she said. Joan got up to finalize preparations for the dinner before calling the family to the table.

~#~

Joan opened the door to find Angie.

"He left." Angie's face couldn't seem to decide between grief and anger.

"Left? You mean, deployed?" Joan asked.

"No. His enlistment ended and he went home."

"Oh."

"He never said a word about it. I called him up to see when he planned to pick me up tonight, and his roommate said he'd gone."

"Wait...you mean, you didn't know he was leaving?"

"I had no idea. But I know where he lives in America. I'm going after him."

Nothing Joan said could change Angie's mind. Over the next few days, the whole family pleaded with her, but the next week she flew to America.

~#~

Joan joined the crowd at water's edge to watch the house floating in Placentia harbor. It was pulled along with ropes by men in boats, moving from some deserted outport to a coastal town. The house bobbed up and down, sometimes appearing to roll over, only to right itself in short time.

If walls could speak, what stories would that old house tell?

The hundred-year-old house had abandoned its birthplace, leaving forever a place of birthdays, weddings, holidays, and burials. Did it take with it the memories of laughing children, romancing lovers, crying mothers, and sweating fathers? Despite all its history on the land it left, the house said goodbye and set sail for a new life in a new homestead. It symbolized the freedom of a fresh start, a new beginning.

Exactly what I need.

Many of Joan's friends had left for America. Father was gone. Vinny was gone. Angela and Mary now lived in America. Her other siblings had married and led new lives.

If I stay here, my life will never change. It'll be dreary and stale forever.

As she watched the house float dreamily across the bay, Joan knew the time had come to leave her own home forever.

But first, she had one final task.

~#~

Joan's boss at the PX, Sam Smith, still harassed her daily. Hourly, sometimes. Try as she might, Joan couldn't figure any reason for it—especially since he treated everyone else just fine.

Guess he's just a nasty, evil rat.

With plans for America set, Joan told the girls as they left after work that she'd be resigning the next day. Rose and Pat Vadors begged to give her a going-away party, and Joan agreed to meet them at the Club the next evening.

Then she went home and wrote out four copies of a two-page resignation letter addressed to Sam. The letter described in detail an itemization of all the effronteries Sam had directed at her over the years, including the sexual harassment that she hated most. She mailed a copy to Sam's immediate supervisor, to the man above that, and to the base commander.

The next day Joan walked into the store and handed the final letter to Sam. "I quit, and I'm leaving now." She turned on her heel and strode away without allowing him time to say a word.

At her party that evening, Joan asked, "So, how was everything at work today?"

Rose's eyes and mouth opened slowly as realization dawned in her eyes. "It was you! I should have known."

"Tell us," everyone begged.

"I sent Sam a going-away present," Joan said smugly. "I went to the post office all the way over in Fox Harbour, just so he couldn't trace the package back to me."

"Did you really?" Pat asked.

"Yup, I wrapped the package nice and tight, and marked it 'Personal' to make sure only Sam opened it."

"You wouldn't believe the commotion that package caused," Rose said with a laugh. "Sam shouted and shrieked and worked himself into such a frenzy that he had to race to the bathroom and throw up. He raved and vomited until he had to go home, all the while shouting that he'd have someone's head."

"What on earth did you send him, Joan?" Pat asked.

"I thought, Sam is a big rat so he deserves to have one of his own. I got my brother Leonard to bring me the biggest dead rat he could lay his hands on. The carcass had just begun to rot before I wrapped it up. I'm glad Sam got sick over it. He'll know it came from me, but he'll never be able to prove it."

Rose piped in. "He'll never forget it, that's for sure.

Gosh, Joan it was some awful looking, and the stench stunk up the whole store. It was disgusting, all right."

Joan laughed in glee.

~#~

Joan made plans with her sisters Mary and Angela. Mary and her husband owned the New York home they raised their family in. Angie had a room there, and Joan would share it. Mary and Angie promised to pick Joan up from the airport at the appointed time.

Next came the difficult goodbyes. Joan made a point to visit the homes of many of her family and friends in town. She hugged and kissed and cried and said goodbye to all of them, one by one. After the last goodbye in town, she returned to the lighthouse to pack for America.

As she packed, Mother came into the room and sat down on the edge of the bed. Tears rolled down her face.

"I hate to see you go. We may never see each other again."

"Sure we will. I'll make sure to have a place for you when you come to visit." Joan continued folding her clothing into the suitcase.

"I'll never go all the way to America. It's too far, and too expensive, and I'm afraid of flying. I won't ever meet your future husband or the lovely children you'll have." Now Mother sobbed uncontrollably.

For the first time Joan fully understood Mother's view of the situation. *She's right. Mother's getting older—this truly might be the last time I ever see her.*

Joan began crying as well. "Don't say that, Mother.

I'll be back. I'll bring my husband and children, again and again. You'll see. I love you, Mother. I couldn't bear the thought of never seeing you again."

Both of them wept all evening and into the night. At one point Lenny poked his nose in to see the commotion for himself, but there was nothing he could do to placate them. Before long, his own eyes filled with tears.

Joan crawled into Mother's bed that night and they slept in each other's arms. Next morning Mother sobbed again, starting Joan off. She couldn't stop until Leonard loaded her suitcase in the car for the trip to the railroad station.

Chapter 24

A New Beginning

Once on the train, Joan grew excited again. In St. John's she'd board a plane for New York.

A plane! Anything is possible now.

After a five-minute delay at takeoff, Newfoundland disappeared below the clouds. Despite that, Joan's anticipation of America kept her eager for the future. She wouldn't waste time mulling on the past.

The flight went well and with so many new things to see and experience, the trip passed quickly. It seemed no time at all before the plane landed and Joan stepped into America.

Holy moly.

Her sisters had told her New York was bigger than she could imagine, but this...this defied description. What Joan had always considered "the city," St. John's, was a tiny backwater compared to this.

Joan followed the crowd and the signs to collect her suitcase, then waited at the passenger pickup area. Hundreds—maybe thousands—of people bustled around, but neither Mary nor Angie were anywhere to be seen.

A few panhandlers approached her aggressively for handouts. Frightened, Joan shouted at them to go away, then went to stand near a service counter. At least if some bum made trouble, there'd be someone nearby who might help.

The minutes ticked by. Joan became more nervous and tired with each one. Where were her sisters? Fear and worry wrestled with anger and frustration for top place.

After an hour, Joan could stand it no longer. She found a pay phone and called Mary's apartment.

"Hello?"

"Jack? It's Joan. Is Mary there? Or Angie?"

"No; they went to see a movie and then pick you up."

"I've been waiting an hour and they're not here yet."

"Why don't you get a cab? You can be here in less than twenty minutes."

Joan made sure she had the address for the cabbie and hung up.

Her emotions already high, they reached a fever pitch on the taxi ride to Mary's. Her mind raced over all the things that could have gone wrong—and could yet go wrong—to a lonely country girl in the big city for the first time.

And now this expensive cab. How can my sisters treat me this way?

She finally reached the house. Jack greeted her at the door. Joan tried to be civil to him, but her anger threatened to boil over with each word. When he suggested she rest until Mary and Angie returned, Joan took him up on it.

Some time later the front door opened and closed. Jack's voice mingled with the women's. Joan went to the front room where they stood talking.

"Where were you?" she exploded. "I was scared out of my mind. People were begging money from me and calling me names. I started crying, which just drew more attention to me."

"I'm sorry," Mary said. "I called the airport this morning. They said your plane would be several hours late."

"Hours? We had a five-minute delay, that's all. I'm the one that waited hours!"

"I'm sorry," Mary reiterated. "We never would've left you waiting if we'd known. It was just a mistake."

Suddenly the humor of the situation hit Joan and she started laughing. She threw her arms around Mary. "I'm so glad to see you, Mary!"

The three sisters hugged and cried and laughed and talked all at once.

~#~

Joan marveled at the amount of traffic and people and noise, but she soon adjusted to the pulse of the city. One thing stood out: she needed some new clothes to look like a cosmopolitan city woman instead of a fisherman's daughter. The fashion and celebrity magazines sold on every corner showed stylish outfits and new hairdos.

Looking glamorous cost money, so Joan took steps to get her Newfoundland hairdressing license validated for practice in the city and took a job nearby at the beauty salon that Mary used. With her first paycheck she went shopping.

"Wow, you really do look like Joan Crawford—except your hair's redder," Angie said when she saw her sister's sophisticated new look. "Weren't those clothes expensive?"

"Not too much. I might look like a fashion plate, but I still have the good sense of a Placentia girl. I find bargains and ways to economize."

"Good, because I want you to save up so we can get an apartment together. With the new baby coming, Mary could sure use our room."

"That's true," Joan said. "We should start looking right away."

~#~

A couple of weeks after settling into their new apartment, Angie called Joan to the phone.

"Hello?"

"Hi, Joan. Want to go to the Newfoundlander Club with me tomorrow night?"

"Andy Ryan, what are you talking about? You know I'm in America now."

"After you left, Placentia seemed boring and lonely. Your mother gave me your address and phone number."

"I understand the phone number, but why do you need the address?"

"To make sure I got a place near you when I got here."

"Got here? You mean, *here*? In New York?"

"Yeah, in Brooklyn. I got a cousin that lives just a few blocks from you. I'm staying here. So what do you say? The Newfoundlander Club is for all of us from The Rock. You'll love it. I'll pick you up at seven, okay?"

"On one condition."

He said it with her: "We go as friends, nothing more."

~#~

The Newfoundlander Club near Prospect Park hummed with life on Saturday night. Joan was surprised to see some acquaintances from the Argentia naval base in the crowd. But the club attracted more than folks from The Rock; many Scandinavians as well as locals mixed in.

Andy's cousin brought Angie, and they sat with Joan and Andy enjoying beer between dances. The club played big band music on a juke box and the dance floor overflowed.

Andy and Joan were doing a swing dance. Joan couldn't swing very well; so many people crowded the floor that she bumped into other dancers if she stepped too far from Andy. She came out of a swing under Andy's arm and her legs tripped a dancer behind her.

Joan's leg tangled under him. He fell to the ground in the middle of the dance floor and his arm slipped under Joan's leg. Down she came, falling right on top of him and pinning him to the floor.

The two struggled to their feet and made their way to the side of the dance floor to apologize to each other.

"I'm Matt," the other dancer said. "Can I make it up to you over a cup of coffee?" His eyes shone with pleasure as he looked at her.

What a gentleman. It was my fault but he's taking the blame. And I sure am glad I wore this gorgeous dress.

She answered "Yes," then dragged Matt over to

the table where Angela sat, introduced them to each other, and said she and Matt were going to step over to the diner next door for a cup of coffee. She bade Andy and his cousin goodnight and off they went.

Matt and Joan talked long into the night. Joan gave him her phone number and they agreed to get together again. Matt walked her home from the diner. At the front door, he seemed to hesitate a moment, then he bent over and kissed her goodnight.

Joan felt every bone in her body melt with that kiss. Her world swirled and she would have sunk to the floor if Matt hadn't held her tightly against himself.

When he finally released her, Joan ran upstairs to the apartment and found Angie waiting for her. Joan bubbled with excitement as she shared the details of her date with Angie. When she got to the end, she said, "He kissed me until I almost fainted."

Angie put the back of one hand against her forehead and fanned herself with the other like a girl from a silent movie. "Oh, I'm faint," she teased.

Joan laughed with her but said, "It's true! I've never been kissed like that. I swear, he has the fluffiest lips on Earth." She swirled around and danced to her room. She dreamed of that kiss.

The next week she turned down Andy's request for a date so she'd be free when Matt called to ask her out.

He never called.

So the next weekend Joan accepted Andy's offer to meet at the Newfoundlander Club for Saturday night dancing. As they danced the first set Matt walked up and tapped Andy on the shoulder.

"Cutting in."

Andy stepped aside, and Matt took his place.

"You have some nerve," Joan said by way of greeting. "When I give a man my phone number, I expect him to use it. I want nothing to do with you."

"Please, forgive me. My mother snatched up my pants next day and washed them—with your phone number still in the pocket. I've been coming back here every night since then hoping to see you again. Please give me another chance."

His face wore the badge of truth. "On one condition. Take me out right now for a slice of pizza and a Coke, and spend the rest of the night telling me how desperately you've been missing me. If you can convince me of the truth, I'll pretend it never happened." Joan smiled so he'd know she already forgave him.

Many hours later, Joan wrote her phone number again. This time she made Matt promise to safeguard it.

He called the next day, and the next, and every day after that. He took her to Club, to the park, to the movies, out to eat. Often Joan invited him to the apartment for dinner. She usually served beans and franks. Paying rent and keeping up with fashions were more important than expensive meals.

"What's the first thing that drew you to me?" Joan asked one afternoon.

"Red," Matt replied.

"Red? What do you mean?" She'd been wearing a green dress that night.

"Your hair. I love red hair. Yours is even redder and more vibrant than Maureen O'Hara's."

"Maureen O'Hara, huh? Is she your pinup girl?"

"Only till I met you. I knew the moment I saw that hair you were the girl for me."

~#~

"It's time for you to meet the rest of my American family," Matt said. "Come for dinner after church on Sunday."

The next Sunday, Joan went to Matt's house for dinner to meet his family. His mother and father welcomed her with broken English but much warmth. "Call us Ma and Pop," they said. "Everyone does."

Matt's four brothers, as well as a few friends and other relatives, already crowded around the table. Bread, salad, antipasto, and wine, sat out on the table. Ma soon added meatballs, sausages, braciole, lasagna, and, of course, pasta with tomato sauce.

Matt's family was affectionate and fun. Joan loved the food and the family and the noise. It brought back good memories of the old days at the lighthouse, when the whole family gathered in the kitchen.

Toward the end of the meal Pop suddenly demanded from the head of the table, "Where's my dessert? Don't you make no dessert?"

Joan looked around uneasily but no one else seemed to notice his tone of voice.

"Of course I make dessert," Ma said. She reached up and slapped the back of his head. "I always make dessert."

Pop curled his hand into a fist and jabbed at her, but didn't touch her. She returned the action.

Matt caught Joan's eye and grinned. Her eyes widened. *Oh, it's a game they play.*

Everyone laughed as Pop pulled Ma onto his lap.

He planted a big sloppy kiss on her lips before she got up and brought anisette, dessert, and coffee.

From the corner of her eye Joan saw Matt's littlest brother Tony, still a young boy, reach his fork toward the meatball platter. He couldn't quite reach.

"Don't put your fork in the meatballs, Tony," Ma said. "You have plenty already. How you eat more?"

Tony's sad eyes stared at the meatballs but he put his fork down.

After a moment, while Ma talked to someone else, Joan took the serving spoon and quickly scooped a meatball onto Tony's plate. He beamed at her with a smile so big it almost split his face.

~#~

At the end of the evening Matt walked Joan down the stairs and out into the front door foyer. It was the one place in a Brooklyn brownstone house that a man could secretly steal a kiss from his girl. The darkened foyer could not be seen from the street thanks to a rolling window shade with a ring pull hanging on a string. Matt gave Joan a romantic kiss with his fluffy lips.

Then he whispered into her ear, "There's a rock in the ocean a thousand miles long, a thousand miles wide, and a thousand miles tall. Every thousand years a little bird flies there and sharpens his tiny beak on the rock. When the day finally comes that the bird wears that big rock down to nothing, only one day of my eternal love for you shall have passed."

He yanked the ring pull of the window shade off

its string, slipped it onto Joan's left finger, and said, "Marry me?"

"Yes."

When they shared the news with their friends and family, everyone congratulated them and happily helped plan the wedding—all except one. Andy Ryan didn't come around or call anymore. In only a few weeks, Joan heard that he'd married a Newfoundland girl he met at the club.

~#~

Joan thought about her sisters' weddings. The whole village had been welcome at a cold plate party. She couldn't invite the entire city of New York. She asked Mary, "What kind of weddings do Americans have?"

"All kinds. You better ask Matt or his mom what they think."

When Joan asked them, Matt said, "I figured we'd have a traditional football wedding, like most Italians around here do."

Football wedding? Joan had no idea what that was but it didn't sound particularly appealing. However, it was Matt's family who would be there. Aside from Mary and Angie, no one from Joan's family would be able to attend. So it seemed right to do what his family expected. Besides, she didn't really care what kind of wedding it was—she just wanted to marry the man she loved.

Since both Joan and Matt were good Catholics, they married in the church. The wedding ceremony itself was the traditional service Joan knew and loved.

At least two hundred people poured in the church dining hall for the party afterward. Tall piles of hoagie sandwiches wrapped in waxed paper—made by Matt's family the day before—sat on a table at one side of the room.

"That's our spot." Matt led Joan to the table. He showed her how each sandwich's wrapper was marked with the kind of filling it had. "We're the designated quarterbacks of this game. When somebody yells for a sandwich, we take turns throwing it to them. Sometimes somebody else will catch it and you have to throw another one."

That turned out to be an understatement. The most fun came from the antics of those who tried to intercept sandwiches—especially when two people tried for the same one! Joan laughed so much her cheeks grew sore, but she kept right on laughing.

Between hurling sandwiches, Joan and Matt joined others on the dance floor. The band played a variety of Italian songs, music from Newfoundland, and American tunes.

A few hours into the party, Andy Ryan appeared before Joan. "Can I dance with the bride?"

"Of course, Andy. I'll always dance with my old friend."

He clutched Joan close and danced her across the floor.

"I met your wife," Joan said. "She's nice—and really pretty."

Andy pulled his head back and looked Joan in the eyes. Tears streamed down his face. As the last measure of the song played, he said, "We both married the wrong people." He dropped his arms, turned, and walked away.

His words squeezed at her heart on his behalf, but he was wrong. Joan married the love of her life. She prayed Andy would find the happiness with his wife that she felt every moment with Matt.

The party went on deep into the night. Finally, exhausted, Joan and Matt left the church hall. Matt's family had made a little downstairs apartment for him and Joan in his parents' three-story Brooklyn brownstone townhouse. There they went, to their own home, to begin their life together.

Joan had a new home, love, and life in America, but the lighthouse remained a beacon. It frequently called both of them back to The Rock and the place Joan used to call home.

~The End

Above:
Convent school in Placentia

Left:
Joan

Below:
An outport

Above: View of the lighthouse from the water

Below: Joan and Leonard

Above: Joan

Below: Monica's husband Charlie and Gussie

Joan's brother Gussie standing left; her brother
Freddie kneeling; her brother Leonard standing left.
Standing in center is Madge's husband Din.

Below left: Bridie with her husband Ben and children.
Below right: Bridie and her daughter Sheila

Gussie with wife Jean and children

Madge with Bridie's children

Above: Joan
Below, left: Joan at the lighthouse
Below, right: Joan with Frank Warren

Above: Matt

Above:
Angela (left) and
Joan (right)

Below:
Joan and Matt's wedding
photo with his family

Above: Joan at far right, next to her is her sister Mary.
Standing is Mary's daughter (also named Mary).
Angela is holding Joan's first son, Gary.

Below, Joan with her sons,
baby Don (the author) and Gary

True Tales and Tall Tales

Spoiler alert: Read the book first.
This following contains information that will ruin the storyline if read first.

This book follows a girl from a large family that lived at a lighthouse. The girl, Hannah (Joan) Greene, later became my mother. My grandfather was the lighthouse keeper.

The stories contained herein are mostly derived from family oral history. However, I have taken artistic license, dramatizing some stories and adding a few fictional ones. Specific family details about my aunts and uncles have been massaged and manipulated to make for a story line that flows.

Here, chapter by chapter, I confess to what was real and what was almost real.

In the prologue, I describe Michael Green's adventure on the sailing ship *Commerce*. The story of the *Commerce* is a true story; and, Hannah's (and my) ancestor Michael Greene did indeed sell his schooner to raise money to buy Point Verde land. But Michael was not a passenger on the *Commerce*, and that drama was not a part of his life.

Chapter 2 and Chapter 7 each contain a fairy story. Although obviously make-believe, these are the actual stories told to my mother. Many fishing communities had real superstitions about fairies, and these folk tales were told in earnest.

As a child my mother believed in fairies, and that the stories about them were true. As an elderly woman, she talked to me about them as if she never doubted them, in the sense that fairies might be departed spirits.

It's possible children were told these stories in an attempt to make them stay out of the forest and away from the cliff as a safety measure to keep the child away from danger.

In Chapter 3, I tell the story of cousin Eddie getting drunk and passing out on top of Grandma in her bedroom. Although a true story, it actually happened to me.

When I was fourteen, I stayed at my Aunt Angela's house (baby Angie in the book) for a week when my folks were on a trip. At the time, I was part of a school play. Aunt Angela drove me to the cast party, where I stupidly got drunk.

When Aunt Angela picked me up and saw how drunk I was, she said, "Your mother will kill me if she hears about this. Let's keep this a secret between us. When we get home, speak to no one. Go straight to bed. I'll punish you in the morning. Go straight to bed."

Once in the house, I walked into the wrong room. It belonged to my fifteen-year-old female cousin. I passed out, right in her bed, without knowing she was there. If you read Chapter 3, you know the rest of the story. We certainly were not able to keep the secret.

Chapter 6 tells Joe's big yarn. This yarn is half true.

The Yank on the boat was me. On one visit to the Rock, I went fishing with some Newfoundlanders. I caused the disaster that could have cost our lives.

The solution to the fishing line wrapped around the propeller was for one of us on the boat to get in the water and clear the line. The two Newfoundlanders were discussing who was going to go into the water. I feared they were about to demand I go or even push me in, but luckily for me, another boat passed nearby, and the operators of that boat were able to free the propeller from their boat.

The rest of the yarn about using a Yank for bait is typical of one of the tall tales Grandpa Greene or any other Newfoundlander fisherman would tell.

Snowstorms at the lighthouse were often mean and fierce. The storm in Chapter 7 is a combination of all the stories my mom told about storms, made into the one storm. The details are accurate, but didn't occur all at the same time, as in my narrative.

Chapter 8 tells the story of a fishing vessel, the *John Leary* owned by Captain Noseworthy, caught in a storm.

There were certainly times when my grandfather gave aid to stranded seamen, including putting them up for the night at the lighthouse. However, I don't know the names and details of those situations. Artistic license surfaced once again as I filled in the gaps with this story.

The young fisherman Andy Ryan was a real person, and he did pursue my mother all his life. But I romanticized the way they met. Andy actually lived in the village and met Hannah in the course of normal village life.

In Chapter 9, I introduce the assistant lighthouse keeper Billy Corbin. There was definitely an assistant lighthouse keeper, but I made up the name Billy Corbin.

Ships were grounded near the lighthouse, and Uncle Leonard and other local men did indeed engage in salvage work on those vessels, selling the goods they recovered from these grounded ships.

However, as Mom's stories did not always come with a lot of details, I once again filled in the gaps. The grounding of the *Esmerelda*, in Chapter 10, came from my imagination, and the story of Billy Corbin's disappearance was inspired by other true stories involving the dangers of salvaging Newfoundland shipwrecks and the men who lost their lives in that pursuit.

In Chapter 13, Tommy, the mysterious American who floated ashore, is pure fiction.

The bit about Sister Georgine and her wrinkles in Chapter 14 actually happened to me. I did not have my homework to turn in, and Sister Georgine did not like my excuse. She called me up and forced me to look closely at her wrinkles.

The regatta in Chapter 17 did not happen. Although rowing regattas were common in Newfoundland, Placentia did not have a regatta until the 1960s, well after the time frame of this book. (And to my knowledge, none were ever "fixed.")

There was a real Ambrose-type character running around Placentia and causing problems. I changed his name so as not to offend his descendants, who may still be around.

The storm in Chapter 19, when Joan is returning for her sister's wedding, is a hybrid story with a little enhancement. My mom did travel to outports by boat, and she suffered some bad trips in poor weather in doing so. While there were some stressful moments in her travels, none were near-death experiences.

The Sore Thumb portion was based on something that happened to me. I was out boating on Long Island Sound as a teenager with two of my friends. We fought a heavy current and stupidly caused the anchor rope to wrap around the engine propeller. We were about to crash against the rocks at an actual place known as the Sore Thumb. Out of the blue, a strong, bronzed young man who looked like Tarzan realized our plight and jumped off the rocks into the heavy surf—with a knife clenched between his teeth. He swam to our boat and cut the anchor rope free of the propeller just in the nick of time before we could be crushed on the rocks or swept out to sea.

In Chapter 20 Gussie cuts the hair of a Nazi. Gussie's widow told this story to a cousin, who told it to me. There's no way to verify it, of course.

Vinny Rizzo, introduced in Chapter 22, was not real. My mom dated men from the military base but never got that serious about any of them. Although she didn't lose a lover to the war, many young women did, so the story isn't entirely fiction.

Some of the details in the story happened to other people—namely me. When I met my wife, I was playing Chopsticks on a piano surrounded by women, and wearing ugly orange clothing.

The love affair, including the marriage proposal, is the story of the romance between my wife and I. However, instead of being on a ship, I was in one car and my (future) wife was in another. We were driving on the highway to destinations that would separate us for a long while. As she took her turn off the road to head to her destination, I shouted out to her, "Marry me." I had to wait a long time to get her answer.

My mom's boss at the PX was an awful man who did indeed receive a dead rat from her when she left, as told in Chapter 23.

Moving houses on the water was part of the great program of outport relocation. These events actually happened after my mom left Newfoundland. Read "The History Behind Her Story" to learn about this wonderful piece of Newfoundland history.

All the rest of the family anecdotes in the book are true accounts of my mom's family.

The Rest of the Story

The last lighthouse keeper in Point Verde vacated the residence in 1992.

Two years before that, the government replaced the lighthouse and residence with a square, steel skeletal tower with an enclosed lantern room on top. This tower, a fog signal, and a shed, all enclosed in a chain-link fence, are all that remain on the Point. Today, computers and satellite communication remotely control the whole facility.

People still drive out to the lighthouse point to enjoy the beauty, solace, and majesty that God bestowed on its surroundings. Emotions swell when you visit there, coming from the ghosts of the people who lived there, and the people impacted by the lighthouse. It's a lonely place. The descendants of Joe Greene are currently involved in funding and building a memorial garden on the site of the old lighthouse.

Point Verde exists today as a bedroom community and the people there are no longer fishermen. They are schoolteachers, pharmacists, construction workers, and more, who make their living on the Rock. There are no businesses in Point Verde and the two-room schoolhouse stands empty and locked up. It no longer calls children to class. The village is still a beautiful place and many Greene descendants still live there.

Placentia is the second-fastest shrinking town in Canada with a dwindling population standing at 3500 residents. The disappearance of the American military base, combined with a cod fishing moratorium in 1992, has caused the citizens to seek a livelihood elsewhere. Many have moved to Canada's mainland. The town is still a charming place with clean air, water, and landscape. Many descendants of the Greenes still live there, as well.

Newfoundland stands today with a population close to 500,000. It is a modern place with modern conveniences, but with wide expanses of empty lands between towns and villages. Nature's beauty abounds there. Fishing has become a memory and the offshore oil business now propels the economy. It is a most wonderful place to visit.

As of the date I wrote this book, all of the Greenes from the lighthouse except baby Angela have passed away, along with their spouses. All nine of Joe and Louise Greene's children went on to great success in life by raising healthy families and entering business. They owned a department store, a convenience store, a night club, a restaurant, and a barber shop.

Joan (previously called Hannah) and her husband Matt, the parents of the author, stayed happily married until Matt's death in 2014. Joan lived another year after that, under the loving care of her two sons.

Joan remained lifelong friends with Andy Ryan. He never lost his crush on Joan, but he accepted the outcome, married someone else, and even became good friends with Matt.

The grandchildren and great-grandchildren of Joe and Louise Greene, many of whom are alive today, also lead successful lives. They have spread out all over the U.S.A. and Canada. They have become authors, actors, bankers, CPAs, police officers, business owners, singers, songwriters, teachers, engineers, and everything else. Many of the granddaughters met and married American servicemen from the Argentia base.

All of these lighthouse family descendants hold the memory of Point Verde Lighthouse close to their heart.

The History Behind Her Story

Historic, Geographic and Personal Perspective
on People and Places in the Book

On Newfoundland in General

The heroine of the book, Hannah, lived in Newfoundland, an island in the North Atlantic off the coast of Canada about the size of the State of New York. At the time that Hannah was born, Newfoundland was a Commonwealth Realm, like Canada and Australia. This meant that it was an independent country with a written constitution and the King of England was its monarch. Today it is a province and part of the nation of Canada.

Newfoundland is a wonderful, beautiful place. It is Canada's fourth largest island, barely touched by mankind, where huge, empty land is dotted with lakes and forest and green fields. The caribou run wild and the air and water are crisp, fresh, and clean. Rocky, wave-soaked shores are commanded by giant cliffs and populated by millions of seabirds native only to this area. Beautiful and happy people live in the small fishing villages and ports that crop up along its coastline and in cities and towns further inland.

Most of the population are of Irish and English descent and frequently speak with an Irish Brogue reminiscent of Old Ireland. Hospitality is the driving force behind every Newfoundland face you see. It is impossible to meet a native Newfoundlander and not be cornered into a friendly conversation, usually leading to an invitation to his home for tea.

The weather in Newfoundland is what you would expect in a northern maritime climate. In the summer there are many brilliant sunny days, in contrast to fierce Nor'easters and massive snowstorms in the long, cold winter. Finally, there is fog. Dense fog is one of the most common weather patterns in Newfoundland. There is a term coined for this type of weather: "It's another mauzy day."

Newfoundland is a beautiful place to visit, vacation, and live. While sparsely populated, it is very civilized, with all the modern 21st-century conveniences you could want. This is one of the places you must see before you die.

On the Greenes

When Hannah was born in 1918, close to 80,000 people lived in Newfoundland. It was not a crowded place. Outside of St. John's, the population lived mostly in little coastal villages. Everyone depended on the cod fishery industry. To survive, people either fished or worked on the land in service to the fisherman. Fishing was life, and it was hard work.

Hannah's village of Point Verde was largely Irish and mostly descended from one family—that of Michael Green and his sons John and Robert.

As seamen, Michael Green and his sons plowed the seas known as the Cod Triangle in Michael's schooner. They squatted on the peninsula of Point Verde in Newfoundland, where they fished for cod. When they had a full ship, they sailed to England and traded it for dry goods. The dry goods they took to Jamaica, and traded for rum. The rum went to Boston. The Greens had many relatives in Boston, and Michael, John, and Robert lived in the city while they sold or traded the rum. Then it was back to Newfoundland to begin the cycle again.

Michael and his sons were British loyalists and non-violent Quakers, so when the American Revolutionary War broke out, they left Boston and moved permanently to Point Verde in 1775. They squatted on the land of the wealthy Placentia fish merchants Saunders and Sweetman until 1803. Michael sold the schooner and saved the money. Eventually he used that money to purchase the land.

His sons John and Robert met and married local Irish Catholic girls from Placentia. As part of the marriage agreement, they were required to convert to Catholicism and change their hated English surname from Green to Greene. The family tradition says, "They were required to burn their Mason's aprons in public before they were allowed to marry." The aprons were a symbol of the Masonic fraternity, which had been banned by the Church due to its alleged anti-Catholic sentiments.

Though Michael Green and his sons settled permanently in Newfoundland, they and their offspring always maintained connections with the family that remained in Boston. Family was important. Many Greene fishermen through the generations went to Boston to trade cod; and in return, Boston relatives came to visit Newfoundland and the Newfoundlander Greenes.

On Cod Fishing and Placentia

Cod fishing off the coast of Newfoundland began soon after Columbus discovered the New World in 1492. In 1496, the English crown issued a royal patent to John Cabot to explore the New World, and in 1497 he came upon a "New Found Land" and named it so. He wrote many letters describing the enormous amounts of fish in the area, saying they were so abundant that one could almost walk across the sea upon their backs.

The British Navy, in the midst of expansion, needed a food source for its sailors—one that would allow the ships to remain at sea for months at a time. When the navy received word of the bounty of fish in the New Found Land, the solution appeared clear as day.

However, the British were not alone in this realization. France, Spain, and Portugal also saw the benefit of the Newfoundland fishing grounds. For a great many years after Cabot's revelation, all these countries employed great fishing fleets to fill their navies' larders.

There was a difference. When Spain, Portugal, and France fished, they did it in the deep waters of the

Grand Banks. They then processed the fish completely while at sea, hardly ever setting foot on the rocky shores of the beautiful island. Britain, on the other hand, concentrated on inshore fishing. They spent much effort over the years to stake a bigger claim of the fishing grounds for themselves. By 1713, Britain controlled the island exclusively, with Queen Elizabeth as its monarch.

The British modeled their hold on Newfoundland after plantations. Hence the name they used for the master merchants in the business was "planters." At the beginning of each fishing season, the British abducted and coerced coastal Irishmen onto their ships, transported them across the Atlantic, and set them ashore to make cod. Once the season ended, the Irishmen were returned home. The British repeated this year after year. Irishmen did not care to be pressed into fishing. Many decided to jump ship and disappear into the forests, creating a free and independent life for themselves.

Codfish proved very popular. During the period of 1530 to 1680 the Newfoundland inshore fishing frenzy grew to great heights. Planters began claiming a spot which no one else could use. They called these areas "rooms." The early arrivers got the best rooms. Some groups came up with the strategy of leaving a few men behind when they left. Those men would be able to claim rooms before other fishermen arrived the next season.

As fishing became more competitive, once-empty beaches became so crowded that many planters had no place on the beach to dry their fish. Fishermen spent more time jockeying for rooms and less time actually fishing. When the navy got less fish than usual, Britain made it illegal for anyone to live on shore in Newfoundland past the annual fishing season. They hoped this would curtail the fighting, but all it accomplished was illegal squatting. The Greene ancestors were among those squatters.

When the new season came, the planters saw an opportunity to get more fish by hiring the squatters who had already staked out good spots on the beach. Years of ship jumping resulted in larger and larger settlements of Irish men and women. They became permanent residents of Newfoundland. Among these groups came the Flynns, the Murphys, the Corbins, the Kemps, and many others who played a part in Joe and Louise Greene's ancestry.

On Point Verde

Hannah's home village of Point Verde sits on a small peninsula and includes Point Verde Island. The whole area is located on the Avalon Peninsula in Southeast Newfoundland. It stands southwest of the larger village of Placentia and sits at the very edge of Placentia harbor. Early fishing settlers (mostly Greene ancestors) dropped rocks across the channel between Point Verde Island and the mainland to make the first land bridge. They built fishing rooms on the land bridge with flakes for drying cod. The bridge created a small but tidy little harbor to shelter their dories from the open sea.

From the 1600s, fishing rooms stood as the only habitations on the little island. It remained that way until 1878, when the government built a lighthouse.

The economy of Point Verde and Placentia depended on the fish. There were good years with big catches and bad years with low catches. When Hannah was growing up, the rest of the world was experiencing the Great Depression. That event didn't affect the fishermen and their families as much as small catches. Every year proved to be a tough year of hard work, but without big catches the people suffered in poverty.

The Great Depression made one difference for Point Verde. The Newfoundland government, like many other governments throughout the world, set up food banks and cash subsidies to help people struggling financially. People who accepted this assistance were said to be "on the dole" and were looked down on by those who didn't.

The small villages of the country, including Placentia and Point Verde, did all they could to rise above the financial crisis. Many citizens left the villages and headed to the big city of St. John's to find work. Some members of the Greene family followed suit as they got old enough to make important life decisions.

On St. John's

St. John's, the capital of Newfoundland and its most populous city, is one of the oldest cities in North America. It started out as a Basque fishing town just after 1497 when first visited by an English ship commanded by John Cabot. The city succeeded due to its magnificent port, which served both the fishing boats and the cargo boats filled with goods for the people of Newfoundland.

People compare the quaint streets of St. John's to those of San Francisco, with many hills that run through town. St. John's possesses homes of many bright colors, painted so to allow fishermen coming home from the sea to spot their homestead from a distance. The town served the British as a supply port in the French and Indian War, the American Revolutionary War, and the War of 1812.

In 1901 St. John's won renown as the site of the first transatlantic radio, broadcast by Marconi. The city was also the starting point for the first transatlantic flight, in 1919. By the time Joan Greene arrived in St. John's to live with cousins from the Flynn Family, the city had become a bustling modern port town with hotels, restaurants, entertainment venues, and of course, the offices of government and institutions of higher learning. The city played a key role in the defense of North America during World War II, housing bases for American, British, and Canadian forces.

On the Star of the Sea Lounge and Tough Economic Times

Newfoundland fishermen suffered turmoil over the poor fishing harvest and the awful conditions imposed by the larger fish merchants. They resolved to unionize themselves against these powerful merchants. This resulted in the formation of a group called The Fishermen's Protective Union, or the FPU. The FPU provided members a social and mutual benefit and financial insurance against the sickness and death of its members. Like many fraternities, the FPU had a "secret club" aspect to it, with secret handshakes and ceremonies.

The Catholic Church took offense at the secretiveness of the group, so it started its own fraternal organization with the same goals and structure. They called it the Newfoundland Fishermen's Star of the Sea Association, or the NFSSA. The church fostered NFSSA lodges in all the fishing towns with large Catholic populations. Placentia had a big lodge and as a result, they built the Placentia Star of the Sea Hall. So the place originally started out as a fisherman's fraternity, but as fishing tapered off it evolved into a social gathering place for all.

Despite these associations, Newfoundland never escaped financial stresses. As the Depression engulfed the world in the years leading to World War II, the disastrous financial state of the country caused it to give up its independence to Great Britain by 1934. A British-appointed commission came in to govern—but neglected to budget a solution to Newfoundland's problems. As a result, little change took place in the financial conditions of Newfoundland after the government's reorganization, but now it no longer even had its own power to solve its problems.

On Outports and Outport Life

Outports are tiny fishing villages on small islands and isolated peninsulas with relatively easy access to fishing. A typical outport might have 60 families or fewer, who settled there because they could get easy shelter and fresh water. Many outports have been around for 300 years or more.

Conditions were often primitive, without even running water. The homes were simple but comfortable. Many outports had no businesses or stores. Sometimes an outport might have a fish merchant with rooms or maybe a blacksmith. Some little towns have only a church and a school. There were no government services, whether medical or personal. It was a hard life.

A boat was the only way to get to most outports. Being so isolated, outport life could be lonely. Residents might not hear from the rest of the world at all unless they sailed to some coastal town. Weather conditions often made that impossible, especially in winter. Thus, some residents owned a second home on the mainland, where they lived in winter.

Most of the outports received necessities by packet steamboats. These packet boats brought the news, mail, supplies, and medical assistance to the isolated communities. They also provided ferry services. In some places the boats came once a week; in others, once a month. Some places had no packet boat at all.

When that boat rolls into port everyone rushes down to greet it. It was a big event for the residents. What the outport fishing families lacked in money, they made up for in spirit, family and community.

Despite the province's recent addition to the Federation of Canada, Newfoundland still had to fend for itself in many aspects. Many outports were ignored by the government and the towns were dying. The salt cod fishing industry continued its downward spiral. In 1992 the government declared a permanent end to the industry. The government found it cheaper to pay residents to leave their island outports than to subsidize their continued existence. This led to the Government Outport Resettlement Program of 1954.

The idea of leaving behind the homes built by their ancestors preyed on the minds of the outport residents. Many decided to take their houses with them to their new towns. Thus began the practice of floating a house across the harbor to a new location.

Residents worked together to jack up the house in question. The men placed log rollers under the house and pushed and pulled the house down to the water's edge using block and tackle. There, they strapped oil drums or tar barrels all around the base of the house so it would float. They pushed the house into the water and one or two gasoline-powered boats slowly pulled the house to its new location. The trip generally took 2 or 3 hours.

Getting the house back up on the ground and rolled to a new location proved to be an even more difficult proposition, as it usually required an uphill effort. A floating house stood out in 1950, but by the time the mass relocations began in 1954, it became a common but compelling sight.

In 1950, one of the first houses to float across the bay into Placentia came from Merasheen. The whole town came out to watch the spectacle and to give a hand in jockeying the house into position when it arrived.

On World War II and Its Effect on Hannah's World

In the years leading up to WWII, no one in Placentia could have predicted such massive changes in the community resulting from actions in Europe. But Germany was already looking at the world for opportunities to advance its power and Newfoundland was a consideration.

Successful naval warfare, especially submarine warfare conducted by U-boats, depended heavily on good weather. Weather systems travel from west to east. For accurate weather data to work with, the German navy needed weather ships and weather stations all over the North Atlantic.

The Siemens Company, a German industrial giant, invented automated weather stations that solved the problem. These compact machines measured air pressure, wind speed, wind direction, humidity, and temperature every three hours, and sent these data via a two-minute Morse code message. The machines ran on a six-month battery pack.

German U-boat commanders were able to sneak these devices into Newfoundland and hide them in various maritime locations. The first and only discovery of one of these many hidden weather stations took place in 1977. Good camouflage techniques helped keep the machine hidden. No one knows where the remaining weather stations in Newfoundland are located.

After Germany invaded Poland in 1939, the British government declared war. Since Great Britain administered Newfoundland, this drew Newfoundland into the war as well. From that day, everything changed for Placentia and Point Verde in significant ways.

In September 1940, the United States and British governments came to an agreement whereby Britain would receive wartime equipment in exchange for free land leases where America could build military bases. Several bases were established in Newfoundland, including one near St. John's and another large one a few miles outside of Placentia, in the town of Argentia. Four hundred families were displaced from Argentia to accommodate the new navy base. Eventually an army and a marine base were built there too. Troops began to arrive in January 1941 and by the height of the war, the base encompassed 3,500 acres and accommodated 12,000 servicemen. This effectively tripled the population of the Placentia area. In addition, the military established an army barracks with 50 men on the grounds of the Point Verde lighthouse.

The Argentia base made profound changes to the town. Besides adding the military population, a sizable civilian population came to work on the massive construction job needed to build the base. A civilian workforce was also called on to perform the many civilian jobs that were created on the base, and these folks came to live both in the town and in the dormitory housing set aside for that purpose on base.

Before the war, the old town never had more than 100 autos. With the base came the traffic of military vehicles and base personnel. Traffic, parking, and road improvements descended on the town. Government money from Britain, Canada, and the USA abounded in great quantities. Local citizens bought autos in response. Overnight, American culture flooded the little sleepy fishing settlement of Placentia and it became a boomtown. Fishermen abandoned their boats and flocked to work on the base, where jobs paid good, steady money. Suddenly everyone in town had a good job and money in the pocket. Placentia changed forever.

The servicemen that came to town needed entertainment and the base commanders built bowling alleys, movie theaters, restaurants, pool halls, night clubs and even a casino. The townspeople with base passes used these facilities. The opportunities for modern distractions greatly impacted the lives of the townspeople.

Finally, the servicemen who received weekend passes frequently visited Placentia, the only town for miles, and spent their military pay. In town they met and dated local girls. These girls were no longer limited to the life of a fishermen's wife. American men gave great promise for a different life in America. Many girls took advantage of the change and joined the men they met to marry and lead American lives.

On the Aftermath of World War II

The British government reeled from the aftermath of World War II, and struggled to keep up with the needs of Newfoundland. They arranged a referendum election giving Newfoundlanders a choice between continuing under British rule, becoming independent, or joining Canada as a province of that nation.

Independence won the majority vote; but then officials met behind closed doors. When the meetings ended, the officials announced that Newfoundland would join Canada. Newfoundland citizens went into an uproar. To this day some old timers remain angry at what they consider a double cross by the British and the Canadians. They fly the flag of the independent republic.

Regardless, Newfoundlanders became citizens of Canada. Many Newfoundlanders rejected the idea, and chose instead to leave the island for other parts of the world. Frequently, that meant the United States of America.

Above: Making fish

Left: Floating an outport house to a new location. Courtesy Library and Archives Canada/National Film Board

Below: A beached iceberg. Courtesy Doreen Dalley, Twillingate Newfoundland

Above: Mummering

Left: One of Joan's paintings

Below: The author being screeched in

Above: Joan as a girl

Below: Joan on her 90th birthday

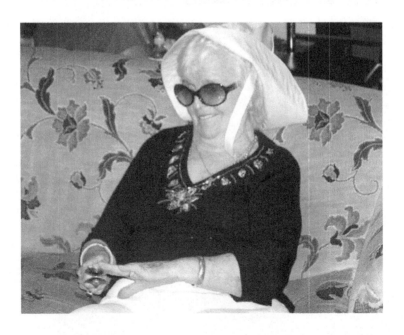

About the Author

Born and raised in New York, Don Ladolcetta lived 40 years in Florida managing a career as a CPA and banker while raising a family. He retired to Texas with his wife and spent five years successfully pursuing his lifelong dream of world travel—until the Covid-19 virus hit the globe. Hindered by the new world of social distancing, he used the time to write his first novel. The semi-biographical story is about a girl who grew up at a lighthouse in rural and isolated Newfoundland, who grew up to become his mother. Don finished the novel about the same time he received his Covid vaccination, so hopes to resume his travels.